Tracey Livesay

Like Lovers Do

A Girls Trip Novel

AVONBOOKS

An Imprint of HarperCollinsPublishers

First Avon Books mass market printing: September 2020

Print Edition ISBN: 978-0-06-297956-8
Digital Edition ISBN: 978-0-06-297957-5

Cover design by Guido Caroti
Cover illustration by Reginald Polynice
Cover photographs © FS Stock/Shutterstock (couple); © Christian Delbert/Shutterstock (lighthouse); © Marc Lechanteur/Shutterstock (rocks); © KRagona/Shutterstock (ocean); © lechatnoir/iStock/ Getty Images (sunset)
Author photography by Abby Braman Photography

FIRST EDITION

20 21 22 23 24 QGM 10 9 8 7 6 5 4 3 2 1

To the staff, nurses and doctors of St. Jude Children's Research Hospital. You do extraordinary work and allow parents to focus on their children without any outside worries. You have our sincere gratitude and utmost respect forever.

Chapter One

Dr. Nicole Allen leaned back on the lounger and let the sun warm her bikini-clad body. Clouds dotted the blue sky, and though her lounger occupied prime real estate next to a pool, she could still hear the crashing of the waves fifty yards away on the beach.

She exhaled and every inch of her body, from the top of her curly bun to the tips of her bright orange-painted toes, gave in to gravity and relaxed into the chaise. Two days into their four-day vacay and she'd finally relegated all thoughts of surgeries, the hospital, and her upcoming fellowship from her mind.

Well, okay, they were still on her mind, just simmering. On the back burner.

It was the best she could do. Her work was never far from her thoughts. She lived, ate, slept, and fucked medicine. She was a doctor. And not just any doctor. An orthopedic surgeon. She'd worked hard for the coveted status, was unashamed to admit it defined who she was. But the privilege came with heavy responsibilities and not a day passed where she wasn't mulling over a possible diagnosis or upcoming surgical procedure.

Which is why she needed this vacation and, more importantly, time with her girls.

The soft whoosh of the sliding glass door—leading from the four-story beach house where they were staying—sounded behind her.

"There you are!" Caila Harris strode into Nic's line of sight, lovely in a bright yellow coverup that looked striking against her dark skin. "Did you enjoy your massage?"

"It was amazing. I haven't had one since our last vacay." It was a luxury Nic couldn't afford to spend money on more than once a year. "How was yours?"

"Magical. And essential. Last month I traveled back and forth between Virginia and Chicago four times!"

Even so, Caila had seemed more tranquil than usual. She still worked hard, climbing her way to the top of the corporate ladder, but she looked happier than she had during their vacation last year. Caila would probably attribute it to meeting the love of her life seven months earlier.

"Did you just finish?" Nic asked, shifting in her seat.

She and Caila had started their massages at the same time but Nic had been done for a while. She'd appreciated the downtime. Caila tended to stuff as much as possible into the vacays she coordinated.

"I finished right after you, but Wyatt called. I was talking to him."

The aforementioned happy-maker.

Caila's beloved grandfather passed away last year, leaving her grief-stricken and distraught. She'd made some mistakes at work, and, to avoid losing her job, had agreed to be sent to a small town in Virginia to close down a factory that happened to be the town's biggest employer. In the midst of the chaos, she'd fallen in love with the town's mayor, whose family was practically Southern royalty. She kept her job, got a promotion, and landed herself the man.

Leave it to Caila to overachieve when it came to finding love, too.

"Aren't you glad we still did this?" Caila asked.

Nic lazily rolled her head to the right to see her friend lifting her face to the sun, her arms outstretched to the side. Just to be obstinate, she wanted to disagree with her, but she couldn't.

"Maybe," she said, one corner of her mouth lifting at her slight accession. "How's work?"

Caila slid out of her sandals. "It's going well. We've completed modernizing the factory in Bradleton. By the middle of January, we'll be able to manufacture products in-house."

All of her friends were smart, successful gogetters. They'd followed different paths after their time together in college: Caila had attended business school and been offered a job with a Fortune 100 company, Ava had gone to law school, and Lacey had pursued her dream career in dance.

But of her three friends, Caila was the most like her. Both were driven by this internal need to succeed that no one else understood.

That similarity was also the reason why they always seemed to clash.

"And you and Wyatt?"

Caila lowered herself to the edge of the pool and slipped her feet into the water. "I wasn't sure how we were going to make it work, I just knew I wanted to. But it's been wonderful. It's exceeded all of my expectations."

She couldn't deny the happiness she saw shining in Caila's eyes or heard in her voice, but Nic wasn't sure she believed her. Caila's job had been her life. Climbing the corporate ladder had excited her more than any relationship. Which is why she and Caila had always been on the same page regarding their life philosophies: careers before dears. Now she'd changed? Just like that? How could she continue pursuing her goal with that same single-minded focus if that time was now eaten up by a man?

Before Nic could voice her question, laughter alerted her to the fact that Ava and Lacey had finished their massages. When they cleared the foliage, Nic's eyes widened and she pointed at Ava's head.

"What is that?"

Ava Taylor touched the brim of her straw hat. "It's to keep the sun out of my face. You know all this brownness doesn't need to tan."

Nic and Caila shared a glance.

"And what look were you going for?" Caila asked.

"Oh come on," Ava said, jamming her fists on her shapely hips. "You've seen this look before. Women wear it at the beach all of the time. I'm trying it out for tomorrow."

Nic shot a look at Lacey. "You let your friend come out of the house wearing that?"

Lacey, her tall, lithe dancer's body showcased to perfection in an emerald green one-piece, held up her hands. "Don't blame me. I sent her the link to the one she *said* she wanted."

"It was four hundred dollars! I wanted Jennifer Lopez's hat. I don't have her money."

Nic motioned to Ava's studded sandals. "How much did you spend on those?"

"That's different. These are Valentino."

Caila brought a fist to her mouth, as if covering a cough. "So you were going for the J.Lo floppy hat look, circa 2002?"

"Exactly!"

Nic capitulated in her own struggle not to laugh. "Unfortunately, you ended up with the Miss Celie hat look, circa *The Color Purple*."

Ava narrowed her brown eyes. "I did not!"

Nic pulled out her phone, did a quick google search, and showed Ava a still from the movie. Then she efficiently engaged her camera app, took her friend's photo, and showed her the screen.

"Dammit!" Ava muttered, tugging the offending item off her head and tossing it onto the nearby table.

"It needs to be more than straw to be fashionable," Caila said. "It should be big and actually floppy. What you're wearing is just sad."

"Screw all three of you." Ava plopped down on a lounger situated beneath artfully planted palm trees. "I'm claiming the best full-coverage spot under the umbrellas when we head to the beach."

"We'll get a cabana," Caila said. "That way, we won't take any chances. 'Cuz I don't do the sun, either."

Lacey shook her head from her spot next to Caila on the edge of the pool. "Nic and I weren't blessed with your melanin. We need to lie out. Plus, cabanas are too big and they block the view. How are we supposed to see the men?"

Nic pursed her lips. "What men?"

Nic hadn't seen anyone worth her time, though to be fair, she hadn't been looking. She wasn't opposed to a vacation fling, but the timing wasn't right. She was two months away from finishing up her residency and starting her fellowship.

"Remember that guy from the club last night?" Lacey asked.

Nic scoffed. "That one? He was alright."

"His friend was cute," Ava said.

Nic jerked her head back. "The one with the chicken legs?"

Lacey raised her brows. "Ava wasn't looking at his legs . . . unless you count the third one that was visible through his too-tight pants."

They all winced in unison.

"Speaking of hot guys . . ." Ava scooted closer

and lowered her voice. "Did you have Randall for your massage?"

"I had Holly," Caila said.

Ava pointed to Nic. "So *you* had him?"

"Uh-huh."

"How was he?"

Nic shrugged. "He was good. Why?"

Ava sighed. "I don't know. I mean, I wasn't sure if he was giving me a massage or courting me."

"What are you talking about?"

Lacey shook her head. "Don't encourage her nonsense."

"It's not nonsense! When I got a massage a few months ago, the therapist didn't have a need to entwine his fingers with mine, like we were holding hands."

Nic sat up. "He massaged my palms, but I can't say it was anything like holding hands."

"See? What did I tell you?" Ava shot at Lacey. "Then he did this move where he rolled me back and forth on the table and everything was jiggling."

Ava shimmied for them to underscore her point that she did, indeed, have curves aplenty.

Nic waved her hand dismissively. "They do that to make sure you're truly relaxed and that all of the tension is out of your body. He did that to me when I was facedown, too."

Ava tilted her head knowingly. "I wasn't facedown."

It took a second for the meaning to sink in but when it did, they all burst out laughing.

Nic admired the smiling faces around her. She could count on one hand the number of people she'd trust with her life and these women would claim three of those fingers. She'd met them their first year of college at the University of Virginia. While everyone else seemed to have their shit together, Nic felt out of place from the moment she'd arrived. It was so different from the small city in western Tennessee where she'd grown up. Her roommate had been from a wealthy Georgia family. Shelby and her friends had swept into the dorm in their pearl stud earrings and floral fit and flare dresses, tongues dripping with sweet Southern accents and malicious gazes that swept over her and found her wanting.

It had taken every ounce of self-control Nic had possessed not to hide her big-box store bed-spread and the worn-out suitcase and nonmatching duffel bag that held all of her belongings. Shelby had talked of little else but partying and pledging Tri-Delt, whatever that was. All dreams Nic had of finally finding "her tribe" had vanished.

One afternoon, she'd headed down to the dorm's TV lounge to watch *Oprah*. It had become a ritual she and her mom performed, their brief moment to catch up after Nic came home from school but before her mother left to start her second job. Nic had sprinted, not walked, away from her home and her past, so she hadn't expected to crave anything that reminded her of there. But she had. And in doing so, she'd met three other girls who'd been trying to carve out their own little space in their new environment. They'd become best friends, and the following fall, when they had a choice in their housing, they'd decided to room together. They'd remained close all four years and during that time, they'd managed to become as important to her as if they were family.

Nic wrapped her arms around her raised knees. "I appreciate y'all agreeing to an earlier and shorter vacay this year and one close to me."

With her residency wrapping up, studying for and taking her boards and her fellowship starting in August, Nic couldn't afford as much time off this year. Additionally, the added bonus of being in the Outer Banks meant driving instead of flying, which saved money and allowed her to detour to her future home in Durham and look at apartments on her way back to Baltimore.

"Anytime," Caila said. "Days of vacay, places of vacay, all negotiable. Missing a vacay isn't."

Two years after they'd graduated from college, Caila had been sent on a weeklong work trip in Florida and given a bungalow on the beach. She'd invited Nic, Ava, and Lacey to come down and stay with her and thus their annual vacay had been born. It was cherished time they never missed.

"Caila, make sure you thank Wyatt for us. Arranging all of this"—Ava gestured to the house—"and the morning of pampering was very nice of him."

Lacey nodded. "He's a keeper."

Nic frowned at her. "Because he's letting us use this house and he paid for some massages?"

"Don't forget the mani-pedis," Ava piped in.

"Shouldn't we see if he treats Caila well, before we, I don't know, pimp her out for future vacays?" Nic crossed her arms.

Caila smiled. "Your concern touches me, Nic. But don't worry. He's wonderful. And I'll pass on your gratitude, Ava. Wyatt was happy to do it. Said it would be his way to introduce himself to my friends. He knows how important you are to me and he's a fan of big gestures."

"Is he now?" Ava smiled. "Anything else big about him?"

"Oh yeah," Caila said, a smile teasing her lips. She tapped a spot halfway down her thigh.

"Damn," Lacey whispered.

Caila nodded. "Girl, yes! He has this big mole, right here and—"

Lacey threw a pillow at Caila.

Caila dodged it, her tongue between her teeth. "That's what you get for being nosy."

"Ms. Harris." A woman strode from the house and set a pitcher of water and sliced citrus fruit on the patio table. "The chef wanted to know what time he should serve dinner?"

Caila looked around. "Seven thirty?"

They all nodded and the woman smiled and left them.

After everyone had their drink, Ava lifted her glass. "To the Ladies of Lefevre and a great vacay," she said, referring to the name they'd given themselves based on the dorm where they'd met.

"And to Dr. Allen, starting her fellowship," Lacey added.

Pride and happiness swelled in Nic's chest. "Dr. Allen. I'll never get tired of hearing that."

That title, and about two hundred grand in student loans, were the only things she could claim at the moment.

"You shouldn't. You worked hard for it."

"You've been in school forever," Caila said, flicking the water with her foot. "You've already done nine additional years past college. I know you're paid during your residency, but with your student loans, it has to be tough. You're officially a doctor. You could start earning money now. Why do a fellowship?"

"The field I want to go into is very specialized."

"Orthopedic sports medicine, right?"

Nic nodded. "An orthopedic sports medicine *surgeon*."

It was a tough discipline and one of the top paying. Unfortunately, it was extremely male dominated, with the lowest percentage of women— about four percent—participating.

"You're a tiny little thing. Ortho requires brute force and more strength than you could possibly have."

A wink and then, "Think about your future. It's not conducive to raising a family. And I doubt your husband will be happy with you working around all of these burly men."

Her husband? Fuck. That. She hadn't worked hard and sacrificed only to get married and give it up because some man couldn't handle sharing the limelight or he'd made promises to her that later, he couldn't be bothered to keep. Her mother had once made that mistake.

Nic never would.

"I'll put off making a doctor's salary for now," she responded to Caila, "but in a year, my starting salary will be several times what I would've made as a general physician."

"What are we talking about?" Lacey asked.

"Mid–six figures."

Silence.

"Shit, Nic, I'd stay in school for that, too," Ava said.

"Except you failed Organic Chemistry," Caila added.

"Oh my God, are you the keeper of all memories?" Ava asked.

"Yes," Caila said, in her "duh" tone.

"You're good," Lacey told Ava. "California Superior Court judges do well."

"Not *that* well," Ava muttered. "But that's great news, Nic. In a year, you'll be able to take care of your mother the way you've always wanted."

Tears scalded the backs of her eyes but Nic refused to let them fall. It was no secret that a large motivating factor in her ambition involved taking care of her mother. After Nic's father had left, Dee Allen worked several jobs to make sure they had everything they needed. Once Nic set her eyes on a goal, her mother never questioned it; she just figured out a way to make it happen.

"This fellowship will get you there?" Caila asked.

"That's the plan."

"And then you'll be done?"

Some note in Caila's tone struck Nic the wrong way.

"Why?" she challenged, aware her own tone held an edge.

"I'm wondering when it will be enough."

Nic raised both eyebrows. "Uh, hello, paging Ms. Pot. Do you remember last year, when I threatened to throw *your* phone in the ocean?"

As soon as Nic's words registered, she regretted uttering them. It was during their vacation last year that Caila had found out her grandfather had died.

"I'm so sorry," Nic said, scooting forward and reaching a hand out to Caila. "That was insensitive as fuck."

Caila accepted Nic's hand and her apology. "It's okay." She dashed away a tear and the action threatened to shred Nic's own composure. "And you have a point. I'm not the same person I was last year."

Nic squeezed Caila's hand before letting go. "Let me guess. The mayor's magic dick stole your ambition?"

"Ooh, the mayor's magic dick. That's a great porno title," Lacey said.

"Oh mayor, what about that proposition? I

have a proposition for you," Ava said in alternating cartoonish female and male voices.

Caila shook her head, the sadness receding from her gaze. "Cute."

"They're joking, but I'm serious," Nic said.

"I know you are. I got my promotion, but I still have goals. I still have my eye on the C-suite. But falling in love with Wyatt helped me to appreciate there's more to life than work. For the first time ever, there's a work/life balance. And I have someone to share my victories with."

"What are we, chopped liver?" Lacey asked.

Caila rolled her eyes. "You know what I meant."

What was it with people newly in love and in relationships? They tried to convert everyone they knew like fanatical churchgoers. Or Scientologists. Caila used to have a fit when her mother or Ava used to pull this same crap on her.

"I'm happy for you." She truly was. For *her.* "But that's not the path we're all supposed to take. I sorta remember hearing that from someone."

"The worst kind of person is someone who quotes you back to you to prove a point."

Nic laughed and blew her a kiss.

"And on that note, we should probably go get changed for dinner," Ava said, rising from the lounger to stand. "I'm looking forward to hitting the club again tonight. They're probably waiting for us to get the party started."

Lacey shuddered. "Can we not go back there? Please? The manager followed me around all night."

No one could've anticipated they'd find Lacey's number one fan managing a small club on the Outer Banks. The man had taken one look at Lacey, recognized her from a national commercial she'd performed in, and had gone out of his way to try to impress her.

"He told me he was dripping so much sauce he sweat BBQ," Lacey whined. "He said it like it was his best pickup line."

"He gave us a VIP section, comped a round of drinks, and told the DJ to play all our song requests. That was worth a smile for one of your fans, right?"

"Weren't you the one just complaining about pimping out our friends?" Caila asked.

"Yeah!" Lacey said. "If it's so easy for you, Nic, you do it!"

"It is easy for me." Nic had no problem doing whatever it took to achieve her goals. "And I'd do it. But he doesn't want me. He wants you."

"Which is unusual in and of itself, since Nic is usually the one fighting them off," Caila said. "Remember our senior break trip when we met those two guys from Cornell? Baby Boy lost his fucking mind over Nic."

A languid heat invaded Nic's body and she bit her lower lip. They'd called him "Baby Boy" because he'd reminded them of the actor Tyrese Gibson. Six feet, shaved head, and sleekly muscled with skin that looked like he'd been double-dipped in expensive dark chocolate; the kind that's nutritious should you want to indulge.

And boy, did she ever indulge . . .

"He would get up early and go down to the pool and reserve loungers for our whole crew just so we could hang together." She sighed. "We had a good time."

Ava frowned. "Then why didn't you keep in touch with him?"

Nic shrugged. "It was a fling. They end. I wasn't interested in making it more than it was."

"Nic! God, who knows what could've developed?" Lacey said. "I don't understand how you can be so intimate with guys, but you don't get to know them or let them get to know you?"

Nic didn't take the rebuke personally. Lacey was their resident romantic. And not in that tragic star-crossed lovers, dying in the name of love bullshit way, but in the love at first sight, eyes meeting across the room, happily ever after way that Hallmark and Lifetime and all those other channels got off on.

"It's my superpower?" Nic asked, facetiously.

Lacey pursed her lips.

"Wasn't he an actor?" Caila asked.

Baby Boy had starred in a popular sitcom when he was a kid, but he'd taken a break from the business to attend college.

"I think I saw him on a show about a year ago," Lacey confirmed.

Ava snapped her fingers. "I knew I recognized that guy! Isn't he in the cast of that new Netflix drama everyone's talking about? Damn.

You couldn't have kept in touch with him? Exchanged emails?"

Nic threw an arm over her head and rested it against the back of her lounger. "He reached out to me a few years ago."

"What?" Ava dropped back down onto her chair. "Why didn't you tell us? What did he want?"

"He found that stupid profile y'all hounded me to put up on Facebook. We exchanged messages for a few weeks. He was getting ready to go to Vancouver to film a small part in a movie." Nic crossed her legs at the ankle. "He wanted me to fly over and spend some time with him."

Actually, he'd said something about seeing if she tasted as good as he'd remembered, but she kept that little tidbit to herself.

"Did you go?" Lacey asked, her hazel eyes wide.

"I would've told you if I had. But it wasn't an option. I'd just graduated from medical school and was about to start my residency. I wasn't going to risk my future for a few months' fling." She curled her lip. "Probably less because he would've eventually gotten on my nerves."

Lacey stared at her for a long moment. "I can't with you. I would kill to meet a great guy. They throw themselves at you and you toss them away."

Nic scratched her cheek. "Well you're in luck, because Came Thru Drippin' is all about you!"

Lacey's posture dropped and she rolled her eyes. "That's not what I was talking about."

Laughing, they all stood and began heading into the house to get ready for the evening.

"Wait!" Lacey shifted her weight onto one foot and crossed her arms over her chest. "I'll go back to the club one more time . . . but only if you let me plan the next vacay."

Silence greeted Lacey's demand. And then—

"Hell no!" Nic said.

"Seriously? You can't deny me. I'm a grown woman."

"Who, until last year, never noticed she hadn't planned a vacay."

"I didn't know it was on purpose." Lacey set her jaw. "I want my turn."

Two pairs of contemplative brown eyes met a skeptical green pair.

"I don't know. Maybe it's time?" Caila said.

"This is a bad idea," Nic warned.

"Come on," Ava said. "Let's give her a chance."

Nic knew they were making a huge mistake, but she was outvoted. Relenting, she threw her hands in the air. "Fine. But when we end up in the middle of nowhere in some broke-down, cracked-out accommodations, I'm not going to blame Lacey. I'll blame the both of you."

Chapter Two

Baltimore
Early June
Six Weeks Later . . .

As Nic had strolled the several blocks from her home to the hospital, the rising sun had gradually lightened the sky and elevated her mood, aided—in no small part—by the travel mug of coffee she'd clenched tightly in her hand. But there were no windows in the doctors' lounge, a design choice probably made for the same reason there were usually none in casinos: to keep people hyperfocused on the reason for being there and unaware of the passage of time.

Still, as she shrugged into her white coat and transferred her stethoscope, pocket references, pen, and hand lotion from her backpack to her pockets before shutting the locker door, Nic embraced the excitement that fluttered low in her belly at the start of each shift. She loved her job and couldn't imagine doing anything else. Or practicing any other specialty. She wasn't interested in puzzling over a medical mystery for years or following patients over time. She preferred results and thrived on the instant gratification of repairing someone, of eliminating their pain, and, almost immediately, improving their quality of life.

And as she became more specialized in sports medicine, her skills would enable her to help an athlete transition from a painful, inactive state to a pain-free active one that allowed them to continue doing what *they* loved. In ninety-five percent of her cases, people had a positive outcome. Not all doctors could make that claim. Most of the time, her patients were happy. She found her work intellectually fulfilling and emotionally exhilarating.

And whenever her body called for a different type of stimulation, she didn't need to travel far. As Caila had pointed out during their vacation, Nic never had a problem finding men who wanted to spend time with her. The problem was the interest wasn't usually reciprocated.

Nic wasn't looking to date. She didn't have the time or the inclination to invest in it. She'd worked hard to get to where she was. Orthopedic surgery was one of the most competitive residencies to match into. So much so that it was one of only four specialties that didn't have enough positions to accommodate all the med school graduates who wanted one. She'd achieved her coveted spot by ranking in the top five percent of her class, having several forms of research and volunteer experience. And the grind had continued through the next five years of her residency to guarantee she'd get into the sports medicine fellowship of her choosing.

That amount of effort meant work had to be her primary focus. Her top priority. But when she was confronted with that inevitable sexual itch that needed a long, thorough scratching, she had her pick of several doctors who were in the same boat. They all understood it wasn't personal. It was purely physical, which was how she preferred her male relationships. It allowed her to concentrate her energy and attention where she wanted it.

On her patients.

She allowed herself one final glance in the mirror hanging on the wall to ensure her curls were tamed into a nape-scraping bun and that her plain white button-down was securely tucked into her gray slacks. It always felt weird to be in the hospital in civilian clothes, instead of scrubs. She lived in the green cotton fabric, but today she'd be doing clinic hours instead of the OR, which meant dressing like a teacher instead of a surgeon. She smoothed a hand over the bumps and ridges where her name was monogrammed into her coat's fabric—"Nicole Allen, MD, Orthopedics Surgery"—and left the room.

She didn't balk at the numbers displayed on the huge digital clock face that greeted her, mounted high on the opposite wall. As chief resident, it was important to her to set a good example, which meant being on time and being prepared. That didn't mean she needed to be at the hospital at quarter to six; morning reports didn't begin until seven A.M. But yesterday, she'd operated on a young girl, a consult from the emergency room. She wanted to check on her before the day began and other tasks took precedence.

Skipping the elevator—the ones in that wing ran twice as slow as the others—she opted for the stairs. She was wistful as she realized it wouldn't be long before she'd have no use for the idiosyncrasies and nuances of these buildings that she'd spent years learning. There were only three more weeks until her last day at Johns Hopkins and though she was excited to begin the final phase of her medical education, she had to remind herself to take advantage of every opportunity to learn while she still walked these halls.

Using her badge, Nic swiped the sensor and opened the door to the surgical intensive care unit. The three women sitting behind the nurses' desk smiled at her approach.

"Morning, Dr. Allen," the nurse in the middle said.

"Ladies. Quiet night?"

"Pretty much. There was a car accident on East Lombard Street and Dr. Cowler had several ortho consults last night."

Anticipation tingled along her nerve endings, heightening her awareness better than all the coffee in the world. Some of those consults might require surgery. Part of Nic's duties as chief resident involved scanning overnight admissions in case she needed to make alterations to the daily OR schedule. Because of the accident, she would probably have to shift a few of the previously scheduled surgeries to make room for any pressing incoming cases. She might even have to scrub in and handle a few herself.

She tapped the top of the counter with a fist. "Thanks for the heads-up. Toland?"

"In twelve."

Nic sanitized her hands and entered the space. The beeps and whooshes of various machines provided a soothing, melodic dampening cloak to the outside noise of the unit. She took a moment and allowed her eyes to adjust to the dim lighting. In the bed, a teenaged girl lay on her back, her chest rising and falling steadily, her face turned to the side, her brown skin slightly ashen. Moving quietly, Nic located the computer contained in every patient's room, and logged on to check Simone's chart.

"Dr. Allen?" A whisper in the dark.

Nic started, her heart pummeling her chest. She glanced over her shoulder to the person sitting in the chair next to the bed.

"Mrs. Toland. I'm sorry, I didn't mean to wake you."

Simone's mother straightened and pushed her hair back from her face. "It's okay. I didn't mean to doze off."

Scanning the notes, Nic pressed a button to

close the file and turned to face the other woman. "You needed the rest. How is she?"

"You're the doctor. You tell me."

Nic smiled. "Her vitals, CBC, and imaging all look good. I'm happy with how it turned out."

Mrs. Toland's expression softened. "I can't believe it. A month ago, we came here because Simone had been having terrible hip pains. We'd been to doctor after doctor who'd told us everything from the pain was all in her head to she'd need a full hip replacement. Maybe more than one. But for the first time in almost a year, we have hope. Because of the surgery you performed. Because of you."

Warmth spread through Nic's body at the praise. She nodded. "Her recovery will take time. She'll be confined to a wheelchair and it won't be easy—"

"But she'll be able to run track again," Mrs. Toland said, pressing a hand to her chest. "And before your diagnosis and this surgery, we didn't think that would be possible. I don't know how we'll ever be able to thank you."

There was no doubt that the money and validation from choosing this specialized field was important, but there was nothing like seeing a patient, especially a child, get better. Eliminating people's pain, helping them to live their best life . . . the feeling was indescribable.

Nic squeezed the mother's shoulder. "I'm happy I was able to help. And if you really want to thank me, make sure I get an invitation to her first track meet after rehab."

Leaving the room, Nic sanitized her hands again, waved to the nurses, and exited the unit. She still had a few administrative tasks to complete before meeting the other residents for morning report in the conference room. Hopefully, one of the junior residents stopped to pick up doughnuts from the place around the corner. She was starving.

Several hours later, in between patients in the ortho clinic, Nic let the receptionist know she was heading to the cafeteria to grab a quick lunch before her next appointment. The junior residents *hadn't* brought breakfast to the meeting and now her stomach was rebelling at its mistreatment. A man had walked through the clinic carrying something with bacon and Nic had grabbed on to the plastic glove dispenser to prevent her body from rising and floating through the air, like a cartoon character following a seductive scent plume toward a cooling pie.

When her phone rang, she barely resisted the urge to scream in frustration.

"Dr. Allen," she answered between clenched teeth.

"I need you down here." Dr. Amalia Ocampo's voice lacked its usual playful warmth.

"Can you page someone else? I was just getting ready to—"

"Now!"

Shit! Nic pressed the call button for the elevator. God help anyone unlucky enough to be on it with food.

Five minutes later, she pushed through the doors into the emergency room. A level one trauma center, the state-of-the-art facility was over thirty thousand square feet and housed the most innovative and advanced medical technology in the world, allowing them to see more than one hundred thousand patients annually.

Amalia was waiting for her, dressed in green scrubs, her straight black hair pulled into a ponytail. "Over here."

Nic followed the senior ER resident down the corridor past numerous waiting areas and triage bays until she stopped next to an exam room. Through the small window Nic spied an elderly black man lying on a gurney.

What the fuck? Amalia prevented her from putting food in her belly so she could see a patient?

Nic shot the other doctor a pissed-off look. "I'm not doing consults today. Cowler is on call."

Amalia continued as if Nic hadn't spoken. "This is Mr. Brant, a sixty-three-year-old male who presented with ten days of progressive pain and stiffness in his left shoulder."

Nic opened her mouth to question Amalia's hearing when she hesitated. Progressive pain in the left shoulder? That sounded familiar. "Didn't you call for a consult on him yesterday?"

"Yes," Amalia said, her dark eyes widening.

"Imagine my surprise and irritation to find him back here with the same problem."

Nic noted Amalia's sarcasm, but she didn't comment on it. "Who came down?"

"Whitaker."

Ugh. One of the interns on her team. Bro, MD.

"Page him and tell him to get his ass down here, stat." Nic waved her hand beneath the wall-mounted antibacterial foam dispenser and entered the room, smiling at the patient. "Mr. Brent, my name is Dr. Allen and I'm an orthopedic surgeon here at Hopkins. Do you mind if I take a look at your shoulder?"

When he gave his consent, she ran through an efficient but thorough examination, then told Amalia, "He'll need an MRI as soon as possible."

Anger at the missed diagnosis licked at her skin. The signs were all there: the diminished range of motion, generalized swelling and warmth, the darker coloration. It would've been obvious to anyone who knew what they were doing. Still, she forced herself to take a deep breath.

Despite your wishes, no one's perfect. Mistakes happen.

Especially with interns. Even though it was the end of Whitaker's first year and the task was something he should've been able to do, Nic told herself to calm down. This would be a good opportunity for a teachable moment.

Three more weeks. Three more weeks.

"You paged me?" Whitaker's blue eyes telegraphed his surprise at seeing her, but he recovered quickly, pasting a cocky smirk on his pale face.

Nic thanked Mr. Bryant, stepped out of the examination room, and motioned the intern over.

"Did you take this consult yesterday?"

He crossed his arms over his chest. "If that's what it says."

If that's what it—

Apparently in his first year the little shit hadn't learned about the hierarchy in the hospital. Pissing off a senior resident was NEVER a good idea. Even if you were right. Which he most definitely wasn't in this case.

Three more weeks. Three more weeks.

"That *is* what it says. It also says you gave him pain meds and discharged him with instructions to follow up with his primary care physician."

"Yeah."

His nonchalance abraded her nerves, like a cheese grater on skin. He acted as if he'd done nothing wrong. As if the fact that the patient he'd seen the day before, who'd come back less than twenty-four hours later, wasn't a cause for concern. No curiosity about why he'd returned. No remorse. Just an exaggerated head tilt and a curled lip that suggested his belief that she wasn't worth his time.

And it was that disrespect that wouldn't allow her to channel Whitley Gilbert and relax, relate, release.

Nic pursed her lips. "What are the six steps of a shoulder examination?"

"Excuse me?"

Did she stammer or stutter? "What are the six steps of a shoulder examination?"

His mouth tightened, but he responded, showing her that arrogance hadn't rendered him completely insane. "Inspection, palpation, range of motion, power, neuro-vascular examination, and special tests."

"Did you do them?"

He shifted his weight and hesitated . . . "Yes."

Goddammit! Nic closed her eyes and pinched the bridge of her nose. He never examined the patient. And when called on it, he'd blatantly lied to her face!

She shook her head. Trust was one of the most important assets an intern could earn from a senior resident. That trust would allow the younger resident additional opportunities and responsibilities because a senior resident had faith that they could handle themselves. But once that trust was broken . . .

"What was more important?" At Whitaker's quasi-innocent look Nic said, "Don't make me have to go around this hospital solving this mystery like I'm on an episode of *Diagnosis: Murder*!"

And she would.

His forehead wrinkled. "What?"

Lord, replenish my reserve of patience . . . "There was something more important to you than doing right by this patient. What was it?"

Whitaker exhaled. "Gorley was doing a lumbar spinal fusion."

You piece of shit! Her throat burned and she struggled to keep the disgust she felt from her expression. "This is your job. People's lives are at stake. You don't get to rush through it because there's something more exciting that you'd rather do."

His detached facade started to crumble. "He stated that he may have fallen, but he couldn't remember, he reeked of alcohol and his clothes were filthy. You expected me to miss a surgery that would actually help my career? The guy's a bum!"

"And that gives you the right to be negligent in his care? Because he doesn't occupy the same tax bracket as your family?"

"What's the big deal? He came back. He'll be treated."

"He shouldn't have had to come back. You should've gotten it right the first time. If you'd actually done the examination, you would've figured out the genesis of his injury was the least of his problems. He probably has septic arthritis of the left shoulder. A delay in diagnosis and treatment could lead to complications of septic shock or osteomyelitis. He presented acutely with all of the classical features of infection and you missed it. Just to watch a surgery you'll probably see several times while you're here." She pointed her finger at him. "You half-ass a consult like that again and you're gone."

Blood flooded his face. "You can't do that."

Watch me.

"Personally, no, but I have access to the people

who can and this is the type of behavior that will get you fired from a program."

And nothing in his attitude or behavior led her to believe he'd learned from this incident and wouldn't repeat it. That feeling was reinforced when he said—

"Do you know who I am?" Whitaker moved into her space and used his seven-inch height advantage to loom over her.

She refused to be cowed. "Do I care? All I know is you're the intern who carelessly misdiagnosed a patient and refused to own up to his mistake. And that makes you a problem resident and someone I'll have to keep my eye on."

"This isn't over. I know people, too," he said, before storming off.

"What a prick," Amalia said, falling in beside her as she headed back the way she'd come.

The encounter left a sour taste in Nic's mouth that temporarily diminished her hunger. "Seriously, somebody save us from lazy, incompetent, irresponsible interns."

"We were interns once." Amalia tilted her head. "Do you think we were like that?"

"Hell no. Neither one of us would've gotten away with that type of behavior."

Whitaker and men of his ilk lived by a different set of rules. If she or Amalia, as women of color, had mouthed off or disrespected a senior resident that way, a chewing out would've been the least of their worries.

"Are you going to report him?"

Nic sighed. "I should."

"You could just leave it alone. Why go through the hassle of the paperwork? In three weeks, he'll be someone else's problem."

True.

"You on call tonight?"

"Nope. After clinic, I'm going home, eating half my weight in food, taking a hot shower, and going to bed."

Amalia elbowed her. "Those would be my plans, too, if I had the rich and sexy Benjamin Reed Van Mont waiting for me."

Nic almost laughed. Ben *was* rich. His grandfather had invented a device that was still used in all medical imaging machines and had parlayed his newfound wealth into a biomedical behemoth. Both of his parents were renowned doctors in their respective fields. The Van Mont family was considered medical royalty. In fact, there was a clinic at Hopkins with his family's name on it.

But sexy?

He was certainly good-looking with dark hair and dark eyes, but she didn't consider him sexy. Probably because she preferred a little edge to her men and Ben had all the edge of a gummy bear. He was also a relationship guy and Nic could think of a million things she wanted more.

"Ouch!" Nic rubbed her side. "He's not *waiting* for me. I rent his garden apartment. He's my landlord."

"This is why I question you being honored

with the designation of chief resident. I thought you were smart. I would've gotten a piece of that from the beginning." She winked. "I might have even offered to pay *more* rent."

"That's why you would've been out on the street after three months looking for another place to live." Nic looked at her watch. "Crap. Now I won't have time to grab something to eat before my next appointment."

Amalia slapped the nurse's desk with her palm and the young man behind it handed her a protein bar. "Here."

"Ah! Bless you!" Nic tore open the wrapper and took a bite.

"Remember this moment when you're the team surgeon for the Ravens and I ask you for tickets."

"The Memphis Grizzlies," Nic corrected.

"Or, since you're not interested in Mr. Van Mont, you can thank me by setting up an introduction."

"Oh no! I'm not going to let you ruin my perfect arrangement. Besides, we're not his type."

"Gay?"

"Traditional. Looking for a woman to stay home, pop out 2.5 kids and live happily ever after."

Amalia winced. "Damn."

"Exactly. Now, stop acting like we're in an episode of *Grey's Anatomy* and get back to work."

Chapter Three

As her day began, so it also ended . . .

The sun was setting, turning the sky a pretty orange and violet, as Nic rounded the corner of her block in the historic Butcher Hill area in Baltimore. Close to the hospital and bordered on two sides by green space, it was a diverse neighborhood with friendly people constantly involved in activities meant to foster a sense of community. She was usually too busy to attend those events and on the rare occasion she wasn't working, she'd much rather spend her time catching up on reading or reviewing notes.

Waving to the retirees chatting outside on their stoops, she sidestepped a father walking alongside his daughter on a tricycle. The smile of paternal pride he directed at the little girl caused a burning ache in her chest.

She'd never known that look.

Nodding briskly to acknowledge their calls of apology, she approached the shiny black door that heralded her arrival at the beautiful brick building she was fortunate enough to call home.

She could never live here on what she currently made. As she'd told her friends, she might be a doctor, but her job was still educational, and with student loans and the money she sent monthly to her mother, she was surviving on a pittance. Hearing about Ben's apartment from a coworker at the hospital and moving in here was one of the best things that had happened to her since meeting the Ladies of Lefevre.

But he didn't need to know that.

She opened the door and stepped into the split-level entryway and was immediately soothed by the exposed brick walls, bright white moldings, and blond maple hardwood floors. The house alarm dinged, declaring her arrival, and a deep friendly voice called out from above, "You have a package on the counter."

"Thanks," she called back.

Her hands skimmed along the wrought-iron banister as she headed downstairs into her "garden" apartment. She dropped her leather tote on her couch and tossed her keys on the dark wood pub table that also housed her mail and several coffee cups. She kicked off her shoes and changed into leggings and one of her favorite T-shirts that read "Unapologetically Brainy Black Girl" before bounding back up the way she came, and going farther, up to the second floor into the main part of the home.

The captivating scent of simmering tomato sauce claimed her attention and alerted her to the fact that Ben was cooking. In response, her stomach growled, demanding that she pick up her pace. The man was a god in the kitchen, possessing the ability to do something Nic had never believed in before meeting him: making healthy food taste good.

Lights from hanging pendants reflected off the dark cabinets and the white marble, greeting her as she walked into the room. Ben stood with his back to her, his tall frame covered in a maroon T-shirt and dark gray sweatpants, tossing vegetables from a cutting board into a stainless steel frying pan.

"How much longer?" she asked.

"Hello to you, too," he said, stirring the contents with a wooden spoon.

She spied the brown parcel sitting on the countertop. "Is that it?"

"Your package? Yeah."

Excitement was a temporary dam for her ravenous exhaustion as she tore open the box and squealed in delight at its contents.

Ben finally glanced at her over his shoulder, a dark brow arched. "What is it this time?"

"Goat milk soap, whipped body cream, and a curl pudding for my hair," she responded absently, checking to confirm everything she'd ordered was in the package.

"Good grief!" He snorted and turned back to the food he was preparing.

"I didn't ask for your commentary, Charlie Brown," she said, picking up each item and inhaling its wonderful scent.

Caila was into designer purses; Ava was all about shoes; Lacey was their resident fashionista. For Nic, it was hair and skincare products. Face cleansers, moisturizers, lotions, hair products—she loved them all. And the more luxurious, decadent, and lusciously scented the better. Sometimes, when she needed a break from studying and researching, she'd surf her favorite beauty brands online and imagine what she'd purchase when she got her first real check working as a team physician.

La Mer Moisturizing Cream, anyone?

"Let me guess: they're from some organic boutique shop you saw online where each delicate, vegan bar cost about twenty dollars?"

"Wrong," she said snidely—but only because she'd gotten the lot on sale. She always waited for the sales.

"Ahhh." His head bobbed. "You got them on sale."

If she didn't value these soaps so much, she'd throw one at him.

"I have dry, sensitive skin"—which was true, but it was also what allowed her to justify spending money now—"and with the constant hand washing and antibacterial sanitizer, I have to take precautions to keep these babies"—she wiggled her fingers—"healthy. They're my money makers. I keep them moisturized and pampered. Now, as a white man who'd never thought about lotion until I moved in—"

"I still don't," he interrupted.

"—I understand moisturized skin may not be important to you."

"Ha. Ha." He smirked, lobbing something in her direction.

She watched as the broccoli floret bounced on the counter before falling to the floor. She pointed to it. "That's from your half of dinner."

"Riddle me this, Queen of Self-care, why don't your insides rate the same consideration as your outsides?"

"Excuse me?"

"You obsess over the glop you put on your skin and your hair, but the food you eat? Jesus. If I didn't feed you, your entire diet would consist of sugary carbs, protein bars, and ramen noodles."

She frowned, taken aback. She didn't know he had an issue with cooking for her. "You offered. I never asked you to, so if it's a bother—"

"Nic, I'm not complaining. Just making an observation. And it's not a bother. If I'm cooking, I'll make enough for you. Don't I always?"

He did. Which was one of the many reasons why, though the rent was a tad more than she could afford, and her budget was tight, she gladly paid what she did to live there. It had been a wonderful three years, especially since leaving the situation she'd been in for the first two years of her residency. The third time she'd come home from an overnight shift to find some random half-naked dude eating her leftover pizza on the couch was the third time too many.

"Those would be my plans, too, if I had the rich and sexy Benjamin Reed Van Mont waiting for me."

The sleeves of Ben's T-shirt hugged his biceps while the muscles in his back and shoulders bunched as he stirred the pan's contents. Nic swallowed. The scenery was definitely better now than it had been at her old place, too, though this was the first time that particular thought had crossed her mind.

And she didn't like it.

"Uh . . . how was your day?" she asked, attempting to get things back on track.

"Busy." He turned off the stove and covered the pan with a lid. "I met with a potential new client. Someone who recently came into a large amount of money and wants help managing it."

Unlike the others in his family, Ben hadn't gone the medical route. He had his own business; was an in-demand financial advisor who operated a successful boutique investment advisory firm. She respected his initiative. His family had enough money that he could've spent his life living off his trust fund. Instead, he'd worked hard to build something for himself.

Ben pulled down a stemless wineglass, filled it with her favorite sweet red blend, and placed it in front of her.

"Thanks." She took a sip and moaned low in her throat. *So good.* "Sounds kind of boring."

Ben's gaze heated and flicked to her mouth before quickly rebounding away. Her lips tingled, as if aware of the drive-by visual caress.

That moment of intensity had briefly altered his face. Or maybe her perception of it. But in that instant, she could see what Amalia had meant.

Sexy.

He smiled and once again, he was Ben, her friend. "Maybe. To the uninformed."

What the hell? Had she imagined that flash of interest?

He was still talking. "Would it change your mind if I told you the client is the creator behind one of the hottest up-and-coming social media platforms?"

Dammit! Amalia's comment was playing with her head. What she'd seen had clearly been a trick of the light. Everything was fine.

"Really?" She wasn't on social media. Especially after the Baby Boy incident. She barely had time to live her own life. She didn't want to waste it reading about anyone else's. But that didn't stop her from being curious. "Which one?"

"Ahhhh," he said, waving a teasing finger in her face. "Not so boring now, huh?"

She grabbed his finger. "Which one?"

He broke from her hold as easily as if she were a wet tissue, which at six foot one to her five-three, wasn't that difficult. "I can't tell you. It's privileged."

"I'll check with Ava, but I'm pretty sure there isn't such a thing as financial planner–client privilege."

"There is such a thing as confidentiality and

my clients expect that of the person they trust with their personal finances."

He was right. And she should know, since he'd helped her figure out her current budget. She'd flip the fuck out if she thought he was sharing her information with other people.

"Well, you brought it up," she retorted. "Will signing this new client be a burden on your workload?"

He was brilliant when it came to money and his talents could help a lot of people. But he insisted on keeping his company small.

"No, I can handle it. But if I need to cull my list, I know where I can start," he said, displaying a sly smile.

"Don't you dare!"

He laughed and the corners of her mouth tilted up in an automatic response. She couldn't help it. Being with Ben, talking to him—it always made her feel better.

"How was *your* day?"

His query brought back her incident with the intern. She rolled her eyes. "Days like today have me counting down until I leave for Durham."

He frowned. "Why? What happened?"

She braced her elbow on the counter and laid her cheek in her palm. "I had an incident with an intern."

He began plating their food. "There's always those first-year residents who graduate medical school thinking they know everything, not realizing they learn best by keeping their mouths shut and listening."

Ben could give advice on that subject. He was a great listener. He provided a safe space for her to vent with someone who understood what she was going through. She never worried about the politics of talking to him, afraid that her opinion would get back to the wrong people. He kept her confidence, which allowed her to keep her sanity. She shook her head and grabbed the can of pecans on the counter, popping one in her mouth. "Exactly. I keep forgetting you're not a doctor."

He actually shuddered. "Fuck no."

"Hey! That's not nice."

He shrugged. "Doctors aren't nice."

She pursed her lips. "Says the person who isn't one."

"Says the person who's grown up around them his entire life." He poured himself a glass of some dry blend that probably cost more than her entire outfit. Which wasn't saying much, but still . . . "So, what happened?"

"It's not worth getting into, but I handled it." She swallowed another sip of wine. "I can't wait until this is all behind me and I'm focusing solely on sports medicine at Duke. I heard some of the fellows actually get to go to the Carolina Panther football games."

Ben stared at her. "You hate football."

"I know, but the possibility of being on the sidelines if an injury occurs?" She gave him a goofy grin and two thumbs-up.

"You're morbid." Ben scooped the plates off the counter.

"Committed," she corrected him, grabbing their glasses and following him past the marble countertop bar and the gorgeous oak wood farmhouse table in the eat-in kitchen to the large sectional in the living room.

Ben set their plates on the coffee table. "You may need to be."

"Ha. Ha." Nic snagged the remote and aimed it at the large flat-screen TV mounted on the brick accent wall above the fireplace.

He settled next to her on the couch and frowned. "What are you doing?"

She engaged the TV guide, looking for her favorite channel. "It's my turn."

"You can't be serious! The NBA finals are about to start."

"In three days."

"So? I gotta see what the analysts are saying."

"Give me a break. You can watch all of those shows on the ESPN app tomorrow."

"It's not the same," he grumbled. "Fine. But I'm not watching—"

"I've been looking forward to this all day," she said, exhaling in pleasure at the two women on the screen getting into an argument in a restaurant.

Scowling, Ben picked up their plates and stood. She jerked. "Hey! Bring back my food!"

"If I can't watch basketball, you can't watch your housewife show. If you want to eat this dinner, you need to compromise and pick something else."

She narrowed her eyes, annoyance settling in and readying her for battle. But she looked at the food on the plate and her mouth watered. All she'd had time for after her impromptu trip to the ER had been a bag of chips from the vending machine. That had been around noon. Then she'd finished seeing patients in the clinic, scrubbed in to do a surgery, prepped the OR schedule for the following day and . . .

Dammit.

Twisting her lips, she put the channel on HGTV. "Same wager as usual?"

"Yup. The person who picks the winning house doesn't have to do the dishes."

"Can you feed me now?"

Smiling, he sat down and handed her a plate. "My pleasure."

Warmth suffused her body and she stiffened at the unexpected and unwelcome response. That smile. The one that carved crinkles at the corners of his eyes, creased lines in his golden cheeks, and showed off his straight white teeth. *That* smile? For some reason, it was hitting her sweet spot tonight.

Unaware—thankfully—of her sudden confusion, he nudged her shoulder before digging into his food. On the screen, the couple was listening as the Realtor listed off the first home's features.

He scoffed. "Nope. It has a pool. The wife clearly said she didn't want a pool."

Nic pushed her food around her plate, her appetite diminishing in the wake of that brief moment of awareness. She enjoyed spending time with Ben. She worked eighty-hour weeks at the hospital and when she wasn't working, she was usually occupied with studying, research, or preparing for presentations. Residency, and being chief resident, left little time for socializing. When she did come home, Ben always welcomed her with food and his company. Or, if it was really late, he'd leave a plate downstairs for her. It all worked because Ben was her friend, nothing else.

She eyed Ben out of the corner of her eye as he shook his head at something on the screen. It's not as if she *hadn't* thought about it. When they first met, she couldn't deny she'd found his tall fit body, dark curly hair, and rich brown eyes attractive. But it didn't take her long to discover he wasn't her usual brooding, bad boy type. The type that fucked well but sucked at any other interaction. Ben was a good guy.

And good guys wanted good girls. He'd never made a move on her or exhibited any behavior that hinted at a sexual attraction. He watched out for her, took care of her. In the beginning, she hadn't expected this treatment to last. Surely, any woman he was dating wouldn't like him feeding his attractive roommate dinner, no matter their claim of friendship. But in the three years she'd lived here, none of the women had ever interfered. Speaking of . . .

"How's Jennifer?"

Ben's broad shoulders stiffened. "I wouldn't know. We broke up three weeks ago."

"Oh!" Her stomach twisted.

In surprise? Or a recently discovered relief?

Nic had liked Jennifer. Kind of. She'd been better than the others, though the times she'd come over she'd been a bit boring. But Ben seemed to have a type. Like Emily the administrative assistant, who'd thought she'd bake her way into his heart, or Gabby the Pilates instructor, who'd enjoyed reminding Nic of how flexible she was. In the middle of the living room.

Bitchy, much?

Yeah, probably. She'd long ago accepted who she was. But Ben was smart, funny, and capable—she didn't understand his attraction to women who didn't seem . . . challenging.

To each his own, she guessed. At least they were nice. Perfectly fine marriage material, something she knew was important to Ben. Not everyone would have her mindset. She'd put in too much time and money to give it up for a man. She had sex when she wanted it, but she was married to her work.

With effort, she shook off that earlier thirst misstep. She wouldn't let any of that weirdness affect them. Dick came and went, but good friends were a treasure and few and far between. You held on to them, no matter what.

"I'm sorry," she finally said, after a pregnant pause so long it was post term.

"It was for the best."

Since he didn't appear to want to talk about it any more than she did, she returned her attention to her plate. She took a bite, and the delicious flavors reawakened her appetite. When she was done, she put the empty dish on the table and leaned back against the couch, pulling her feet up beneath her.

"That was great, as usual. Thank you."

"No problem. You were clearly hungry."

"Because you probably won't have to wash that plate? Or because you know I barely eat at work?"

"Well, both and because"—he pointed to her head—"you didn't pause to take your hair down."

"You're right. I got sidetracked by my packages and the food."

She gently pulled the elastic from her hair and immediately sighed, closing her eyes as the weight of her ringlets was released from her head and fell around her shoulders. She dug the pads of her fingers in and began massaging her scalp, grateful for the reprieve. She didn't even try to contain her moans of relief. When she opened her eyes, she found Ben staring at her, the muscle in his upper jaw twitching.

"What?" She let her hand fall from her hair.

He started and cleared his throat, pink tinging his cheekbones. "Nothing."

That earlier trace of awareness skittered through her again. Was she horny? She'd been flirting with an anesthesiology resident, and one night when they'd both been on call they'd made use of one of the on-call rooms to scratch that particular itch. When had that been? She thought back. It was before she'd gone on vacation, there had been snow on the ground . . .

Good Lord, it had been six months!

Damn.

Maybe that explained why she was suddenly thinking about Ben in a way she shouldn't.

He leaned an arm along the top edge of the sofa and they continued watching the show, shouting out comments and suggestions as the couple visited the final two houses. In the end, the couple picked the first house.

"What the fuck? She said she didn't want a pool," Ben said, picking up their plates and carrying them into the kitchen.

Nic snuggled back against the cushions. "But it had the best master bedroom suite. That walk-in closet was incredible."

"When's your next day off?"

She yawned. "I'm on call tomorrow, so Thursday."

"You have any plans?"

Why did her eyelids suddenly feel as if they weighed fifty pounds each? "Gotta finish up my presentation on osteochondroma."

"What's that?"

"Benign bone tumors," she said, exhaling as the sofa welcomed her into its plushy depths. God, it had been a long day.

"Are you listening to me?"

Hadn't she just responded to him? She'd told him what osteochondroma meant. "Uh-huh."

"What was the last thing I said?"

Nic wanted to respond, but exhaustion arrived on an express train, offering her first-class accommodations and ready to drag her down into slumber. The last thing she remembered as she succumbed to mindless fatigue was being covered with a comfy throw, her curls gently brushed off her face.

Chapter Four

Ben scanned the list of dependents displayed on his computer screen. It was part of his intake questionnaire, the form he had potential clients fill out with information about their income, assets, expenses, and other finances.

"Is this real? There are more than ten names on here. You can't take care of everyone."

The large black man sitting on the other side of Ben's desk exhaled an audible breath and shook his head. "They never listen."

The words were uttered so low, Ben wasn't sure if he'd imagined them. "Excuse me?"

"I'm not trying to take care of everyone. These people are important to me."

"If you're going to spend like this, there isn't a financial planner alive who can help you hold on to your money until your next contract, let alone retirement."

Quentin "Q-Ball" Miller had been picked early in the first round of the NFL draft. His rookie contract was projected to be thirty million over four years with nineteen five guaranteed. That

was life-changing money. Money that, if managed properly, could be the basis for a genera-
tional wealth shift. And yet Quentin had just
given him a list of ten people he wanted to immediately cut checks to. In large amounts.

Quentin straightened and looked at him, the
smiling face and charming persona he'd shown
throughout his collegiate football career notice-
ably absent. Instead, his dark eyes were flat, the
angles of his face sharp. "This isn't going to work
out."

Ben nodded. "If that's how you feel."

"It is. I've worked hard for this money. Sacrificed time, relationships. My body. My health.
I have to be careful who I trust my finances
with. Mr. Ashford said you might be that person,
but . . ."

Quentin shook his head and stood, his six-
five, two-hundred-forty-pound frame an obvious
giveaway to his position as a wide receiver on
the football field. They'd attended the same prep
school—though over a decade apart—and Ben's
old guidance counselor had reached out to him
and asked if he could offer the young man some
advice on his upcoming contract.

Ben rose from his chair and held out his hand.
"When you find someone who does work, let me
know and I can forward your file to them. Or, I
can have Ezra put everything together and send
it to you."

"The latter," Quentin said. He briskly shook
Ben's hand, efficiently maneuvered between the

two chairs situated in front of the desk—a mini display of what he could do on the field—and left the office.

Ben shoved a hand through his hair. This was why he'd made the decision to not handle athletes. The player who came from a background of poverty, made a lot of money, and blew it all before the end of his first contract, filing for bankruptcy within ten years of retiring was a cliché because it was true. He'd seen it time and time again. Sure, the lump sum sounded like a lot of money. It *was* a lot of money. But once you deducted half for federal and state income taxes and another ten to twenty percent to handlers, the rest could go quickly due to lack of planning and unsustainable lifestyles.

And unlike athletes in other sports, football players had a shorter playing window. Quentin had only two to three years to prove himself to his team and the league, to get a second contract that would definitely take care of him forever. The more he gave to his mother, cousins, and friends, the less he'd have to live on for himself.

Ezra, his assistant, came into his office. "That sounded intense."

Ben exhaled and retook his seat, leaning back and staring at the ceiling. "It was."

"I don't understand." Ezra's brows strained to meet despite the ridge between them. "Athletes talk. If you did a great job for Q-Ball, he'd tell his teammates and associates. With as many professional teams as there are in this region, you could have a nice practice area managing players. Instead you let him walk. Why?"

In his experience, dealing with athletes was never fun. Their egos made them nightmare clients. Add to that an unwillingness to learn about money, a disrespect for him, and a resistance to his ideas and he hadn't met one he was willing to break his rule for.

He'd thought Quentin was different.

He shook off the dissenting thought. It didn't matter. The idea of being inundated with athletes, as Ezra had mentioned, and expanding his business beyond what he could handle was the reason he hadn't fought to make the football player his client.

Ezra braced an arm on the back of a chair. "Analysts are saying he's the steal of the draft. He's going to make an immediate impact."

"I hope so. I really liked him." Ben motioned to the iPad on his desk. "That's his information. Can you forward everything to him?"

"Will do," Ezra said, grabbing the tablet.

Ben collapsed back, replete with gratitude for the many tasks he no longer had to perform. Ezra was working on his MBA at the University of Baltimore. Ben had hired him part-time when the administrative work began to take time away from the actual work he needed to do on behalf of his clients.

Ezra's phone rang and he hurried out to his desk. "Reed Financial Services . . ."

Ben swiveled in his chair and gazed out at the

Inner Harbor. From this height in Baltimore's World Trade Center, the colorful boats that dotted the water looked like toys, the tourists and residents strolling the plazas resembled insects. It was a gorgeous view and one of the main reasons he leased the space for his offices.

In the past five years, he'd turned an urgent desire to leave Van Mont Industries—his family's business—into a thriving boutique financial planning firm that provided him a great living, while not having to rely on the money he received from the Van Mont family trust. He could've chosen from numerous offers, but his comotivation for leaving was freedom. He'd spent years immersed in his family's drama, where fourteen-hour days and a nonexistent social life were the norm. He wasn't keen to cede control of his life to total strangers; to trade one type of dysfunction for another.

His parents had vehemently opposed his decision, but then, being on the receiving end of their disappointment wasn't a novel experience for him.

"What do you mean you don't want to go to medical school? Are you insane? Your father's a doctor. I'm a doctor. Medicine is in your genes."

"You're choosing to leave a prestigious business empire your family has cultivated for over one hundred years for a little financial start-up? All this time, your mother and I must've been wrong about your intellectual aptitude."

But Ben had made up his mind, knew the split was in his best interests if he ever wanted to have a family.

And there's nothing he wanted more.

Not a family like the one he'd had growing up, with parents who were either engrossed in their demanding careers, leaving him to be raised by nannies and housekeepers or, when they deigned to come home, preoccupied with outdoing one another with tales of their medical genius. No, he wanted more for his children than the manic display he'd witnessed and survived. He couldn't wait to show them the unconditional love he'd never experienced.

Unexpectedly, an image of Nic crashing on the sofa last night surfaced in his mind. In repose, the lines, furrows, and aura of toughness faded away, leaving a loveliness one might mistake as fragile. She'd fallen asleep so quickly he'd known she must be exhausted. In her fifth and final year of residency, she had a lot to shoulder. But he had no doubt she could handle it all, even excel. She was one of the smartest, hardest-working women he knew. She was also one of the most beautiful. A fact that hadn't escaped his notice when she'd dropped by to inquire about the basement apartment he had for rent.

Since his row home was close to Johns Hopkins Hospital, he'd expected to get flooded with applications from med school students and young physicians. Their long hours, awareness of his last name, and steady employment made them ideal roommates, even if they weren't people he'd want to socialize with.

When he'd opened the door, a shocking pain had flared in his chest, as if an invisible force had punched into the cavity and gripped his heart, giving it a squeeze for good measure. She was stunning. Pale, creamy skin, and mounds of caramel-colored coils and curls that tumbled to just beneath her shoulders and gave her an energy and intensity that made her appear more imposing than she actually was. Then he'd noticed the look in her mesmerizing green eyes and his burgeoning interest shriveled on the vine. That same arrogance and certainty saturated his parents' expressions and declared her a doctor before she'd ever introduced herself.

That made her off-limits. No matter how gorgeous, smart, and funny he'd eventually found her, people with demanding careers—especially doctors—made the worst type of parent. He'd experienced it firsthand. And it wasn't something he was willing to subject his future children to.

But allowing her to rent his apartment had been a wise decision. She was a good roommate and a better friend. She was loyal to those she cared about and honest to a fault. She listened without judgment and accepted him for who he was as a person and not by his last name. Not to mention they always had fun spending time together at home. He stood by his choice to keep things platonic, but it hadn't been easy. And he was going to miss her when she left for Durham.

Ezra knocked on the door and stuck his head in. "You don't need to worry about losing Q-Ball as a client! That was April Ingham's rep. April heard you'd signed the co-creators of the Celeb-Link app and she wants to come in for a meeting."

Adrenaline coursed through him, lifting his lips into a shocked, but pleased, smile. Handling April Ingham's finances would be a major coup for any firm. Her family had made their fortune in oil, but, like him, she'd trod her own path. She'd gotten involved in the fashion industry as an early influencer—a term he couldn't believe was an actual job!—and now ruled a billion-dollar empire.

Ezra frowned. "I wonder how she heard about CelebLink? You just finalized the deal yesterday."

"It's a small world," Ben murmured.

It was true. Inhabitants of a certain tax bracket might not know each other personally, but they all ran in the same circles. Seven degrees of the insanely wealthy. The Rockefellers may not know the Johnsons but they knew the same people. If one wanted to contact the other, it could happen in a matter of minutes. It wouldn't surprise Ben to learn that April knew the co-founders of the social media app.

"Why aren't you more excited? If you land her account, you will up your portfolio by several hundred million dollars! You'd better start hiring now," Ezra said, drumming his hands against the wall. "You're going to need a full-time assistant and more staff to handle that amount of funds. And, just like with the athletes, if it's such a small world as you claim . . ."

Ben would be introduced to a new pool of impressive clients with which to grow his business.

Dread sank like an anchor in his stomach, inhibiting his earlier elation.

"I'll find an opening in your schedule and set up the meeting with Ingham's team for the week after you return from Martha's Vineyard."

"No."

"Oh. Do you want me to fit them in *before* you leave?"

He'd managed an entire department of finance executives, as well as handled his own multi-million- and billion-dollar accounts at Van Mont Industries, and the work had consumed his existence. He'd left because he'd wanted more for his life, like getting married, starting a family and being present in his children's lives. How could he hope to achieve that if he allowed his business to expand beyond its current comfortable confines?

"Thank April's team for their interest but alert them we're not accepting any new clients."

Ezra's incredulity was meme worthy. "She owns one of the hottest fashion companies in the world. Adding it to our portfolio is a no-brainer."

"I'm not interested in growing this business for growth's sake."

"You've taken this company as far as you can

on your own. You should hire more people and expand. You can train them, make sure they share your perspective and way of operating. There aren't a lot of finance professionals who have your vision. Or who care about more than just making money at any cost. You could help so many people. Why does growth have to be a bad thing?"

It didn't. For most business owners, growth on that scale would be a dream scenario. But he wasn't most business owners. He didn't want to take his company to the next level. He wouldn't be like his parents, prioritizing his job over having a family. No, he was fine with Reed Financial Services the way it was.

Profitable. Manageable. Prudent.

Chapter Five

Ben was still mulling over Ezra's words several hours later at home when his doorbell rang. Engaging his home's smart app, he rolled his eyes at the devilish, grinning face of his best friend, Davis Yates. Striding from his home office, he crossed the living room and kitchen and descended the short staircase to open the front door. "Look what the cat dragged to B-more!"

"Benji!" Davis held up his curved palm and Ben took it, pulling the other man in and slapping him on the back. "How's it going?"

Ben winced at the dreaded nickname, but let it slide. "I'm good. You?"

"I can't complain. Well, I could, but no one would give a fuck."

"Truer words . . ." Motioning for Davis to enter, Ben waited for the other man to pick up the duffel at his feet, before closing the door behind him. "Dude, you're always welcome to my guest room when your latest kicks you out, but it's a long way from New York."

"Ha. Ha. I had a meeting with a few lawmakers in DC. Thought I'd stop by to see one of my best friends on my way back home."

Ben wasn't fooled by the calm tone or the considerate words. Especially because Davis wasn't known for either trait. Davis was loyal, charming and always down for a good time, but one didn't go to him looking for comfort.

That was Ben's forte.

He turned and headed up the stairs knowing Davis would follow. "You want a drink?"

"Hell yeah. I always need to take the edge off after dealing with fucking politicians."

Ben laughed and headed into the kitchen. "I guess water's out. Beer, wine, bourbon, or tequila?"

Davis leaned an elbow on the counter. "Yes."

It was barely five thirty. Knowing he had a couple hours of work ahead of him and Davis still needed to travel home, Ben opened the fridge and grabbed a local brew. He popped the top off the bottle and handed it to Davis.

"Should've known you'd play it safe. Join me?"

Ben grabbed one for himself and leaned back against the island, crossing his feet at the ankle.

Davis took a long pull. "I needed that." He cleared his throat then loosened his tie while surveying the space. "I haven't visited since you moved. This is much nicer than the place you had in Annapolis. Bigger, too."

"Thanks." Ben studied Davis, noting the way he pulled on his ear, scratched his shadowed jaw, and fidgeted with the bottle's label. "Why are you *really* here?"

"I told you, it was on my way—"

"Bullshit. I'm seeing you next week, so this little detour wasn't necessary."

"So, you *are* planning on coming?"

"Of course. Why would you doubt it?"

He exhaled. "Because my mother spoke to your mother, who didn't know you were going to be on the Vineyard."

Fuck! Ben shoved a hand through his hair. He kept communication and contact with his family to a minimum. "What am I, fifteen? My parents don't need to know my comings and goings. There was never a question about me being there next week."

"I hope not. Palmer and Bronwen would be upset if you didn't show. It'll be a while before we're all in the same room again."

Which was why Ben wasn't going to miss this trip. He, Davis, and Palmer had known each other since they were children, their parents having all met while vacationing with their families during the season on Martha's Vineyard. Palmer had met Bronwen in college and it wasn't long before they were a package deal.

In two weeks, Palmer and Bronwen were both traveling across the world for three years to head up bridge and water projects, respectively, through Engineers Without Borders.

"I don't understand this need you have to ignore your family. You already separated from the business and proved you can be a success on your own. What purpose does it serve to keep them ignorant of your life?"

"Dealing with my parents is like engaging in a game of mental chess. It's tiring and I refuse to play any longer."

"But they're the only parents you have. My parents have their issues, but these past few years, I've noticed they're not as invincible as I thought. Especially my dad." Davis lifted a shoulder. "I know you. You'd be gutted if you didn't settle the discord between you while you still had the chance."

He appreciated Davis's perspective, but they'd had different experiences growing up. Despite their issues with each other, in the eyes of the Yateses, Davis could do no wrong. Ben's parents believed wrong was all their son did.

"So"—Davis trailed his fingers in the condensation streaming off his beer bottle—"are you still seeing that preschool teacher?"

Jennifer?

Hadn't Nic asked about her, too?

He'd met Jennifer at the gym. She was pretty and sweet, and he'd enjoyed being with her. In the beginning. Though she'd possessed many of the characteristics he was looking for in a wife and partner, he'd had to admit he'd begun finding her company . . . unstimulating. When he'd realized he preferred staying home to meeting her at the ballpark, or the aquarium, or the museum, he'd known it was time to end things.

"No. We broke up a few weeks ago."

And she'd taken it with the same graciousness she'd exhibited the entire time they'd dated. What was wrong with him? Jennifer was the type of woman he wanted to be with.

Then why weren't you still together?

"Is there anyone else you're spending time with?" Davis pressed.

His mind spun through a roulette wheel of images and quickly settled on Nic. He preferred spending time with her more than anyone else, but Davis's question seemed to imply something beyond the scope of friendship. Which wouldn't describe him and Nic. The more Ben thought about it, the more he realized their association was contained within these four walls. Granted, she didn't have a lot of free time, but as far as anyone outside of this house was concerned, their friendship didn't exist.

He kneaded a spot on his chest to ease the sudden tightness. "No."

"You're single, then?" Davis confirmed, his innocent expression incongruous with the sharp planes and angles of his face.

Ben narrowed his eyes. *What the—*

He straightened and deliberately placed his beer on the counter behind him. "What's going on?"

"Nothing."

He wasn't buying it. "If you don't spill, I will post the picture of you on the beach wearing that lime green Borat mankini."

Davis scoffed. "You don't have that picture."

He was right, but . . . "How do you know? Are you willing to risk it?"

Davis tilted his head. "You wouldn't."

Ben didn't flinch. "Try me."

Davis's icy blue eyes—the feature women seventeen to seventy had deemed "dreamy"—widened.

In their group of friends, Ben was the keeper of the peace, the ringmaster of resolutions. He wasn't one for seeking out conflict or making waves. He was even-keeled, easygoing.

Until he wasn't.

They stared at each other for several long drawn-out moments. Ben almost expected to hear an ominous twanging instrumental score followed by the sight of tumbleweed drifting across the room.

Davis broke first.

"Damn you! Sometimes I think you're a fucking robot!" He sighed. "I don't know the specifics, but Bronwen invited Tinsley."

Ben closed his eyes and squeezed the bridge of his nose between his thumb and index finger.

Fuck.

Tinsley was the girl everyone thought he should marry, and, for a time, he'd agreed. She was from a prominent New England family and like him, she had certain ideas about what her future would look like. Unfortunately, her picture of her future hadn't been with someone who'd left their family's guaranteed fortune and struck out, unpredictably, on their own.

"Jesus Christ! You're a Van Mont! Why would you give that up to start over?"

She'd broken off their engagement a month after he'd opened his business, informing him she had no interest in "struggling."

"And Palmer didn't say anything?" His friend had to know how Ben would feel about this development.

Davis waved off his words. "What was Palmer going to say?"

Not much.

Palmer adored Bronwen. Had from the moment he'd seen her long dark ponytail streaming out behind her on the lacrosse field. If she wanted Tinsley to come, Palmer would make it happen.

And why shouldn't he? Ben and Davis weren't the couple's only friends. It wasn't Ben's place to curate Palmer's guest list. But dammit! A week in a house on Martha's Vineyard with his ex was not Ben's idea of fun.

"Are you still in love with her?" Davis asked.

"No."

Had he *ever* been in love with her? He'd thought so. She was beautiful, cultured and well-traveled. She'd wanted to get married and have children. *And* his parents had approved of her.

Wholeheartedly.

"Are you sure? Because she seems to think you are."

Ben jerked back. "What did she say?"

"She told Bronwen you asked her out when the two of you ran into each other in Manhattan."

Ben wanted to grind his teeth. This is what he was afraid of. Tinsley wasn't interested in just celebrating her friends. Not when she could stir up mischief, too. His ex loved drama, would create it for herself even if none was present.

"It wasn't in Manhattan. I saw her when I went skiing in Vail with Rick and Hunter."

"I remember that trip! I was going to crash it but I ended up having to go to London."

"It was the first time I'd seen her since we'd broken up the year before. I didn't want things to be awkward, so I invited her to have dinner with a group of us, hoping we'd be able to get along. She agreed but bailed at the last minute."

Typical Tinsley move.

Drama.

When they'd been together, that particular stunt had usually been followed by Ben searching her out and convincing her to spend time with him. Sometimes the convincing took an hour or more and when she eventually conceded—as she always did—she'd make it seem as if she'd generously granted him a favor. Looking back on it, he realized that dealing with Tinsley had been just as tiring as dealing with his parents. Maybe that's why he'd stayed with her so long.

The dysfunction had felt familiar.

"She seems to have regretted that action," Davis said.

Ha! Because she hadn't gotten the response she'd wanted. He hadn't chased after her.

"All she could talk about during her lunch with

Bronwen was your business and how well it was doing."

"I was raised to expect a certain standard of living, Ben. Now you want me to live beneath that? When I don't have to?"

He flicked a glance skyward. "Not interested."

"Then good luck. Tinsley was always ruthless when it came to getting her way."

He gestured palm up toward Davis. "I'll hang out with you. You can be my reverse wingman."

"Yeah, about that . . ." Davis grimaced and pawed a hand through the hair at his nape.

"You're bringing someone?"

It had never occurred to him to ask. Bringing a date for the week seemed to imply more commitment than Davis had ever seemed interested in exhibiting before. Not a surprise considering his parents' acrimonious divorce when Davis was a teenager and his father's subsequent multiple marriages.

"Yeah. Sabine."

Davis and Sabine had been hooking up casually for the past few years. According to Davis, it was an arrangement that worked well for them.

"Wait. Everyone will be boo'd up?"

Except him.

And Tinsley.

Maybe he could fly out and surprise Palmer and Bronwen in Fiji . . .

Davis pointed at him. "I can see your brain working. Don't you dare back out now. Why don't *you* bring someone?"

"For what?"

"To discourage Tinsley!"

"You think that'll work?"

"No, but it'll be better than if you show up alone."

When had his life turned into some teenage rom-com? That wasn't him. He didn't like playing games.

"I'm not dating anyone."

"It doesn't have to be serious. You're rich, good-looking. It shouldn't be hard to find someone who'd be willing to spend a week with you in a beachfront house on the Vineyard." Davis glanced at his watch. "My train leaves Penn Station at seven thirty. Let me hit the bathroom and then you can treat me to dinner at the Capital Grille before you drive me to the station."

"What if I had plans?"

"Do you really want me to answer that?"

Ben shook his head and laughed. "Fine. There's a half bath back near the door."

Davis loped off and Ben searched for his phone and keys. He was slipping into his shoes when the front door opened, and the heavy tread of footfalls running up the wooden stairs thundered through the space.

"Ben!" Nic's husky tone was brimming with anger. She rushed into the kitchen, dressed in black tapered pants and a white collared shirt, her cheeks flushed and her eyes flashing as they skittered around the room.

He'd never seen Nic look so totally out of control. "What's wrong? I thought you were on call tonight. Are you okay?"

"You won't believe what that little fucker did! He ran to his daddy! And now they've sent me home while they look into the 'situation,'" she said, curving her index and middle fingers in the air.

"Hold up." He gripped her upper arms to still her incessant pacing. "What are you talking about? Who's the little fucker?"

She continued as if he hadn't spoken. "There was nothing inappropriate about my actions. And they want to take that intern's side over mine? I've never heard of that. Ever!"

She was talking so fast—frustration swamped him. How could he help her if he didn't understand what happened?

"Slow down, Nic. Please. It'll be okay."

"No! It won't!" She pulled away from him. "I did the right thing. Whitaker deserved to be reprimanded. And to think I hesitated to write him up, considered the ramifications on his career, and that motherfucker went and reported me!" As hot as she'd burned, she suddenly cooled, her shoulders slumped, and her chin trembled. "I've worked so hard to get where I am and I'm damn good at my job. Doesn't that count for anything?"

Without a second thought, he opened his arms and Nic stepped into them. She gripped his T-shirt in her fists and rested her forehead against his chest. Her trim body shook and he hugged her close, hating her distress and wishing he could take it on himself.

However, even in the midst of consoling her, he couldn't help but acknowledge how great she felt against him, fitting him perfectly, like a newly found puzzle piece. The faint scent of honeysuckle teased his nose and he inhaled, drawing in her fragrance.

"What's this froufrou lotion in the bath— Well, well, well. What do we have here?" A grinch-like smile creased Davis's face. "Benji, I thought you said you weren't dating anyone."

Dammit.

Nic froze in his embrace and then jerkily, as if some invisible being was controlling her movements, she backed away and turned to face Davis. Her eyes narrowed and she tilted her head to the side, staring up and down at his friend, as if assessing him. Curling her lip, she jammed her hands on her hips.

"*Benji,*" she said, placing special emphasis on the nickname, "who in the hell is this and why is he using my expensive, specially ordered castanha oil hand cream?"

Chapter Six

*N*ic stalked up and down the space in her apartment, her blood simmering beneath her skin. She still couldn't get past the idea that an intern had gone over her head to the attending and *she'd* been the one chastised! Especially because she'd been absolutely within her right to reprimand Whitaker.

It was infuriating!

Disagreements between interns and senior residents happened, and in the medical hierarchy, the senior resident's word ruled. The same would be true if there had been a dispute between a resident and an attending. Legally, the attending physician was in charge of a patient's care, so if they opposed a medical decision she made, she'd have no choice but to defer to their opinion.

But this hadn't been a dispute over a plan of treatment. Whitaker hadn't given the proper care to a patient and she'd called him on it. And for her trouble, she'd been blindsided by some bullshit power play where she hadn't been informed of the rules.

Nic clenched her fist so tightly, her short nails dug into her palms. What she wouldn't give for a good surgery. The mental focus required along with the physical exertion of tool usage usually settled her spirit.

But thanks to Whitaker, it would be a while before she'd be in the OR again. And definitely not an OR at Hopkins.

When the attending physician had called and stated he'd wanted to see her, she'd been slightly annoyed. She didn't have the time for the unscheduled meeting and, if she were honest, she and this particular attending had never gotten along.

She'd headed up to the fifth floor, her mind on the rest of her duties more than the impending meeting.

She knocked on his door. "You wanted to see—"

Dr. Nigel Agner held up a finger to indicate she should wait as he continued perusing something on his computer screen. After two minutes, she considered turning around and leaving, but he pressed a button on his keyboard, minimizing the screen, and finally giving her his full attention. Agner considered himself a gentleman physician, from his hard side part and comb-over, to his bow tie, suspenders, and monogrammed initials followed by "MD" on his shirt cuff.

He stared at her, his pale eyes giving nothing away. "Thanks for stopping by, Dr. Allen. I heard you had an issue with one of your interns yesterday."

She nodded. "I wouldn't say it was an issue. But I did have to talk to Whitaker about how he handled a case."

"And you didn't think I should be called in?"

Nic pursed her lips. "No. Whitaker took a consult and failed to conduct a basic shoulder examination just so he could attend a lumbar spinal fusion. I reprimanded him as warranted and moved on."

Agner braced his forearms on his chair. "I received a complaint regarding your handling of the case."

Shock slackened her facial muscles. "From whom?"

"Doesn't matter. But you need to know we're going to look into this situation further."

She forced herself to remain calm. "My behavior wasn't inappropriate or out of line. I've dealt with similar situations before."

His jaw tightened. "Well, this time was different."

"Why?"

"Because this time you admonished the son of one of our regular charitable donors!"

His ragged breath was audible, and splotches of color materialized on his cheeks. He ran his hands down the front of his shirt as if the motion would decrease the cortisol surging through his system.

It did dick all for her own stress level.

She wanted to scream! If any other intern had made this mistake, and Nic had done the exact same thing, she wouldn't even be here. Why should it matter that Whitaker was the son of a hospital donor?

"Look," he said, his tone unexpectedly weary and his starched posture drooping, "you're a great doctor, Allen. Truly gifted. But success isn't based on talent alone. I don't doubt you were in the right, but we need to appease this donor. We can't be seen as taking his concerns lightly."

She tried to swallow past the dread obstructing her throat. "What're you going to do?"

"Whitaker rotates off your service in two weeks. I want to eliminate the possibility of any interaction between the two of you. So . . . take that time off."

Was he serious?

She was right. Whitaker was wrong. Yet he was being allowed to stay and she . . . she was being exiled from doing the thing she loved most in the world.

How was that fucking fair?

Agner's parting shot, "Consider it an extended vacation before your residency ends," almost sent her through the roof.

When she'd left Agner's office, Whitaker had been standing nearby with a couple of other interns, a smirk creasing his entitled face.

Walk away, Nic. He isn't worth it.

But her feet weren't in the mood to do what was reasonable. "If you think you've pulled some boss move here, you're wrong."

"Not so tough now, huh?" He jerked his chin

upward. "I guess all it takes is getting that ass chewed out."

Like henchmen extras in a bad action movie, the group surrounding him laughed.

Nic turned her attention to them. "Are *your* last names Whitaker? Then you might want to think twice about adopting his behaviors. I doubt his father will bail *you* out when you get in trouble. In fact, like most people who're drowning, he'll drag you down to save himself."

Their amusement faded and they blinked, sliding considering looks at each other and Whitaker.

"Accept defeat, Nicole," Whitaker sneered, the disrespectful use of her name instead of her title hitting its mark, as he'd no doubt intended. "You're too pretty to be so bitter. Though, if you want to slip into the on-call room for a minute, I've got something that'll calm you down."

She actually threw up in her mouth a little. Yeah, a minute was probably an accurate accounting of time.

"You're an asshole. And you've just shown every doctor and nurse here that you're a spoiled little dick who went crying to Daddy when things didn't go his way. No one will want to work with you. They will, because this little stunt ensured it. But it'll be from obligation, not desire." She curled her lip in disgust and eyed him from head to toe. "Of course, men like you never understand the difference."

Squeezing her eyes shut to block out the memory, Nic sank down on her couch and allowed the soft microfiber to cushion her as she slid her fingers into her curls and clutched her skull. The feeling of uselessness engulfed her, adding to the turbulent mixture of her emotions. She stood by her handling of the situation, but because this kid came from a connected family, *she* was being punished? The patient could've died, and Whitaker still failed to understand that.

Or maybe he understood, but he didn't care.

Nic remembered the first time she'd actually gathered the courage to speak the words she'd held close to her heart for years:

"I want to go to college, and I want to be a doctor."

It hadn't been an easy road. She'd been constantly bombarded by images and messages that led her to believe that goal wasn't achievable. That someone like her—black, female, poor, raised by a single mother—could never amount to anything that prestigious. But she'd worked her ass off in high school, college, med school, and beyond. She'd put her head down and moved forward against the almost constant barrage of doubt, skepticism, and hostility.

"I think you're reaching, dear. That's a nice dream, but maybe you should try to be more realistic."

"Just because you have an advantage getting in med school doesn't mean you should be there."

"Are you sure you don't want to go into peds or obstetrics/gynecology?"

She'd fought against those words, and all the others like them, intent on proving she was good enough. That she could make it. And she'd be damned if she didn't. The cost of the gamble had been too high for her to fail.

The sting of tears burned Nic's eyes as she grabbed her phone.

Her mother answered on the second ring, her image alarmingly close on Nic's screen. Dee Allen was still a strikingly beautiful woman, with light brown skin and dark eyes, though years of anxiety and hard work had taken their toll, causing lines to fan out from her eyes and brackets to deepen around her mouth. "Nicole!"

Nic was warmed by the pleasure in her mother's voice. "Hey, Mom."

"How's my brilliant doctor daughter? Working hard?"

No one was more responsible for Nic's often-praised work ethic than her mother.

"Trying to," she muttered. At Dee's slight frown, Nic cleared her throat. "Do me a favor? Move the phone down. I don't need to check you for nasal polyps."

Dee laughed and adjusted the phone so that her entire face and neck were visible. "Better?"

"It'll do. How are you?"

"Wonderful, now that I'm talking to you."

Nic smiled. Everyone deserved a mother like Dee. She never shied away from showing her pride and unconditional love for her daughter.

But Nic didn't let that distract her from what she was seeing. "Are you okay? You look exhausted."

Dee's eyes flickered. "That's a nice thing to say to the woman who gave birth to you."

"I'm serious. You need to take care of yourself."

"So am I. And I'm fine."

"If I call Mr. Harrison down at the diner, what will he say?"

"If he has sense, he'll stay out of it." Dee huffed out a breath and her curls, so like Nic's own, except liberally laced with strands of silver, fluttered in the air. "Okay. I worked two weeks straight. But I'll get a few days off soon."

Guilt exploded in Nic's chest. Her mother had been grinding for as long as Nic could remember. Dee had given up her own scholarship to college when she'd gotten pregnant with Nic because Nic's father had professed his love and promised to take care of her. He'd left when Nic was ten years old.

"I'm sorry, Mom."

"Don't you start," Dee warned, her features and tone hardening.

"I'm not," she protested weakly.

"Yes, you are. I know this song by heart. 'Maybe I should've stayed in Covington,'" her mother said, in an annoyingly accurate imitation of Nic, "'and taken that job with social services.'"

Nic closed her eyes and massaged her forehead. The idea that she'd been selfish by insisting on pursuing her dream to become a doctor, even as her mother continued to struggle, plagued her.

"Since I was little, you've always worked at least two jobs to support us."

"Because I'm your mother. That's what I'm supposed to do."

And as a daughter, wasn't it Nic's responsibility to give back to her mom? To show her respect and gratitude? To not make things harder for her?

"I just hate the thought of you laboring so hard for almost thirty years. You deserve a break."

"And you think if you'd stayed here I would've had one? Instead of bragging about my daughter the doctor while shopping at Goodwill, we both would've been there." Dee tilted her head. "I would've been fine with that if *you* would've been content. But you wouldn't have been."

Dee was right. If her mother had asked her to stay, Nic would've. But she never would've been happy.

"What's going on?" Dee asked. The camera shifted and Nic could see the faded cream-and-floral fabric of her mother's favorite pillow top recliner. And gracing the otherwise bare walls behind her? Nic's framed college and med school diplomas. "It's been a while since you've brought up this concern. I think the last time you worried if you'd made the right decision was during your first year of residency after medical school."

Nic managed to laugh through the fog of hurt in her chest. "I can't believe you remember that?"

On Nic's first day, the chief resident had given her four patients to see before rounds. She was no longer a medical student. She'd been a doctor, the one making the decisions. The awesome responsibility had floored her. She'd taken too long to go through their files, not wanting to miss any detail that might make a difference. As a result, her presentations had been long, rambling, and barely coherent.

Dee shook her head, a tender smile brightening her face. "You were so worried they'd kick you out for making a mistake."

And that she would've let her mother down. Over Nic's objections, Dee had worked to cover any college expenses not covered by scholarships and financial aid. The heft of all Nic owed—more than the hundreds of thousands of dollars of med school loans—had weighed heavily on her shoulders.

"So what is it?" Dee pressed. "You know you can tell me anything, even if I don't completely understand it."

Nic swallowed. Despite what her mother claimed, she wasn't going to drop this worry on her. Two weeks, and she wouldn't have to deal with Whitaker or his father. She'd be on her way to her fellowship at Duke and one year closer to fulfilling her lifelong dream.

"It's nothing. I just miss you."

"I miss you, too, honey. And I'll see you soon."

That's right! Her mother was coming to her residency graduation ceremony in three weeks.

Nic inhaled a fortifying breath. This is what she'd needed; a reminder of why she'd pushed herself, why she had to succeed despite Whitakershaped roadblocks in her path. Pretty soon, her mother would never have to work another day in her life. Nic would take care of her, the way Dee had always taken care of her daughter.

"I'm looking forward to it."

Tears pooled in Dee's eyes. "Have I told you lately how proud I am of you?"

Only a few dozen times . . . in the last month.

"Thanks, Mom." A thought suddenly occurred to Nic. "Why don't you take some more time off and stay after the graduation? You can go down to Duke with me, see where I'll be working, help me settle in. Like our own mini vacay in Durham."

Her mother's brows rose. "Really?"

"Yeah. It'll be fun."

Nic couldn't think of anyone she'd rather share that experience with. And maybe she'd do a better job of convincing her mother to move to Durham. The job opportunities there had to be better than what she was doing in Covington. And she'd be close, so Nic could keep an eye on her. Make sure she was doing okay.

Dee rubbed her chin. "I'll have to look at my bills after I get paid next week. If I pay half on the electric, they won't cut it off. Then I can put aside a little extra for the next few weeks to pay the extra next month. It wouldn't hurt to not get my morning coffee from the cafe for a little while . . ."

Her mother's voice trailed off and Nic knew she was playing a round of "bill bingo" in her mind.

She remembered it well from growing up. Had done it herself during college and med school to survive on as little money from her mother as possible.

"I could pick up an extra shift at the diner or a few more houses to clean . . ."

Nic's stomach squeezed as her mother strategized how to afford a trip.

While she went away with her friends to fabulous places every year.

"Don't worry, Mom. I'll cover the trip and give you extra to cover what you'll lose in income."

"You don't need to do that, honey."

Yes, she did.

"I know. But I'll do it anyway."

Dee laughed. "That should've been your middle name."

"Excuse me?"

"Nicole 'I'll do it anyway' Allen. When you were three, you almost pulled the bookcase down on top of you because you kept crawling up it to get the toy I hid from you. When you were nine, you climbed to the top of the monkey bars even though I forbid it after you fell the first time—"

"And when I was eighteen, I decided to go to college and med school, instead of staying home to help you."

"Nic—"

A brief knock had her swinging a startled gaze over to find Ben standing in her doorway, a glass of wine in his hand, his dark hair disheveled in that way that told her he'd raked his fingers through it repeatedly. He started to back away, but she shook her head.

"I have to go."

"Okay. I'll see you soon. I love you, Nicole. I'm so proud of you."

Number thirty-seven.

"I know. And I love you."

Ben entered her space after she disconnected the call. "I thought you'd need this."

"I do. Thanks."

She took the glass and when her fingers grazed his, it drew her attention to his hand. As a surgeon, she spent a lot of time studying people's hands. An occupational hazard. Ben's palms were large, his fingers long and slim with blunt-tipped ends. They looked strong and capable, like they could dribble a basketball, suture a cut . . .

. . . or bring a woman to pleasure with a few well-placed strokes.

What the hell?

"Are you okay?" Ben asked. "Did I interrupt something?"

She tilted her head at his pinched expression. "No. Why?"

"You're blushing."

"No I'm not! I never blush."

"If you say so," he murmured, unconvincingly.

Probably because she could feel the heat blazing in her cheeks. Like a neon sign proclaiming, "I was thinking about youuuuuu . . ."

"I was just talking to my mom."

"Oh." He sat down next to her. "How is Ms. Dee?"

She smiled. It was cute that he referred to her mother that way. "Working hard, as usual. She doesn't know how to take a break."

"It's genetic then?"

She narrowed her eyes at him, but said, "I invited her to come to Durham for a little while when I leave for Duke."

"When's the last time you saw her?"

"When she came here to visit just after I moved in."

"She was so protective of you. Wanted to know my intentions," he said, smiling.

Dee had left satisfied that Nic would be okay.

"That Ben is a lovely young man. If someone"— Dee's pointed tone and exaggerated eye movements had made it clear who she was referring to—"were interested in getting married, he'd be a wonderful husband."

Since getting married was the last thing on her mind, she hadn't paid her mother's comment any attention. But after three years of living with him, of witnessing his kindness, his compassion, and his capacity to nurture the people he cared about, she had to admit her mother was right. Nic was excited about Duke, but she couldn't deny that part of what she'd miss when she left was Ben. He'd become extremely important to her in the past few years. She hoped she didn't lose his friendship.

"I'm sure she'll enjoy the trip."

"She will. I just have to convince her not to worry about the cost."

"Van Mont Industries has several condos in a building close to the campus for when any of the executives are in town for meetings or guest lectures. If any of them are free, you can stay there while you look for your new apartment."

Was he serious?

"We couldn't."

"Why not? It makes no sense for you to pay for a hotel when we have a perfectly good place you could stay."

"Thank you." She stared into his expressive eyes. Were those flecks of amber in the dark depths? How had she never noticed before? Or the thick dark lashes that framed them. The heat she saw reflected back at her stole her breath and she looked away, her eyes stinging as if she hadn't blinked in minutes. She cleared her throat. "But enough about me. Where's your friend?"

"Davis?" His voice held a rough edge. "He left."

"Not on my account, I hope?"

"Oh no, your accusation and cool demeanor made him feel quite at home."

Considering what Ben had just offered her and the fact that she'd been rude to his friend in his home, she winced. "I'm sorry. Do you want me to apologize?"

He waved a nonchalant hand. "I'm just messing with you. He's catching the train back to New York but we're having dinner first. I told him I'd meet him there."

She cradled the glass of wine in her hand, stared down into its contents. "I don't think I've met him before."

"You haven't."

Giving in to curiosity she asked, "Was he planning to stay longer?"

"No. Some of my friends will be out of the country for a while, so a group of us are getting together for a week on Martha's Vineyard. Davis felt a need to inform me of the updated guest list."

"Isn't that the mythical coastal town where old money summers and rubs elbows with the Kennedys and the Bushes?"

One corner of his mouth curled upward. "Not exactly."

Nic studied his expression and tone of voice and took into account that his friend came all the way from New York to give him this information in person . . .

"Who are you trying to avoid?"

"Who says—"

"Ben, we can do this the easy way or the hard way."

Once the words were in the air, she wished she would've chosen another expression. The words "hard way" seemed to linger between them, stoking a blaze that, until yesterday, she hadn't been aware was simmering. Those gorgeous eyes dropped to her mouth and the amber flecks seemed to gleam as they followed the movement of her tongue darting out to moisten lips suddenly parched.

"Tinsley. My ex," he said.

Nic inhaled a sharp breath, a sting piercing her chest as she imagined Tinsley. Tall. Angular. Blond. Impeccably dressed in couture.

She took a sip of wine. "And what happened with Tinsley?"

"She broke up with me."

Come again? Why would anyone break up with Ben? He was sweet, smart, rich, and good-looking. He was the perfect catch.

For anyone looking to receive.

Which she wasn't.

"Why?"

"Because it became clear that I wasn't going to become a chip off the Van Mont block."

Nic felt indignant on Ben's behalf. "But you're extremely successful at what you do! Last year you were named Baltimore's Financial Services Champion of the Year and you've been named as one to watch in cash management by *Fortune* magazine!"

"Thank you for your defense, but this was years ago. When I first decided to start my business."

"Let me guess. She's having second thoughts?"

"I don't know, but she's been stirring the pot and Davis wanted to give me a heads-up." He laughed. "He even suggested I bring the person I'm dating to prevent her from getting any ideas."

"That seems extreme. Have you considered just telling her you're not interested?"

"If you knew Tinsley you'd know she doesn't always allow words to get in the way of what she wants."

And she wanted Ben.

"Are you reconsidering the trip now? Because of Tinsley?"

He braced his elbows on his thighs, his hands falling between his knees. "Maybe."

Ben wasn't an in-your-face arrogant guy, but he always projected a complete confidence in himself and his decisions. This uncertainty was new.

"You remember me talking about my friend Caila, right?"

"She's one of your friends from college. The ones you go on vacation with. Caila, Ava, and Lacey."

Warmth spread throughout her chest. She mentioned them often and it was nice to know he listened.

"Last year, while we were on our trip, Caila lost her grandfather."

"Shit. That must've been rough."

"It was. They were very close. She was fucked-up over it for a while. Almost lost her job."

Though, in the end, it all seemed to work out for her. As it usually did. Smart and beautiful, Caila had never met a goal she couldn't achieve. And when it looked like she finally had, she ended up with a promotion and a sexy new man.

"If she had the opportunity to spend time with him again, she'd take it, no matter what she had to do. And that's how we feel about our vacations. These are your friends. Don't let something as petty as an ex get in the way. You never know how much time any of us has."

She saw it constantly in her work.

As if on cue, her phone rang, and she checked the caller ID.

Ben sighed and pushed to his feet. "I'll leave you to take your call."

"No, it's only Amalia." She raised the phone and answered the voice call. "What's—"

"I wanted to give you a heads-up," Amalia said, the urgency in her voice alarming.

"About what?"

"I was upstairs when I saw Whitaker's father in Agner's office."

"He already talked to me about it. Told me to take a couple of weeks off."

"No. Just now," Amalia said. "Whitaker Sr. was apoplectic. Ranting that what you did could follow his son and ruin his career. He said you wouldn't like it if someone did that to you."

What could he do? She was leaving Hopkins in a few weeks, and now, thanks to Agner, she wouldn't be there for most of it.

She said as much to Amalia.

"Whitaker Sr. said he knew Dr. Newman."

Nic hissed in a breath. "James Newman? As in the head of my fellowship program?"

"I'm afraid so. Whitaker threatened to call him and demand he rescind your fellowship offer."

Dread dragged its cold, gnarly fingers down her spine. "Motherfucker!"

Chapter Seven

"And here I believed you when you said you were leaving Van Mont Industries because of the terrible work hours."

Ben looked up from his desk to find Dr. Fallon Rothschild Van Mont standing in the doorway to his office. His mother was the personification of old Baltimore money, from the top of her chignon-coiffed dark hair to the upturned collar of her white tailored button-down shirt to the tips of her Italian loafers.

Ben stiffened, unease coiling in the pit of his stomach. "How did you know I was here?"

"I didn't. It's after six thirty so I stopped by your house first and when you weren't there, I decided to try here."

That was more effort than she usually put into anything involving him.

"I wasn't expecting you."

Fallon arched a finely drawn eyebrow. "Clearly. Maybe if you were, I'd get a better greeting."

He clenched his jaw at the rebuke, but rose and

went over to her, pressing a kiss on her cheek. "Hello, Mother. Please have a seat."

"Thank you, Benjamin." She examined the space, her eyes lingering on the plaques on his wall that broadcast the same awards Nic had referenced yesterday. "It looks different from the last time I was here."

Oh, you mean the time you'd breezed through here on your way to London, took one look at my new office and declared, "Quite a downgrade from your suite of offices at Van Mont Industries"?

He fought back the bitterness being in her presence evoked and cleared his throat. "What are you doing in town? I thought you were in New York for several months assisting on a research project?"

Fallon crossed one trouser-clad leg over the other. "I am. I'm only back for a couple of days. Hopkins called me in to consult on a case."

His mother was a world-renowned cardiothoracic surgeon whose skills and expertise were still in high demand, though she was in her late sixties.

"What can I do for you?"

"I wanted you to know the board voted to add a new strategic arm to Van Mont Industries at our last quarterly meeting."

Since they were still practicing physicians, his parents weren't involved in the day-to-day running of Van Mont Industries, though they, like a few of his relatives, were on the board of directors.

He leaned back in his chair and crossed his

arms over his chest. "You tracked me down to inform me of something I could've read in the annual shareholders report?"

"I wanted to see your face when I told you the news."

That would be a first.

Growing up, he'd seen his housekeeper more than his parents. On the rare occasions they were home, they ignored his presence unless they needed him for a publicity photo or an event to promote their family.

He had no idea why his mother thought he'd be interested in anything that had to do with Van Mont Industries, but he'd learned the sooner she was able to complete her task, the sooner she'd leave. And he could get back to the work he did and the life he'd created where his wishes mattered.

He waited, knowing it wouldn't take long. Fallon was never one to take the circuitous route when a direct one was available.

"We've decided to establish a charitable foundation."

Shock stiffened his posture. For years, he'd asked his family to consider doing that very thing. The company had been in a great financial position for several decades and it made sound business sense from a public relations and taxes perspective.

But his requests had always been met with an avalanche of excuses that had added up to not a chance in hell. The most used rationalization?

The business's sole responsibility was to engage in activities to *increase* its profits, not give them away.

He wondered, why the change?

Instead he asked, "What will your mission be?"

"To fund research into the development of medications to fight disease. Additionally, we want to look at offering programs to help offset the cost of certain prescription medications."

He nodded. "I'm glad the company has finally decided to go this route. You'll help a lot of people."

Fallon eyed him. "We want you to come back and run it."

Her statement rendered him speechless.

If he were still working at Van Mont Industries, he would've jumped at the opportunity. He knew setting up a corporate charitable program of that magnitude would not be easy. He'd have been looking at intensive fourteen-hour days, six to seven days a week. But the chance to use his family's wealth and influence to effect change on a massive scale? Worth it.

But not now.

It had taken a lot of hard work to build a business he loved and was proud of. And though he'd known leaving Van Mont Industries was the right thing to do, making that break from his family had been stressful and difficult. He wasn't willing to give up everything he'd achieved, including his peace of mind, to get sucked back into the family's dysfunction.

He shook his head. "I'm sorry you came out of your way, but I'm not interested."

Her brown eyes, so like his own, widened. "Why not? You'd be CEO! And we're talking an initial funding of a quarter of a billion dollars! The power and prestige you'd have would be immense!"

"Which is why you'll have no problem finding someone to take the position."

"I will never understand you. You'd rather stay *here*"—she said the word as if they were sitting in the city dump—"than come back to the company your family started and take your place—"

"Mother!" He could recite the words by heart. There wasn't a conversation with Fallon that didn't end up back down this road. "It's not happening. I made my choice."

"I'm allowed to have an opinion, Benjamin," she said.

He recognized the tone. He'd been on the receiving end of her displeasure for years.

I don't have time to attend your science fair, Benjamin. I'm accepting an award. Enter again next year and we'll see.

Please let go of me, Benjamin. You're getting dirt on my coat. I don't have time to make brownies for your school. That's what our housekeeper is for.

Stop complaining, Benjamin. Haven't we given you everything? I don't have time for your awards ceremony. Do we have to be there to witness your excellence? Especially when it's expected?

He knew a lot of what his mother did and didn't have.

In abundance.

Fallon exhaled and shifted in the chair. "Why did I have to hear from someone else that you're going to be on the Vineyard next week? Is it true?"

Talk about conversational whiplash.

He nodded, thankful Davis had given him a heads-up. "Yes, I'll be there. Though I don't understand why you needed to know. It's just a trip."

"A trip you've been unable to make the past two summers when your father and I have asked," she said, clasping her hands together on her lap, her chin trembling ever so slightly.

Ben narrowed his eyes. He didn't believe for one second his mother was hurt by his refusal to join the family at their compound. In truth, he had no interest in spending time with them, either shrugging off verbal slights or defending his decision to work outside of the family business. But—

Could his hostility have led him to make the wrong assumption? His parents were still sought after professionally, but they were getting older and he'd been surprised to notice how much more time they spent traveling. Was it possible they actually *wanted* to spend some time with him?

"*Martha's Vineyard Magazine* has been after us for an extended family profile and . . ."

Heaviness settled on his chest like a weighted blanket. There it was. They *were* interested in him . . . for promotional purposes. Would he ever stop being that little boy, constantly getting his hopes up only to be disappointed?

He pinched the bridge of his nose. Hard. "I've been busy."

His mother scoffed. "I doubt this little accounting firm of yours kept you busier than any of us and we still managed to show up."

Her derision stung.

"At the time, 'this little accounting firm' seemed to benefit from my time and attention more than anyone in the family."

"Apparently. Since I heard about your trip from Dina Yates, I assume Davis is going, too?"

"Yes," Ben said shortly, checking the time.

"Dina can't stop talking about how well Davis is doing. It's her favorite topic of discussion." Fallon rolled her eyes. "You're much smarter than he is. Always were. What does he do, decide whether to renovate or construct another building in Manhattan?"

Despite her words, he knew his parents' social circle placed a high regard on offspring who took over the family business. They revered the notion of perpetuating their legacy. Children who lived like they had no job, who spent money like it was a never-ending resource?

An embarrassment.

Children who turned their back on the family business to start their own?

Just as bad.

"What day do you get in?" Fallon reached into her purse and pulled out her cell phone. "I'll call ahead and have your suite of rooms readied."

"I'm staying with Palmer."

She brightened. That got her approval. "How *is* he? I haven't seen his parents in ages. He went into engineering, right?"

"Yes. That's part of why we're all getting together. Palmer and his wife, Bronwen, are heading over to participate in a construction and infrastructure program in East Africa."

Her appreciation dulled. "I enjoy travel as much as the next person, but your generation takes it to the extreme. It's not enough to go to Kenya and enjoy the scenery and culture. You're too busy hurrying off to help the rest of the world. What about here? There are people in this country in need. I'm not sure Sybil and Howard would've spent all that money on an Ivy League education for Palmer if they thought that's what he'd do with it."

"If Palmer's parents have an issue with his career, I'm sure they won't hesitate to inform him. You don't possess any qualms on that front."

Fallon leveled a displeased glance at him and he knew she'd probably reached her limit. He figured she was a second away from leaving, but she surprised him by changing the subject.

"So, your entire group of friends will be getting together?"

"Yes."

"What about Tinsley?"

"What about her? We broke up years ago," he said cautiously.

"I always liked Tinsley. Ambitious, beautiful, and from a great family. When you announced your engagement, I was certain you were finally making a smart decision."

As opposed to the other ones you'd made.

The words didn't need to be said aloud. They hovered in the air, like gathering storm clouds.

His parents' approval was part of why he'd stayed with Tinsley long after he knew things weren't going to work out. It had been strange but heady to receive his parents' esteem for something in his life. And it made family social engagements more tolerable.

But even that benefit hadn't been enough after a while.

"I'm not getting back together with Tinsley."

Fallon waved a dismissive hand in the air. "Of course not. That, like coming back to run the foundation, would make sense."

He was a grown man. He owned his own home. He'd single-handedly started an asset management firm that was consistently lauded as one of the best in the state.

And yet, he could still be affected by his mother's opinion of him. If Nic was here, she'd tell him to get over it. She didn't take shit from anyone.

Speaking of Nic—

"Mother, do you know a James Newman? He's in Ortho at Duke."

"Ortho?" She tapped a manicured finger—

buffed, no polish—against her chin. "Your father and I don't deal much with that specialty. But if he's any good, I'm sure I could get his information. Why?"

"Just something for a client," he murmured, the genesis of an idea forming in his mind.

He'd been right about his mother's tolerance for chitchat once she'd achieved her aim. Five minutes later, she was gone, having revealed a prior dinner engagement with the director of the Department of Medicine. Putting the drama and tension of that visit aside, he concentrated on drafting proposals for several of his clients.

He loved his work, appreciated the precision of numbers. Accounting was black-and-white; digits either added up or they didn't. But that didn't mean he wasn't able to exhibit a bit of creativity. That's where the financial planning came in. What to invest in, how to spend money, the best way to save; all strategies that were unique to each client and their specific goals.

He stretched and attempted to ease the ache in his neck. Glancing at his phone, he was shocked to find he'd been working steadily for over two hours. It was almost nine o'clock! He'd gotten a lot done, but he wasn't ready to leave, still feeling wired from the work and his conversation with his mother.

Turning off the harsh overhead lighting, he opened the bottom drawer of his antique, kidney-shaped executive desk—something he'd inherited from his grandfather—and pulled out a bottle of tequila and a tall, narrow shot glass. He poured himself a drink and swiveled in his chair to stare out of the window at the nighttime Inner Harbor view. He took a sip from the glass, enjoying the aroma and the flavor. Damn, that was good! There was nothing like the taste of high-quality tequila. He leaned his head back and let the alcohol work its magic, smoothing out rough edges, paving over uneven surfaces, until he was level. Fluid. Relaxed. He took another sip. Interacting with his mother wasn't pleasant, but the real reason he hadn't been in a rush to get home was he knew Nic wouldn't be there.

He hadn't realized how much he'd been looking forward to seeing her until he'd received her earlier text. She'd decided to meet her co-worker Amalia for a drink to discuss what she'd heard last night and to come up with a strategy to handle it. Nic was one of the most determined people he'd ever met. She hadn't responded well to the news that her coveted fellowship could be in jeopardy, but he knew she wouldn't accept defeat. She'd fight with everything she had. And he wanted to help her. He needed to find a way to make it all better.

When he'd been talking with his mother, he'd come up with an idea. Ordinarily, he'd hurry home to run it by Nic, but knowing she wasn't going to be there bothered him more than he'd expected. He'd gotten used to her presence. Even when she was on call, he'd known it was only a matter of time before he saw her.

Not anymore. This time next month, she won't be here.

He'd known that, but for the first time, the reality of her departure loomed large. After three years, Nic would be gone. No more eating dinner together, teasing her about her bougie soaps and lotions or watching basketball games and house-hunting shows. No more bright smiles, side glances from her amazing green eyes, or pulling on her soft, bouncy curls.

He'd offered to let her and her mother stay in one of the numerous condos his family owned in the Durham area. Maybe he could look into their availability on a longer basis? See about offering her one to live in during her fellowship?

Is that what you're reduced to? Offering her places to live so you won't lose her in your life?

His phone dinged and, without turning away from the view, he reached for the device where it sat on his desk. His stomach flipped in anticipation when he saw Nic's name on his home screen. He clicked on the message.

She'd typed: What u doing?

He smiled, set his glass on the desk, and dashed off a response: Nothing. Sitting here, having a drink.

What a coincidence. So am I.

He entered a smiley face emoji.

She responded: I've had a hellacious few days & I was wondering if you could help me with that?

Of course he would. Nic was his friend and he knew how much this situation aggravated her. He'd do anything to help.

What do u need?

Her response was almost immediate: U.

He froze, unable to believe what he'd just read. If any other woman had responded to his question in that manner, her intent would've been plain. But this reply from Nic? She didn't see him that way.

Did she?

The capital letter loomed large and bright in the light gray bubble. Tone didn't always come through in text. The "U" could preface an action she wanted him to take, like "U" please bring me my wallet. Or, she could've meant it literally, "U" let's chill, hang out, and watch a movie. Before he jumped to any conclusions, although the blood vacating his brain and making its way south had already made its mind up, he should offer her the opportunity to elaborate or clarify her answer.

Excuse me?

Three dots, the longest delay in his life, and then—

A picture of pale golden skin and perfect, pert breasts with erect light brown nipples appeared on his screen.

The remaining blood fueling his common sense executed a fast break straight to his dick. What the hell?

There was no question about her intent, but this had to be a mistake, right? Or a prank? There's no way Nic would send him a sexy selfie . . .

Where are u? he typed, though it took his suddenly clumsy fingers several tries.

The bathroom at The Taphouse. It was too loud, too crowded for what I want.

Though he was reading the words, he could hear her voice in his head, and it cast a spell on him, entangled him in a web of intimacy. He licked his lips and leaned back in his chair, adjusting his slacks.

And what do u want?

Your hands, lips, tongue, dick. Doesn't matter. I need at least one of them on me, stat.

Fuck!

He'd fantasized about doing all of the above and more to her for years. From the moment they'd first met. And though he was grateful for the friendship they'd formed, one he'd protect at any cost, he hadn't been able to completely snuff out his attraction. He scrolled back up to the picture she sent. Though her face was cut off, he knew it was her. He'd seen her chest countless times when she wore a sports bra to work out or a tank top on warm days. He was familiar with the smooth expanse of skin, the little mole just below her clavicle.

His mouth watered in anticipation. And now he was being invited to partake of it. Hell, she wouldn't have to choose between the four options. He'd give them all to her, if that's what she wanted.

His fingers flew over the keyboard. What if I start with my hands? Gently cover those breasts, then press them hard against you, as your nipples pebble against my palms?

Hmmmmm… What else?

I'll use my tongue.

You know my nipples are supersensitive. I can come just from you pulling & sucking on them.

He didn't know. But now that he did, he'd never be able to forget it. Or think about anything else.

Then that's what I'll do. I'll swirl my tongue around them, savoring their feel & taste. But I won't take it into my mouth until you're moaning loudly & your hot body is writhing against me.

Yesssss. It'll feel so good. God, my skin is tingling & I'm so wet.

He closed his eyes and flexed his hand, already able to imagine it sliding against her torso and down into her welcoming heat.

He typed: Can I feel?

My pussy can't wait!

Damn. He licked his lips. She'll have to. I won't be rushed.

Can I come over?

"Can I come over?" Four words that took this from merely talk to action. He shook his head, straining for clarity, knowing there would be serious consequences if—

Please?

Her plea was like a steel door slamming shut on any attempts to be careful or thoughtful. He wanted her more than his lungs wanted fresh air, but if they were finally going to do this, he didn't want some quickie in his office.

How about I meet you at home?

He pressed the blue arrow and waited, anticipation and desire strumming in his blood, roaring in his eyes, drowning out everything save the bright rectangular screen on the device in his hand.

Three dots.
They vanished.
His stomach clenched. *Son of a bitch!*
Three dots and then—

Ben?

Wait, what? Ben, question mark? Was she rethinking the situation or was it . . . oh no, don't make it be—

Shit! I'm sorry. I thought u were someone else.

Disappointment doused his desire like an icy bucket of water and his heart threatened to shatter into pieces.

Goddammit! He scrubbed a hand down his face. It had been too good to be true. Of course those messages weren't for him. He'd sensed that the moment he'd received the first text. But he'd allowed himself to pretend, to imagine she'd wanted him as much as he'd always wanted her.

Three dots, and then—

Can you delete that tit pic?

He scrolled back to the photo she'd sent. The picture wasn't for him; he shouldn't keep it. But damn . . . Even in the limited light, against the dark walls of the bathroom stall, it was a stunning image.

One he'd never have again.

What if he saved it? He could have this piece of her forever, could indulge in his desire for her safely and from a distance. He wouldn't lose his friend even as he stroked himself to completion thinking of her.

Ben?

He held his breath and let his thumb hover over the image . . . before he exhaled and pressed the screen, erasing the picture as she'd asked.

Chapter Eight

Awareness sprang forth like a steamroller, flattening Nic like the filling in a smushed ice cream sandwich. Her head felt as if it had been decapitated, stuffed with cotton, and glued back on while her mouth was drier than an ancient Egyptian sarcophagus.

It didn't take long to diagnose her condition. Veisalgia. The medical term for the disagreeable physical effects that occurred following the excessive consumption of alcohol. And though she knew what was going on with her body, it didn't make dealing with her hangover any easier.

She took a moment to take stock of her situation. She was lying on her belly, her cheek flat on her mattress instead of on a pillow. She flexed her fingers and the nails of her right hand grazed the hardwood floors and got tangled in some rough fabric.

Getting drunk wasn't something she did. A glass of wine. A beer. A cocktail. One was usually the extent of her drinking. She rarely had the time off to indulge without the possibility of it affecting her work.

And she'd let nothing affect her work.

But last night, she'd decided to meet up with Amalia to discuss the whole Whitaker debacle and get the specifics of what the other doctor had observed regarding Whitaker Sr. and his meeting with Agner. Ava would've been proud of her, because Nic had questioned the other woman like she was Annalise Keating reborn.

"Where did you see him?"

"What did he say?"

"How did he look?"

She'd been determined to get all of the facts. Treat it as a medical issue she needed to diagnose. Nic was so close to all of her dreams coming true. With the successful completion of the Duke fellowship, she'd be able to write her ticket. And she wasn't going to let some insecure, privileged, lazy asshole and his blowhard father take it away from her.

She hadn't intended to get rip-roaring, panty-melting drunk, but Amalia had bought a round of shots, suggesting a Slippery Nipple might get their creative thoughts going.

A Slippery Nipple. Nic had giggled like a prepubescent schoolboy.

And thus began their journey through suggestively named shots land, that took them from Blow Jobs, to Screaming Orgasms, to Circle Jerks to Cunnilinguses. Each progressive shot made ordering the next even funnier, until she was laughing so hard her cheeks ached and she couldn't catch her breath.

Would it still have been funny if she'd known she would end up in hangover hell?

Rolling over onto her back, Nic grimaced as the contents of her belly shifted and the light in the room pushed to get past the barrier of her closed eyelids. With effort, she lifted one hand to lay across her eyes, delaying the inevitable pain she knew would come.

She took a breath and lifted her lashes. Agony sliced through her and instinctively, she slammed them closed again.

Damn you, Sex on the Driveway!

But she couldn't go around with her eyes wide shut and years of an intense work ethic made lying in bed all day a nonstarter. So she sucked it up and opened her eyes again, allowing the agony to infiltrate until she could actually see the ceiling. The three wooden blades on the modern ceiling fan confirmed she was in her bedroom and sent relief coursing through her. She knew she'd come home, but there *was* a brief chance she'd imagined that.

What she hadn't imagined were the pictures she'd taken in the bathroom of the bar and the drunk sexting to Carlos and . . .

No, that wasn't right. She hadn't texted Carlos, though that's what she'd intended. She'd texted—

Oh shit!

She jerked up in bed, causing her brain to explode and ooze from her ears, or at least, that's how it felt, and the contents of her stomach to rebel and revolt. She scrambled off the bed—falling hard on her knees—and searched for her phone. She found the thin white charging cord and followed it, until she located the device, connected and charged but on the floor behind the nightstand. With trembling fingers, she powered on the screen and went to her texts, immediately bringing up her last interaction.

And what do u want?

. . . swirl my tongue around them, savoring their feel & taste . . .

. . . I'm so wet.

Can I feel?

Oh God. Oh God. Oh God.

She'd drunk sexted *Ben*!

And sent him a tit pic!

She wanted to curl into a ball and hide among the debris and dust bunnies floating beneath the bed. Instead she scooted backward on her ass until she was propped up against the side of the mattress.

What must he think of her?

Nic wasn't ashamed of her body and she didn't have a problem engaging in fun, flirty sexy talk. She'd shared both with prior lovers. But her relationship with Ben was special. When she thought about it, he was the most important man in her life. She leaned on him and depended on him in a way that she usually reserved for her mother or her friends. It was different from any relationship she had with any other man. Hell, he'd watched her put her curls into two strand twists before stuffing them all into her satin-lined bonnet. She considered that more intimate than sex.

What if I start with my hands? Gently cover those breasts, then press them hard against you, as your nipples pebble against my palms?

Even now, remembering the words he'd typed, heat pooled at the apex of her— Wait a minute! She'd thought she was texting Carlos, a resident she'd hooked up with a few times over the years. But Ben had known she was on the other end of the texts.

Had known and responded.

Had Ben thought about her in that way? Imagined his hands on her body, his tongue laving her nipples? And now that she saw those words attributed to him, could hear his voice saying them to her, she didn't know if she'd ever be able to forget it. But she had to. As she always said, dick came and went but true friends stood the test of time.

Despite the sexy promise of those texts, they weren't worth losing him. And if they took their friendship beyond its platonic bounds, that would be its inevitable result. She couldn't give him the kind of relationship he was seeking. She didn't want to.

What a complete and utter fucked-up mess! She lifted her phone and checked the time. 9:47 A.M. On a typical day she would be hours into her shift at the hospital. The good news was that Ben had already left for his office. He was diligent about his schedule, meaning he probably wouldn't return until early evening. She planned to be long gone by then. She couldn't face him, not when her humiliation was still so fresh. She wouldn't avoid him forever, just long enough to get her head around what had happened and figure out how to best act.

Because if she did that, if she spent valuable brain activity worrying about Ben, she couldn't dwell on her fellowship. Her shoulders slumped. The fellowship that she'd worked hard for. That would make her one of the most sought-after orthopedic surgeons in the country. That would imbue her with the financial security and respect she'd sought her entire life.

Stop feeling sorry for yourself! This isn't over!

Damn straight. She wasn't going to take this situation lying down. If they thought she was going to slink away quietly and let them get away with this shit, they had another think coming. She could do both, figure out how to deal with her fellowship *and* her relationship with Ben!

Her stomach roiled.

Later.

She couldn't do anything until she dealt with this hangover. Exhaling deeply and resigned to the fact that this was going to be unpleasant, she forced herself to stand and waited for the world to stop spinning. Then, with slow, cautious steps, she headed to the bathroom.

Next time, order yourself a Shirley-fucking-Temple and stay away from the exotic drinks with dirty names!

Thirty minutes later, feeling marginally better after a hot shower and clad in leggings and a T-shirt that read "BAE: Black and Educated," she trudged upstairs to Ben's kitchen in search of Gatorade. He bought cases of the electrolyte drink for after he worked out. Usually, she loved the light-filled space but this morning she was grateful she'd grabbed her shades to counteract the sun's rays.

Nic placed her bottle of Advil on the counter then went into the small pantry and snagged a bottle of Gatorade and a loaf of wheat bread. Returning to the counter, she exhaled at the exertion. Her head throbbed and she regretted her decision to put the shower first. She was wasting her time on this whole orthopedic surgery thing. Imagine the money she could make coming up with a pill to instantly cure the effects of a hangover?

Popping the cap, she took two pills and downed them with almost half a bottle of the drink. That would take care of the pain and the lost electrolytes. Some toast to settle her stomach and then she'd lie down and let the measures take effect. She slid a slice in the toaster, then went for a plate. Ben kept them on the second shelf, which normally wasn't a big deal, but today, her arms felt like concrete and stretching on her tippy toes to reach the dishes was sapping what little energy she had.

Sometimes, she hated being short.

Fuck it, she'd grab a paper towel and try not to get crumbs on the floor.

"Let me get that for you."

At Ben's words, her heart practically triple-jumped out of her chest. But before she could fully register the shock at his unexpected presence, the heat of his body seeped into hers, rendering her boneless. Thankfully, the hardness of his chest pressed against her back anchored her or she would've melted into a puddle on the floor. He rested one hand on her hip, and reached up to grab a plate with the other.

"Here you go," he said, setting the dish on the counter.

Was it her imagination, or did his hand flex and tighten on her before he stepped back?

"Thanks," she croaked, then cleared her throat. It was the hangover, not Ben. She turned to face him, glad he couldn't see her eyes behind the tinted lenses. "I thought you'd be at work."

"I'm going. But I wanted to wait until I knew you were okay." He hooked a finger around her glasses and tried to slide them down her nose. "That bad, huh?"

His touch sent her insides scrambling, like the time she'd ridden the Tilt-a-Whirl at the Tipton County Fair. That had to be the hangover, too, right?

She reached up and grabbed them, holding them in place. "I've been better."

She scooted away from him, though the deliciousness of his cologne followed her, in torturous glee. He was dressed for the office, in heather gray slacks and a baby blue button-down shirt. A smile lit his face, causing his soulful eyes to crinkle. Damn, that grin was lethal. How had she remained immune to it all this time?

And "soulful"? Since when had his eyes become "soulful"?

This hangover was having one hell of an effect on her.

"I'm sure you have." He nodded toward her head. "Indulging in a new beauty treatment?"

Her hand flew up and her eyes closed at the squishy sound confirming the plastic cap she wore. Great. Could embarrassment flush the hangover toxins from her body?

Funnily enough, this was better than what she'd seen when she'd glanced at herself in the mirror this morning. She'd forgotten, or had been unable, to tie her hair up last night and had awakened looking like the bride of Frankenstein, minus the Hollywood special effects. She'd had no choice but to wash it. "Deep conditioning my hair."

"Priorities," he said, amusement coating his features. The toaster popped. "Go sit on the couch. I'll bring it to you."

She shook her head and regretted it immediately. Wincing, she said, "You don't have to do that. Go to work. I'll be fine."

"I've got it. And I'll make you my special hangover remedy."

In spite of herself, she laughed. Not good, either. She seized the plate he'd gotten down. "Thanks, but no. I took Advil and drank some of your Gatorade. The rest is just time."

"Spoken like a doctor." At her furrowed brow, he elaborated, "No imagination. Trust me?"

Other than her mother and Ava, Caila, and Lacey, she couldn't think of anyone she trusted more.

"Yes."

His expression softened. "Then go sit down and let me do this for you."

He grabbed her wrist and pried the dish from her hand, then set about gathering ingredients. She shivered and looked at her arm, certain there had to be some physical manifestation of the sensations stirring just beneath her skin. Slowly, she turned and headed over to the sofa. She could joke about the hangover being responsible, but she knew it was all her fault. She'd roused this newfound awareness of him. Ben was her friend. Why had she ruined everything by sending those texts and that damn picture?

"What happened last night?" he asked.

Dammit. He wanted to talk about it *now*? Before she could get her bearings? Was that going to be the price for his magical hangover cure?

She must've taken too long to respond because he elaborated, "About work. Did you find out anything new?"

Thank God! He was talking about work. *That* she could handle.

"It's as bad as I thought. Whitaker's father believes I unfairly reprimanded his son, and despite several accounts that support my actions, he's threatening to reach out to Newman."

Ben came into the living room, placed everything on the coffee table, then sat on its edge facing her. "I'm sorry, Nic."

His shirt hugged his broad shoulders and the fabric of his slacks stretched over his leanly muscled thighs. She drank some Gatorade to replenish the missing moisture in her mouth. "Yeah, me, too."

He started as if to speak then stopped and turned his head to look off toward the kitchen.

Aww, hell.

"What?" She already felt like shit. She couldn't feel any worse. She might as well deal with this now and get it all out of the way.

"I want to say something but I . . . I don't want you to take it the wrong way."

They needed to talk about it. The longer they didn't, the more awkward it would become. That didn't mean she had to like it.

"Look, I was trying to text my co-worker Carlos—"

"I can ask my parents to make a few phone calls—"

They spoke at the same time. Nic pressed her palms to her heated cheeks as his words broke through.

". . . *ask my parents to make a few phone calls* . . ."

"What did you say?" she asked.

He stared at her, his gaze intense, and for a moment she thought he wasn't going to respond.

The energy emanating from him suddenly felt hot and dangerous and she waited, with bated breath.

What are you going to do, Ben?

Something shifted in his dark brown eyes and though he didn't physically move, it felt like he'd taken a step back.

"That intern isn't the only one with pull. The Van Monts know everyone, including a lot of influential people at Duke. I can ask my parents to make a few calls on your behalf."

Astonishment stole her breath. She'd expected several things. *That* hadn't been one of them.

She pressed a hand against her chest. "You'd do that for me?"

"If it would help," he said, his tone solemn.

If it would help? Hell yeah, it'd help! Having one of the renowned Van Monts speak to Dr. Newman on her behalf would demolish whatever some random donor said about her.

Talk about meeting clout with clout.

"I don't know what to say."

He shrugged, but she wasn't fooled by the nonchalant gesture. Ben didn't get along with his parents and tried to keep as much distance as possible between them. She knew how difficult it would be for him to make that request.

For her.

Nic bit her lower lip. "Why was that so hard for you to say to me?"

"Because you don't like asking people for help

and I didn't want you to feel beholden to me. That's not why I offered."

Tears clogged the back of her throat at his generosity. He knew her so well. Understood how she thought. And he was right that accepting his assistance would be difficult for her. But she'd take him up on his offer. She wasn't stupid. Still, there had to be something she could do for him. To take this from a favor that *would* hang over her head until she paid him back to a sort of quid pro quo . . .

"I'll do it," she said loudly.

And then immediately regretted her exuberance.

Attractive furrows dotted his brow. "Do what?"

She lowered her voice. "I'll be your pretend girlfriend."

"What are you talking about?"

"Remember, when your friend Davis came here to tell you about Temperance—"

He huffed out a laugh. "You mean Tinsley."

She waved her hand. "Whatever. You were worried about her being there and you didn't want it to ruin your time with your friends. Davis said you should bring someone and since you're not dating anyone, take me. I'll do it. It's not exactly an even trade, but—"

He pulled her close and she froze, her arms hanging at her sides.

She was hugging Ben. No big deal. They'd hugged before. But why did this feel different?

Why was she noticing things she hadn't noticed before? Like how great he smelled? She nuzzled her nose against the base of his neck and inhaled. Damn. Could she manufacture his scent? Make that a part of her hangover cure? Cautiously, she wrapped her arms around his waist and returned his embrace.

"Thank you," he said, his voice rough with emotion. "It isn't necessary, but I do appreciate it."

"You're welcome." She cleared her throat. "Now, you need to go into the office and I need to get some rest. I am never drinking again."

She didn't want to let go. But she did.

He studied her face, then nodded. "I'll give you a call later, to check up on you."

"I'm not sick. I'm being punished for making horrible decisions last night. You're being too nice."

"Of course. Because one shouldn't be too nice to their friends," he said, bracing his hands on his thighs and pushing himself to his feet.

"Exactly. I'll be fine. Go to work and try not to lose your clients' life savings, please. Including mine. I may need it earlier than anticipated."

She settled back into the sofa's cushions, happy that things seemed to be back to normal between them. Maybe she hadn't ruined things by sexting him last night. He hadn't mentioned it and he was willing to do her a wonderful favor.

"Alright, I'm going. But if I can't call," he said, his confident stride sounding against the hardwood floor, "how about I text a dick pic? I hear sending naked pictures is how all the cool kids are communicating with their friends these days."

She grabbed the nearest pillow and threw it at his retreating back.

"Too soon?" His laugh echoed as he closed the front door behind him.

Chapter Nine

Ben pulled to a stop in front of the oversized four-car garage on the large concrete driveway. He cut the engine of his car and twisted in his seat to face Nic. Guilt tightened his chest at the picture she presented. Her eyes were closed, body curled in the fetal position—as much as she could in the front seat, and her head rested against the leather, her lips slightly parted. Last week, her nausea had been caused by her actions. Today, it was caused by his.

He still couldn't believe she'd agreed to do this for him. He hadn't intended to hold her to the proposition she'd made. He'd been willing to chalk it up to the gratitude she'd felt for his offer to talk to his parents on her behalf and he'd told her as much the following day.

"I'm going. You do for me. I do for you."

That was part of the problem, too. He wanted to do *for* her; do *to* her. Lots of things. Things that friends shouldn't do to or for one another. And though, other than his joke, they hadn't spoken of that night again, Ben couldn't deny that something had changed.

In the past, when he'd let his guard down and thought about her in that way, he'd been able to overcome those urges because of their friendship and because, as great as Nic was, Ben knew he could never be involved with a doctor. But after their sexting session, it was getting harder to ignore that voice, harder to stand firm behind "hell no!" and not to edge over into "maybe?"

Reaching across, he touched the curl that lay on her cheek, projecting a softness he knew she'd hate, and tucked it behind her ear. "We're here."

Her lashes fluttered, then opened and in that rare, unguarded moment, he saw so much in their stunning green depths. Softness, warmth, pleasure, discomfort, pain, and realization. She uncurled from her position and his mouth watered at the length of creamy light gold skin. Nic was petite, but even in her small form, she was mostly legs. And he appreciated every inch.

She touched the back of her wrist to the corners of her mouth. "If I'd known about this, you would've been on your own."

"I didn't know you get seasick. The only way to access Martha's Vineyard is by boat or plane."

Her eyes widened comically. "We could've flown?"

He coughed to cover his chuckle, certain she wouldn't appreciate his amusement. "I'll make arrangements to fly back. I promise."

He'd stopped at a drugstore as soon as he could and picked her up some Dramamine. Unfortunately, they'd had only the drowsy formula in stock, but he thought the nap might restore the energy she needed to get through the day.

He handed her the small plastic bag. "The next time we're in town, we can check some other stores and find you a nondrowsy version. Just in case."

She shook her head. "In case of what? I'm not getting on another boat. And if that was your sneaky plan to try and off me to get out of all the *House Hunters* bets you've lost, you're gonna have to do better."

He laughed. Now that was the Nic he knew and lo—

"Do you still want to do this?" he asked, not allowing that thought to fully form. "I wouldn't be upset if you changed your mind. You could stay at a B and B in town and fly back tomorrow."

"I'll be fine. You're willing to talk to your parents for me. Helping you send the message to your ex is the least I can do."

"If you're sure?"

She nodded, then winced. "I am."

"Okay. Then let's go over this one last time."

Nic sighed and rolled her eyes. "Good god, man! I've gone over lifesaving surgeries less often!"

"If we're going to do this, we're going to do it right."

The words echoed back to him in the confined

space of the car. They were the words of a teen-ager or the protagonist in some romantic com-edy. What was he doing?

He straightened and faced front, bracing his hands against the steering wheel. "This is ridicu-lous. I'm a grown man. Why am I resorting to these games?"

Nic reached out and brushed his shoulder. "Be-cause you love your friends and you have the right to enjoy time with them without being dis-tracted by an ex who's set her sights on you."

Well, when she put it like that, the sitcom caper seemed reasonable. Responsible, even.

Her touch seared through his shirt, his skin to his very bones.

"Your hands, lips, tongue, dick. Doesn't matter. I need at least one of them on me, stat."

The words were branded on his brain. When he closed his eyes, they were scripted in the fi-ery red of the darkness. All he could think about was putting each of those items on her breasts and so much more. His palms ached to squeeze the pert mounds. His lips yearned to roam over the smooth skin, following their natural curves, paths, and valleys. His tongue throbbed to lick her nipples until they stood at attention.

And his dick?

His dick wanted to learn all the textures every other part did. It wanted to feel the smooth tight channel between her cleavage. Know the feeling of sliding in and out, over and over, as a prelude to the place it really wanted to go . . .

Dammit! Now he was as hard as a rock and if Nic happened to look down, his cargo shorts wouldn't hide it. She'd certainly see it. And just because he couldn't keep a lid on his fucked-up lust didn't mean he wanted to ruin their friendship over it.

"Alright then, let's get moving," he said, tossing the words over his shoulder as he exited the car and went around to the trunk of the rental luxury sedan.

Nic took her time getting out, but when she did, she stared in wide-eyed amazement at the house before them. "I've never seen a house like this in person. It's incredible."

Ben glanced at the rambling eleven-thousand-square-foot shingled mansion with its classic New England coastal architecture. Against the bright, partly cloudy sky, the picture presented an elegant refinement he'd probably taken for granted since their families had been summering up here together for years.

"It belongs to Palmer's family. His parents aren't here. They're spending the summer in Italy and France."

"As one does," she murmured, grabbing the handle of her suitcase.

Watching Nic roll her bag toward the white double doors beneath the columned portico, Ben marveled at the notion of his two worlds colliding. Their relationship had been cultivated in a bubble. The two of them together in Baltimore, away from everyone else in their lives, their connection had strengthened and thrived. Though he counted her as one of his best friends, this was a part of his life she didn't know. A huge part. And he was consumed with the sudden desire to rectify that deficiency.

"Wait. Come with me."

He took her hand and led her to the back of the house, past five Adirondack chairs grouped to take advantage of the breathtaking vista.

The property was situated high on a hill with over 180 degrees of unobstructed water views of the bay, the harbor, and the Atlantic Ocean beyond. Over two acres had been landscaped with several groves of trees and bushes. He guided her over to a relaxing spot where a hammock had been anchored and a fire pit had been positioned in front of several tree stumps.

"Um, it's a nice view but I think I could've waited to see it later."

"I know. But we went from the boat to the car. I thought you'd like a second to breathe in some fresh air."

She settled on one of the stumps and for a few minutes they sat in silence, enjoying the slight cool breeze as it blew in off the water.

"Feeling better?"

"I am. Thanks."

He nodded then looked around, instinctively smiling as memories unpacked themselves from his subconscious and spread out before him.

"What brought on that smile?" Nic asked.

"I had some good times here."

"Really?"

He laughed. "Yeah. The summer after we graduated from high school, we had a party here while Palmer's parents were still in New York. We'd only invited a few people, but it's a small island. Word got out and this place was packed. We turned this area into a VIP section. Ran some rope between these trees and invited all the pretty girls to party with us."

"Slick. I never imagined you as a player."

"I did okay."

"Huh. I thought I knew you pretty well. And I guess I do. About your life now, in Baltimore. But you have an entire history of experiences that I know nothing about," she said, echoing his thoughts from earlier.

He braced a hand against one of the trees and pointed to a large twisted oak fifty yards away. "You see that tree right there?"

She nodded.

"When I was fourteen, Davis bet Palmer and me to see who could climb the highest."

They'd stolen a six pack of beer and come out here to goof off and throw a football around.

"Are you crazy? That tree is huge. You could've broken your neck!"

He warmed at her concern. "I didn't do it. I thought it was stupid. But Davis convinced Palmer. And Palmer did it—he beat him! But when he got up there, he froze. Couldn't come back down."

Palmer had been terrified while Davis had been at the bottom laughing hysterically. Davis's sarcastic bent turned full-blown asshole when he drank too much. Ben had pulled off his shoes and chucked one at Davis, hitting him in the eye.

"I scaled the tree on the other side of Palmer and helped him down."

Nic stared at him, one hand covering her mouth. "Were you okay?"

"I would've been." But Davis had thrown his shoe back up at him, startling him. "I fell. Broke my arm."

The three of them had been a sight: him cradling his broken arm, Davis with a black eye; and Palmer, shaking, white as a sheet.

She gasped. "Your parents must've been so worried."

He'd thought they might be. Hoped . . .

"More like annoyed that I'd interrupted their dinner with some Van Mont Industries' executives."

She stood and walked over to him. "Which arm?"

Ben held out his left one and showed her the scar.

"I'd always wondered about that," she murmured.

Her brow furrowed and she pursed her lips while studying the old injury, stroking her fingers back and forth along the thin, slightly puckered pinkish line. He swallowed back the moisture that flooded his mouth and watched her, noting their similar skin tones, though hers had a depth and creaminess to it that his lacked.

She asked him several brisk questions and he

answered them as best as he could, considering it was almost twenty years ago.

She clucked her tongue in sympathy. "Sounds like a partial non-displaced fracture."

Though the skin around his scar had been sensitive for a while after his injury, it'd been years since he'd felt that phantom pain. So what could he blame for the tingly sensation he was now experiencing?

His heart pounded in his chest and he allowed his gaze to skim up her body, to the small gold studs in her earlobes and a few stray tendrils that had escaped the bun on the top of her hair. She was so petite and angular, she looked brittle, like she could break with a brisk wind. In the early days of their acquaintance, he'd mistakenly assumed she was fragile. It hadn't taken him long to learn how strong she really was. How her small stature belied the force of her personality.

The pulse at the base of her neck throbbed, like she was panicked or . . .

His gaze flew to her face to find a becoming flush dotting her cheekbones. Her tongue darted out and the action drew his attention to her full, luscious lips.

"It'll feel so good. God, my skin is tingling & I'm so wet."

What if he said, "Fuck it"? Just picked her up, wrapped those slim, strong thighs around his waist, and devoured that mouth?

"Hey!"

Shocked, like he'd been abruptly yanked from

a deep dream, he looked toward the intruding sound and found Davis running across the lawn toward them.

Ben exhaled and shifted away, rubbing a hand down his face and attempting to shake the cobwebs of desire that still clouded his brain. Sliding a quick look at Nic, he watched her blow out a long breath and smooth loose hair up into her bun.

Davis lumbered to a stop and strolled the remaining distance between them. "I saw a car out front. I thought it might be you."

They slapped hands before hugging. "We just got here and I wanted to show Nic this spot."

"Ahhh, the scene of the infamous tree-climbing bet." Davis shoved his hands in the pockets of his navy crew-line shorts.

"And the parties with our VIP section."

"Oh God, I forgot about that. One of your best ideas ever, Benji."

"You left that part out, *Benji*," Nic said.

He hated that fucking nickname. Hated it even more hearing it come from her mouth.

"Oh yeah. He was key to that plan working," Davis said. "None of the girls really trusted me and they thought Palmer was a nerd. But Benji here, with those eyes and that face? The girls totally trusted him. Wouldn't you?"

Nic turned the full force of her green gaze on him and his chest tightened.

"I would," she said quietly.

"Palmer's younger brother was always begging to let him hang with us, so we put him in charge of manning the section." Davis laughed. "He was very diligent in his duties."

That was true. A Manhattan bouncer couldn't have done a better job.

"Y'know, Palmer never claimed his prize from the bet," Davis said. "Which was great, because my father would've shit a brick if I'd given him my Xbox."

Nic frowned. "Couldn't you have bought another one?"

Davis wrinkled his nose in horror. "No. It officially went on the market several months later. I got one early because my father provided some of the seed capital for Microsoft."

"My bad," she said, rolling her eyes, and Ben could only imagine the inner monologue she was having.

"We'll forgive you this one time." Davis held out his hand. "Good to see you again."

She shook it. "You, too. Thanks for letting me crash the party."

"No problem. It's for a good cause."

Nic glanced between the both of them. "Is she really that bad?"

"Yes!" Davis said, nodding, his eyes comically wide.

"Damn! What does that say about your taste in women, Van Mont?" Nic teased and bumped him with her hip.

"Not much, apparently." He sighed and squinted his eyes upward. "Tinsley isn't bad. She's just the only child of well-meaning but indulgent parents."

"Which means," Davis interrupted, "she's always gotten everything she's wanted, whether she deserved it or not."

Nic slid a glance in Ben's direction but lowered her lashes before he could read more. "And now she wants you."

"It'll pass," he said, with the utmost confidence. "Until then, I don't want it to ruin our time with Palmer and Bronwen before they leave."

"It won't. Don't worry. I'll do my part. We won't leave any doubt that you've moved on," Nic said.

"You know how much I appreciate this."

"I do."

Their gazes met and held and he could feel it, the connection they'd always had that somehow had changed in the past week. He knew she'd noticed it, too, but like him, she seemed hesitant, unsure of whether they should acknowledge it.

Davis cleared his throat. "Palmer and Bronwen are in the master suite on the main floor. You guys can take the one on the second floor. I took the suite above the garage. As far away from the drama queen as possible."

"Your snide comments aren't helpful, man. I may not like the situation, but we don't have to be dicks about it."

"And that's our Benji, always being nice," Davis said with a wry tilt to his lips.

Because Ben knew that "nice" was not the first word that came to mind when referring to Davis.

"That's one of the things I like about him," Nic

said. She stared at Davis. "There's enough cynical assholes in the world."

Davis's smile turned genuine. "It's going to be an interesting week. Come on, let's go get you guys settled. Before I saw you had arrived, Palmer texted me they were fifteen minutes out."

They headed back across the lawn, grabbed their bags, and went inside the house. Ben could see Nic taking in their surroundings: the grand sweeping split staircase, the architectural focus of the main floor's open plan, the bright kitchen with its white cabinets and butcher block countertops, the four striped upholstered armchairs encircling a wide round table, and the comfy couches situated in front of the large stone fireplace.

Other than the three of them, however, the great room was empty.

"Where's Sabine?" he asked.

"Her flight doesn't get in until tomorrow morning."

"I'd heard something about flying in as an option," Nic said, narrowing her eyes at Ben. "A little too late for it to be useful, but it's still good to have that confirmed."

Crap. She was probably still feeling off from the seasickness and the Dramamine.

"I'm going to take Nic to the room so she can lie down for a bit. I'll be back."

Davis opened the refrigerator. "Cool."

Ben grabbed both of their bags. "C'mon."

"I'm not an invalid. I can carry my own bag," she said, hurrying over to take one from him.

"Watch out for the corner of that area rug—"

The warning came too late as Nic's toe caught on the raised fabric and she stumbled. She probably would've been able to save herself, except she tripped over the bag and would've fallen hard on the wooden floor if he hadn't dropped what he'd been carrying and grabbed her.

She clutched his arms and stared up at him, her pupils dilated, her lips slightly parted in surprise. In that moment he wanted to kiss her so badly, he actually shook from the effort of refraining. Her chest rose and fell, matching his own rhythm. He took a shaky, steadying breath and righted them both, though he didn't step away from her and she didn't move out of his embrace. They stood there, his arms around her waist, her hands gripping his biceps.

"Thank you," she said. "I guess I must still be off-balanced."

"No problem."

The corner of her mouth tilted upward. "You can let go of me now."

"You can move away from *me* now."

Neither withdrew.

One of the glass-paned double doors banged open and, simultaneously, they turned their heads toward the commotion.

"Who are you and why are you hugging my fiancé?" Tinsley asked, a scowl marring her patrician features, her furious gaze focused on Nic.

Shit.

Chapter Ten

Fiancé?

Though Nic knew she hadn't been doing anything wrong, she instinctively shifted away from Ben. He'd said they'd dated. He'd said nothing about them being engaged!

Not that it would've made a difference. She would've offered to help him either way. After all, this was payback for possibly saving her fellowship. But the idea that Ben, her . . . friend, had felt enough for this woman that he'd asked her to be his wife? That they might be married if she hadn't called it off? A prickle of unease quivered in her belly.

Tinsley stood framed in the door, the sunlight glinting off her flaxen tresses.

Flaxen tresses . . .

Okay, that was a tad dramatic, but Nic hadn't been too far off the mark when she'd imagined the other woman. Tall, thin, and beautiful, wearing white denim capris, a navy-and-white top, and matching wedges, she oozed class and wealth.

Suddenly, Nic was fourteen again, standing outside of the sorority where her mother worked, staring at the pretty girls with their long straight hair, designer labels, and expensive jewelry. She almost gave in to the urge to smooth her hands down her bright yellow boatneck top and khaki shorts.

Don't you dare!

Ben pressed his lips together and reached for Nic, slinging an arm around her shoulders and pulling her close. "I'm not your fiancé, Tinns. Not anymore."

His words—not to mention the heat from his body—were what she needed to get her head back in the game.

This isn't personal, Nic. You're here to show Ben's ex that he's moved on. Now do your job.

Summoning a bright smile, Nic slid her arm around Ben's waist. "Well thank God for that, or this would've been an extremely awkward situation."

Davis laughed, as did the couple who stood behind Tinsley, though they glanced at each other with wide eyes.

Tinsley turned her head slightly, as if suddenly aware she had an audience.

"I was joking, darling, of course," she said, the corners of her mouth tilting upward.

Ha! Nic didn't believe her for one second. She'd witnessed the shock and rage on Tinsley's face. The other woman had meant every word she'd uttered in her posh, used-to-being-obeyed voice.

Ben's lips brushed the top of her ear as he whispered approvingly, "Good one."

And then there were no more opportunities for private asides as the space was filled with friends greeting one another.

Nic stepped aside, allowing them room to embrace. At their obvious affection, tears threatened the corners of her eyes and she blinked them away. The display reminded her of her friends. Of that intense happiness, joy, and giddiness that overwhelmed her when she finally saw the women who were closer to her than any blood sisters could be.

"Nic," Ben said, gesturing her over. His hand was warm when it came to rest on the small of her back. "Everyone, this is Nic. Nic, this is Palmer, Bronwen, and Tinsley."

Palmer stepped forward to shake her hand. He was handsome, in a studious way, with blond hair and bright blue eyes showcased behind wire-framed glasses. "Welcome. We're so happy you could join us."

"Thank you," she said, responding to his genuine friendliness.

"We're just surprised. Ben hadn't informed us he was bringing someone." Bronwen's tone was brisk and her words direct, but the striking brunette's blue eyes were curious.

"Yes," Tinsley said, her arms crossed over her chest, "you weren't expected."

"I knew she was coming," Davis offered from

the well-stocked wet bar tucked into the corner, where he was pouring drinks.

Tinsley rolled her perfectly made-up eyes. "That and one hundred dollars wouldn't buy me a pair of shoes worth wearing."

Since Nic had purchased the sandals she was wearing for about half that amount, she struggled to keep her inner irritation from appearing on her face.

"Are you both excited?" Ben asked Palmer and Bronwen, his smile easy and affectionate.

"Excited, nervous, scared, sad." Bronwen laughed and threw her hands up. "We're going to miss you guys, but this has been calling us for a couple of years."

Nic glanced around. "For the newbie, what's been 'calling' you?"

Ben's chagrined expression was actually adorable. "Sorry. They're doing Engineers Without Borders."

"Wow." Nic knew, of course, about the medical equivalent, and while she believed it was a worthy cause, it wasn't something she was inclined to volunteer for. Still, she respected those who gave of themselves to help others. "Where are you going?"

"Kenya," Palmer said.

"That's really important work. I'm impressed."

"Enough about us. How long have you two been dating?" Bronwen asked.

"We've known each other for three years, but

we've only recently started dating," Ben said, responding with the story they'd decided on, sticking as close to the truth as possible.

"So, it's not serious?" Tinsley asked, her eyes gleaming.

Nic slid a look at Ben and smiled. "We live together. That seems pretty serious to me."

"Living together?" Tinsley stiffened and reached out to squeeze Bronwen's arm.

Close your mouth, girl. It's not a becoming look for you.

"Congratulations," Palmer said, grinning and slapping Ben on the back.

"Thanks."

"Three years can seem significant, but it takes time to get to know someone," Tinsley said. "History is so important."

Nic narrowed her eyes. "You know another word for 'history'? Old. People change and grow. What's important is how Ben and I relate to one another. Now."

"Are we done with twenty questions?" Davis slapped the bar top then spread his hands over the six shots lined up like a creator unveiling his masterpiece. "The party doesn't start until our ceremonial toast!"

Just the sight of those little glasses filled with liquid sent Nic's stomach into backflips in an effort to retreat. The hangover last week, the seasickness earlier today. She couldn't do that to her body.

Ben reached for two but before Nic could protest that she didn't want one, he dumped them into a highball glass he'd taken off a stack.

"Hey!" Davis objected.

"The sun hasn't even set, man. I think Nic and I will hold off a bit." Ben quickly refilled their glasses with ginger ale and handed one to her with a wink.

Their fingers brushed as she took the drink from him and a shiver traveled down her spine. Just like earlier, when they'd been standing next to the hammock. With the breeze rustling through the strands of his dark hair, and him looking down at her, she'd been struck once again by how gorgeous he was. His demeanor wasn't overt like Davis, because that wasn't Ben's personality. He was intense, loyal, and fine as fuck.

Her lips trembled into a smile and gratitude settled her turbulent belly. She could've kissed him in that moment. Not in service to their ruse, but for being the considerate person he was.

"Your loss," Davis said. "Now, who wants to do the honors?"

"Why don't we let our guest do it?" Tinsley said, turning to face Nic with another fake smile and a brow raised in challenge.

Davis shook his head. "You don't have to—"

"No, it's okay. I don't mind."

It wasn't rocket science. A quick "here's to a great week" would suffice. But Nic wasn't looking to offer mediocrity, precisely because she knew that was expected.

"Benji, this is why it's bad manners to show

up without telling us you would be bringing a guest," Tinsley said. "If we'd known about Nic, Davis could've picked up some Hennessy or Courvoisier to make her feel at home."

Nic stiffened, instantly comprehending the slight leveled at her.

Hennessy and Courvoisier. Two drinks synonymous with black culture. In this setting, Tinsley might as well have offered to bring Nic some purple Kool-Aid and watermelon!

Outrage pounded in Nic's ears adding a red tint to the edges of her vision. That bitch! The audacious nastiness of the dig stunned her. But when her gaze spied Tinsley's triumphant smirk, she forced herself to relax.

Did the rest of them comprehend what just happened?

"Tinsley! That's rude," Bronwen said. "Ben, it's fine."

Apparently not.

But Ben sensed something else was going on. He frowned and placed a hand on her back, his touch providing comfort. "Are you okay?"

Truthfully, no.

"And the queen of the bitches makes her appearance," Davis muttered, a look of knowing exasperation on his face.

That got Nic's attention. Because Davis had it wrong. Nic was the Queen Bitch. And not because she was spoiled or because it was cute or popular. But because she *had* to be. To survive. To attain the things this woman took for granted.

"What?" Tinsley asked, sliding on a look of innocence, with a tilted head and too-wide eyes. "It was a joke."

Sure it was. The other woman's picture of perplexed sincerity didn't fool Nic for one second. She saw the spite beneath the surface.

Tinsley knew exactly what she was doing. She was "othering" Nic, putting her in her "place."

Nic was familiar with females like Tinsley. Girls who'd zipped around the college grounds in their BMWs or convertibles, young women who uttered rude remarks in mild tones sugared up with smiles, believing no one would call them on it, and grown women who looked straight through her unless they thought she was the help and they needed something.

Daughters of privilege.

Tinsley deserved to have her ass kicked for that comment, but what might feel good—and right—in the moment could have a lasting impact on Nic's life. She wouldn't give Tinsley that satisfaction. Plus, she had more important things to consider. Her fellowship was on the line.

Eyes on the prize, Dr. Allen. This time, you go high.

"Was it?" Nic asked. "I thought jokes were supposed to be funny. Between this one and the one you made when you first got here, you're oh for two."

Palmer exchanged another look with Bronwen and Davis whistled. "Damn."

"And while your concern for my comfort is . . . staggering . . . I'm not drinking. If I were—" Nic scanned the label. Catoctin Creek. She'd had an attending her second year who loved that stuff. "—it's clear that Davis has great taste."

For a second, no one said a word. Then—

"Can I marry you?" Davis asked, clasping his hands together beneath his chin.

"She's taken," Ben said, his eyes molten as they met hers. He entwined their fingers together and tugged her close. He lowered his voice. "Wanna tell me what that was about?"

"Not really," she whispered back. Nic suddenly recalled a salute some of her med school classmates used to make. "Do you still want me to give the toast?"

"Only if you want to. It's tradition," Bronwen said, shooting a heated look at Tinsley, who'd turned slightly away from them, a sweep of red coloring her cheeks and her neck.

Nic raised her glass and waited until the others followed suit. "If the ocean was beer and I was a duck, I'd swim to the bottom and drink my way up. But the ocean's not beer, and I'm not a duck. So raise your glass high and shut the fuck up!"

Nic aimed those last words at Tinsley and when the other woman narrowed her blue eyes, Nic knew her message had been received.

You want to play? Bring it.

"Woo-hoo!" Davis tossed his shot back. "Excellent toast. I'll need to remember that one."

"Tinsley, can I have a word with you?" Bronwen asked.

"Fine." Tinsley began running her fingers through the ends of her hair. "Benji, do you mind taking my bags to my room? You know which room, right? The one we stayed in together the last time we were here."

This chick was a piece of work!

Nic glared at Ben, telegraphing her message hard. *Don't do it.*

She could carry her own damn bags. If Ben was going to jump and do her bidding every time she asked, what was the point of pretending to have a girlfriend?

Ben shook his head. "Sorry, Tinns, you're on your own."

Tinsley's mouth tightened into a pout. "Davis, make yourself useful and put my bags in my room."

Davis was sipping the bourbon shots Ben had discarded. "You look more than capable of carrying a duffel and a rolling suitcase."

"You are not a gentleman," Tinsley huffed.

"For once we agree," Davis said.

Palmer sighed. "I'll take care of it."

"Thank you, honey." Bronwen gave them a tense smile, then looped her arm around Tinsley's. "Excuse us. This'll only take a moment."

She practically dragged the other woman from the room.

Ben took Nic's hand. "Are you okay?"

"What? You mean that?" She jerked her thumb over her shoulder in the direction the other two had exited. "She's just showing her ass. She wanted attention and to get a rise out of me. I can handle Temeculah."

"Tinsley," he said absently.

"Whatever," she countered softly.

His gaze flitted over her features, as if conducting his own diagnostic for a second opinion. Grabbing an escaped curl, he twined it around his finger, before smoothing it back behind her ear. "Are you sure? You look tired."

Nic tapped him on the chest with the back of her hand. "That's no way to talk to your live-in girlfriend."

But he was right. It was all catching up with her and dealing with Tinsley's foolishness was like the cherry on the top of the shit sundae.

"Can you tell me where our room is?"

"I'll do one better. I'll actually carry *your* bags to the room."

They headed to the staircase, passing Bronwen and Tinsley reentering.

"Where are you going?" Tinsley asked.

Ben kept moving. "Nic is tired. We're going to rest a bit before dinner."

Tinsley laid a hand on the gleaming banister. "I hope it wasn't something I said?"

Nic stopped midascension and turned to look down at Tinsley. "Trust me. I didn't pay attention to you at all."

The room Ben escorted her to was bright and airy, with a curved beadboard ceiling, white-painted beams, and windows that presented gorgeous ocean views. Nic was certain she would appreciate the loveliness of her accommodations. Later. Right now, she had a bone to pick with her "boyfriend."

"Fiancé?"

Ben set their bags on the loveseat in the small sitting area that adjoined the bedroom. "I know what she said bothered you. I wish you'd tell me why."

"Fiancé?" Nic repeated.

"I mean, she can be a piece of work, but . . ." He put one hand on his hip and rubbed the back of his neck with the other.

Was he being serious?

Nic walked up to Ben and jabbed her index finger in his chest. "Fiancé!"

"Oh." Her point must've finally penetrated. His chin dipped down and he cleared his throat. "Uh, yeah. Tinsley and I were engaged."

Obviously.

"And you didn't mention it because . . ."

"Because it didn't seem important. It was years ago."

Didn't seem import—

"I'm your girlfriend and you're supposed to be so in love with me, she's discouraged from thinking that she could have a second chance with you. How realistic would that be if I didn't know the extent of your relationship with her?"

"Excuse me if I didn't want to go in depth on one of my life's biggest failures!" He slashed a forceful hand through the air.

Now it was her turn. Ben never got angry or raised his voice at her. She blinked. "Oh."

As quickly as his irritation sprang forth, it seemed to recede. "It's not something I like to discuss, but you're right. I should've told you."

"You're not a failure," she said. "You made a mistake. It ended. Would you have preferred for the breakup to happen after you'd gotten married?"

"No," he confessed, sighing and sinking down onto the edge of the king-sized bed, "but it doesn't make it any less embarrassing. I thought I knew her, that she was the one. I was ready to spend my life with her. I guess it's hard to admit I'd made such an error in judgment."

His distress tugged at her heartstrings. Most of the time he was so positive and confident that when he wasn't, it was jarring.

She sat next to him. "In college I had a crush on my bio lab partner. I blame it on that class. It made me crazy in more ways than one."

The anguish faded from his expression. "Random, but okay. What happened?"

His brown eyes sparkled, and, in the sunlight, the shade was almost translucent. Like dark fossilized amber. She stared, mesmerized by the different striations of color.

"Nic?"

She closed her eyes, breaking the spell. Damn, he was potent. And he wasn't even aware of the effect he was having on her.

"I thought the feelings were returned. Turns

out, that was his move. Seduce a girl in his class so she'd end up doing all the work for him."

He frowned. "How'd you find out?"

She ran her fingers over the woven patterns in the white coverlet spread on the bed. "I'm ashamed to admit it took me a little longer to figure it out than it should have." Especially for someone who'd prided themselves on their bullshit detector. "I saw him with a girl in the library stacks. I eavesdropped and heard him telling her the same things he'd told me, but about a different class."

"Fucker."

She smiled at his supportive indignation. "He was. But I took care of him."

"What did you do?"

"Since we usually worked off my lab notebook, one day he asked me to just copy the work into his. He said his handwriting was crap, and the TA would never be able to read it. He'd told me about the extra credits he was taking that semester, how much stress he was under, and if I could help him this tiny little bit, we could spend more time together." Remembering, she huffed out a disbelieving laugh. "After I agreed, he never opened his book. Ever. He assumed because he'd asked, I was doing it. And since our labs always turned out perfect . . ."

His upper body shifted closer to her. "Did you leave it blank?"

"No. I copied the labs into his book. I just made small changes throughout for the remainder of the semester."

"When did he find out what you'd done?"

"When he got a D in the class and I'd gotten an A." She shrugged, felt the satisfied smile crease her face. "He was furious, but he had no one to blame but himself. If he'd looked at his notebook even once during the semester, he would've seen what I'd done. It was obvious. But he never did."

"He didn't try to hurt you, did he?"

"He got loud. Threatened to go to the professor. And do what, admit that he'd expected me to do his work all semester?" She curled her lip. "I heard he ended up retaking the course that summer."

"This story confirms why I vow to never get on your bad side." His grin faded. "Still, you weren't engaged to your error in judgment."

"But I told my friends about it. And it comes up occasionally. The point is, we've all suffered from rose-colored glasses syndrome when it comes to people we like. You could've told me the full story. I wouldn't have judged you." She placed her palm on his cheek. "You're my friend."

His skin was hot where it met hers and they were so close, she was consumed by the scent that was uniquely him. She didn't know how long they sat there, staring at each other, but she eventually dropped her hand. "So, is there anything else I need to know about dear old Tallulah?"

He laughed, and the flash of white against his tanned skin did funny things to her breathing. "Tinsley."

"Whatever."

"And no."

"Good. What's on the agenda for later?"

"Dinner. But I don't know if we're eating in or going into town. I'll ask Davis."

"Okay." She stood and yawned. "Do you mind if I take a little nap? Meeting your friends has exhausted my reserves of patience."

"Of course not." He cleared his throat. "I guess we should discuss the sleeping arrangements. Do you want me to sleep on the couch?"

She paused in the act of going through her bag. "Why?"

"I don't want you to feel uncomfortable."

"Ben, we're not teenagers. We're in our early thirties. We're friends. And this is a . . . big bed."

"If you're sure?"

"I am. Aren't you?"

"You're right. We'll be fine. Get some rest and I'll check on you shortly."

He closed the door behind him and Nic's gaze immediately swung back to the bed and superimposed the erotic image of the two of them entwined, kissing.

"Then that's what I'll do. I'll swirl my tongue around them, savoring their feel & taste. But I won't take it into my mouth until you're moaning loudly & your hot body is writhing against me."

Crap.

Chapter Eleven

"I guess we should discuss the sleeping arrangements."

Jesus, he'd sounded like a teenage boy on his first overnight trip. He honestly hadn't given a thought to where they'd sleep, strange considering a day hadn't gone by where he hadn't relived their text exchange in vivid detail.

"We're in our early thirties . . . And this is a . . . big bed."

It *was* a big bed. And Ben knew exactly how he wanted to utilize the space. It began with laying her down and kissing every inch of her sweet body and ended with him buried so deep within her neither could imagine ever parting again.

Knowing that's how he felt—that he was a hair trigger away from bursting back in and lobbying to make that fantasy a reality—were they tempting fate by sharing that bed?

Groaning, he let go of the handle and headed down the hallway. He'd give Nic an hour to settle down and get some rest before he went back to check on her.

Tinsley had upset Nic and the fact that he

didn't understand why irritated him. He'd felt her instinctive reaction; the anger had roiled off her so heavily, he was surprised it wasn't visually observable. But Nic had handled it with her usual plain-speak, take-no-shit attitude, something he admired about her. She stood up for herself. Was strong.

Which is the very reason things would never work out between the two of you. She's worked hard to become a doctor. She's not going to give that up. And you can't accept anything less.

When Ben descended the stairs he found Davis sitting in one of the armchairs, a tumbler dangling from his fingers.

"Back so soon?" Davis asked, his tone unusually solemn.

"Clarifying the plans for dinner."

"Initially, I think Bronwen wanted us to go into town, but now . . ." He raised his brows and tilted his head.

Ben exhaled. It was probably best they stayed in tonight. "I'll let Nic know."

But his feet didn't move.

"Join me?" Davis asked.

He had some time to kill. "Why not?"

"Good. Yours is over on the counter."

Ben eyed the waiting snifter. "How did you know?"

"A woman as gorgeous as Nic and you're only friends but pretending to be more?" Davis took a sip of the dark brown liquid. "It was only a matter of time."

Bastard.

Ben strode over, took the glass, and turned to brace his back against the bar. To his right, large French double doors led to a screened porch that overlooked the expansive back lawn where he and Nic had stood only a couple of hours before.

"It seemed so simple at the time. Nic and I are friends. We get along great. We could have a fun little mini vacation and discourage Tinsley at the same time."

"Except you can't stop thinking about the non-platonic good times you could be having."

You know my nipples are supersensitive. I can come just from you pulling & sucking on them.

"I can't," he admitted.

"Then why don't you do it? I've seen the way she looks at you. It's not one-sided."

If only it were that easy.

"She's my friend. These days she's one of my best friends."

"Ouch," Davis said, staring into his glass before taking a drink.

"Stop it. I see her almost every day. We talk. We share things." Ben pushed away from the bar and maneuvered around the coffee table to drop into a chair. "What if we sleep together and it ends badly?"

"Damn, dude, you gotta have more faith in your skills."

That's not what he'd meant. He had no worries on that score. It would be good between him and Nic. He knew it. That much heat mixed with their connection, how could it not? And therein lay his problem. It was hard to deprive yourself of something when you knew it could be great short-term. It was the long-term ramifications that concerned him. But then, he'd always been someone who focused more on the future.

"I'm serious. Sex changes things."

Expectations. Feelings. Regrets.

Palmer walked into the great room and sank into the chair next to Davis and across from Ben. "Fuck me!"

"You wish," Davis laughed.

Did everything have to be a joke with Davis? "Must you be so juvenile?"

"Says the man who's playing games with two women."

Palmer lifted his bare feet and put them on the coffee table, crossing them at the ankle. "I just spent twenty minutes listening to Bronwen fuss about Tinsley."

"I thought Bronwen invited her?" Ben asked.

"She did, but she didn't mean to. She'd seen Tinsley at the Hope Gala and had mentioned how we were all gathering up here for one big hurrah before we left."

Ben winced. He could imagine Tinsley hadn't been happy to hear Bronwen's announcement. She never liked to think of herself as missing out on anything, having exemplified FOMO before it became a hashtag.

Palmer sighed. "She said Tinsley sort of invited herself"—he looked at Ben—"after declaring you'd want her to be here since you'd recently asked her out."

What the hell? How often was she going around spreading that inaccurate story? How many people now thought he'd been sitting around pining after his ex-fiancée? That's what he'd meant. Drama.

Ben shook his head. "It was years ago. In Vail. And I didn't ask her out on a date, I invited her to join the group I was with for dinner."

"Oh. Well, Bronwen was annoyed because she realized Tinsley had basically lied to get here and then when she kept making rude comments about Nic being uninvited . . ."

Just remembering those comments caused Ben's pulse to spike. He gripped his glass so tightly, his knuckles whitened.

"Do either of you know what that remark was about?"

Palmer frowned. "What remark?"

"The one Tinsley made about Nic and the alcohol for her." What was it? "Hennessy and Courvoisier?"

Davis shrugged. "I assumed she was getting on you for bringing Nic."

Palmer nodded. "Courvoisier? Wasn't that an SNL skit?"

Ben clinched his jaw. No. There had been more to that comment. Nic's reaction told him that, even if he'd been the only one who'd noticed. He'd figure it out and once he did, he'd determine how to handle it. There was no way he would let Tinsley get away with insulting Nic. But he'd have to be careful. Nic would hate knowing he'd said anything on her behalf, the insinuation being she'd needed the help. Still, he could stand up for her without implying she wasn't capable of handling herself.

"That's the type of shit Tinns pulls," Davis said, straightening from his slouch to put his empty glass on the table. "Addressing every bitchy, inappropriate thing she says can be exhausting."

Ben agreed. It was the reason he'd been willing to overlook most of those statements when they'd been together. This time, ignoring her rudeness wasn't an option.

"Anyway, Bronwen is in no mood to be reasoned with, so if you're counting on a group dinner . . ." Palmer pressed his lips together and used his hand to make a slicing motion in front of his neck. "Maybe one of you would have better luck. In addition to everything else, she's mad I didn't tell her you were bringing Nic."

"You didn't know," Ben pointed out.

"That's what I said! But she doesn't believe me." Palmer pointed a finger at them. "Because one of you *should've* told me!"

"We had a very valid reason for that," Davis said. "You can't keep a secret from Bronwen. She's your kryptonite."

"She's my wife!"

"Same thing," Davis muttered.

Ben shot him an exasperated look. *This isn't the time.*

"I'm not supposed to keep secrets from her."

"And that's why we have to keep secrets from you," Davis said, spreading his hands out, palms facing upward.

"You're both assholes."

"Hey! That's not nice," Ben said.

"That's also not a secret." Davis settled back and linked his fingers together over his stomach. "You want back in the club?"

"What are you talking about?"

"What if there's another secret we can let you in on?"

Palmer blinked, his glasses momentarily lending him an owlish look. Ben lowered his chin to his chest and pressed his thumb and index fingers against his temples. The tree-climbing bet, the VIP party, racing cars along one of the many narrow back roads. This is how it always started. When he looked up, Davis was watching him, his brows raised.

What the hell?

Ben shrugged a shoulder in acquiescence.

"Nic isn't Ben's girlfriend. They're pretending, to get Tinsley off his back."

"You're joking. Please say you're joking."

Ben shook his head. "I'm not."

"And you can't tell Bronwen," Davis reminded him, gleefully.

Palmer slammed his hand against the chair's arm in a rapid rhythm. "Fuck. Fuck. Fuck. Fuck."

Well, that had been a mistake.

Ben sighed. "If this is going to be a problem, Nic and I can leave in the morning."

"Wait! Do you even know her, or did you pick some stranger to bring to my parents' house?"

Irritation tightened Ben's jaw. "She isn't a stranger. We're friends. Everything I said earlier is true. We've known each other for three years."

"You live together?"

"She rents my basement apartment."

"Oh." Palmer relaxed. "Well, now I don't feel so guilty that I find her *very* attractive—"

"I know! Those green eyes, right?" Davis slid a look at Ben.

"Oh yeah," Palmer agreed.

Ben gritted his teeth and tried to stem the acidic jealousy blazing through him.

"But I should've picked up on it. She's not your usual type."

"Why? Because she's black?"

Ben realized he'd never sat down and considered if the people in his life were racist. He'd never had to. Would Palmer have a problem with him dating Nic because she was black? And if so, what did that knowledge do to their friendship moving forward?

An "are you serious?" expression altered Palmer's face. "Don't be a dick. In the five years since Tinsley you've gravitated toward even-tempered, undemanding women and Nic seems more . . . intense. Like, she's just standing there, but she's . . . vibrating." Palmer let his head fall back against the top of the chair. "I don't know how to explain it."

"Nothing about her is still," Davis added.

"She's always in motion, even when she's not moving."

Ben understood. "She's cool. She's beautiful, funny, and she's smart as hell."

"What does she do?" Palmer asked.

Ben paused. "She's a doctor."

His pronouncement shocked Davis out of his lackadaisical demeanor. "Say what now?"

"You hate doctors," Palmer said emphatically, as if Ben had needed reminding.

Ben laughed a little. "Come on, I don't *hate* doctors."

They stared at him, unblinking.

"Okay, they're not my favorite career professional."

"A doctor. How many times have you railed against your parents for putting their high-powered careers ahead of you?" Davis asked. "You think having one as a girlfriend will be better?"

Palmer chimed in. "Maybe we're jumping the gun. What kind of doctor is she? Pediatrician? Allergist? Family practitioner?"

Ben exhaled. "She's an orthopedic surgeon with a specialty in sports medicine."

They exchanged a look and Davis burst out laughing. "Oh man, you're screwed."

"I don't know what you're talking about," he said.

He did. He knew exactly what they were getting at because it was the issue that plagued him most about getting involved with Nic.

"This is new to Palmer, not me. I've seen you with her. I'm the one who interrupted you when you were seconds away from screwing each other on the hammock out there. You want her but having her would go against everything you've said you always wanted."

Ben cradled his head in his hands. "I know."

"Does this have to be a big deal? You're both smart people. Talk to each other, set some boundaries. It could be a good thing," Palmer argued.

"Or it could blow up in our faces." Ben looked at his two friends. "And I'm not sure it's worth the risk."

"She's that important to you?"

Ben didn't hesitate. "Yes."

Palmer offered him a sad smile. "Then that's a problem. Although I never understood your insistence on ruling out a large number of women based on their occupation."

"Of course you don't. Your parents were pretty traditional. You never had to worry about them being there for you when we were kids. They made you and Pete a priority."

"It had nothing to do with their careers. They made us a priority because they wanted to. The same way Bronwen and I will when we have kids."

"Spouses, parents, kids. Can we stop talking about this? Damn, we sound like a bunch of women on a daytime talk show."

"What the fuck's wrong with you?" Ben said, eyeing Davis's sullen expression.

"When does Sabine get here?" Palmer asked. "You need to chill out."

Based on Davis's current attitude, it wouldn't be fast enough. Sabine had a way of curbing Davis's prickish tendencies.

"She isn't coming."

"What?" Ben sat up. "Why?"

"Work. She was offered an opportunity she couldn't pass up. It doesn't matter. I'm fine. It's better this way. Leaves me free to see what the Vineyard has to offer."

Despite Davis's words, Ben saw beneath his bravado to the distress he couldn't hide. Pinged a disappointment he knew all too well.

"If you want to talk about it—"

"I don't."

Ben held up both hands, palms out. "Cool."

"Do you want to talk about Tinsley?" Davis asked.

Distaste burned the back of Ben's throat. "What about her?"

"She's not going to give up without a fight. She's always been possessive. But more than that, she doesn't like being denied anything she wants."

"I'm not a toy or a piece of meat."

"Boo hoo. Ben's torn between two beautiful women."

Palmer pushed to his feet. "I'm going to try and talk to Bronwen again."

"Don't tell her about Nic," Ben warned.

"I won't. Even though you both have made my life more difficult." He strode away murmuring,

"I told her we should've left and just sent you fuckers postcards from Kenya."

Ben laughed but his smile faded as he considered Davis's remark.

"Ben's torn between two beautiful women."

He wasn't torn. It was no contest. Nic would win every day and twice on Sundays. Apparently, he needed to make sure Tinsley got that message.

Chapter Twelve

The warmth against Nic's back was deliciously welcome though unfamiliar. Still, she snuggled into it, murmuring in appreciation when her nose registered a recognizable scent. She couldn't quite place the origin of the fragrance, but she knew she liked it. A liquid heat crept through her inducing her to heed her body's unconscious urge to squeeze her thighs together.

The steel band beneath her breasts tightened and hauled her backward against a solid, muscled mass. A puff of air feathered against the nape of her neck, raising goose bumps on her body. She trailed her hand along the arm, loving the crisp feel of hair beneath her fingertips.

She never slept at her lovers' homes and she definitely didn't bring guys here. But she felt so comfortable in this position. In his arms. It felt right. She shifted, decreasing the space between them, needing to get as close as possible.

Lips nuzzled the base of her neck where it met her shoulder—her spot!—and she shivered. Her nipples budded against the material of her camisole and she undulated her hips.

Maybe she was dreaming. *If so, please, please, please don't wake up.* When she was on call, her sleep was often irregular. Some nights she'd be roused from a deep sleep with no concept of her unconscious state. Other times, she'd been living her best life in slumber and had mourned the loss when awakened. She knew this would be one of the latter circumstances. She wanted to bask in the heady sensations she was experiencing and fight off the cold realism of awareness for as long as possible.

Nic reached behind her, her palm encountering a bristled scruff and hot skin before her fingers slid into the crisp silk of hair. A strong hand smoothed down her arm and cupped her breast. Fire seared through the thin silk of her top and the fine scrape against her sensitive bud sent sparks of pleasure pinging through her. She ground her hips, seeking to be filled. Instinctively knowing what she sought was behind her.

The hard ridge against her ass told her she was right.

"Nic?"

The voice was gruffer than she was used to, with an enticing rumble that would've had her turning on her back and spreading her thighs wide in invitation.

It also alerted her to the fact that she was no longer dreaming.

Ben!

Her eyes flew open and she took in the white cafe table and wicker chairs set beneath the three windows that framed a gorgeous ocean view and an incredible morning sky. She wasn't home. She was in Martha's Vineyard. The memories came roaring into her consciousness: everything that had happened with Tinsley, the stress of her work situation, her fellowship being in jeopardy, her motion sickness. It had finally caught up with her. After her conversation with Ben, she'd taken a couple of aspirin before lying down. She vaguely remembered him coming back and urging her to change into PJs, put on her hair scarf, and brush her teeth before she once again gave in to the sleep her body seemed to desperately need.

Sleep and other things. With Ben. In a bed.

She'd been grinding against Ben! What was wrong with her? What had happened to all of her self-talk of keeping her hands to herself and their friendship intact?

With the speed, if not the gracefulness, of a Hollywood stuntwoman, she threw the coverlet off and rolled across the wide mattress until her feet landed on the hardwood floor.

"I said we could share the bed. I didn't say you could cuddle!"

Ben shifted up onto his elbow, brown hair tousled over his brow. He nodded at the bed. "Um, I'm on my side."

Embarrassment toasted her cheeks. Ben was still on the far end of the mattress. She'd been the one who'd broken the treaty and crossed the invisible wall of Jericho.

Shit.

She crossed her arms over her chest, shifted on her foot, and huffed out a breath skyward. "Sorry."

"Don't worry about it," Ben said, sitting up and yawning.

He stretched his arms over his head and the blanket fell to his waist. Her already dry morning mouth went sub-Saharan.

Had she never seen Ben with his shirt off? No, she hadn't. Good Lord, why had she been denied such a sight? She'd known he was in good shape; he had a membership at a downtown gym and he ran several times a week. She'd assumed he was more on the wiry side. But damn! Clearly defined deltoids, pectorals, biceps, abs, and obliques, he was leanly muscled, not bulky. Like a sexy hand-drawn diagram from her human anatomy textbook come to life. But with skin. Lots and lots of tanned, lickable skin.

When exactly did he find the time for that body? Because *all of that* didn't come from just eating right. It was hard work. The results suggested he'd devoted all of his waking hours to achieving his goal.

She'd gladly dedicate all of *her* waking hours to appreciating it.

"Give me a minute and I'll grab you some coffee," he said, apparently unaware of the internal upheaval he was causing her. "I know you're practically catatonic without it."

He was right. She hadn't had her coffee. Try informing her body of that fact. Her heart raced and she was alert and focused.

On him.

"Thanks. I—"

Nic broke off as Ben swung his legs over the side of the bed.

"I'm going to take a quick shower," she screeched, hurrying into the adjoining bathroom and slamming the door behind her, but not before she saw the confused look he gave her over his shoulder.

Nic stared at her reflection in the mirror. Her green eyes glittered, a flush reddened her cheeks, and she was breathing heavily through parted lips. She looked like she was still experiencing remnants of motion sickness . . . or she wanted to fuck.

What is wrong with you?

She wasn't some bashful, demure woman prone to fits and giggles at the sight of a naked man. She'd seen more than her fair share of nude male bodies, and usually viewed them with the same dispassion she reserved for an arm, elbow, or ankle. Not for titillation, but for diagnosing a problem or as a means of ensuring the part worked properly.

But when Ben had moved to stand, she'd been overcome with this urge of self-preservation. For three years, and a host of reasons, she'd carefully crafted a barrier to prohibit any thoughts of them as anything other than friends. Doing so had enabled her to allow him into her life in a way that no one, save her mother or the Ladies of Lefevre, ever had. Certainly no man. But since the day of her initial encounter with Whitaker, every inter-action between them had been like picking at a loose thread on a cable-knit sweater. And now, the mental obstruction she'd erected was on the verge of falling apart.

Get ahold of yourself!

Ben was one of her best friends. There was no way she was going to risk that. Especially with her fellowship on the line. She'd already received two calls from Duke Medical School but she hadn't answered them, petrified it was Dr. New-man attempting to revoke his offer. She needed Ben to ask his family to intervene on her behalf. And for doing so, she'd vowed to help him keep Tinsley at bay. There was nothing more impor-tant to either of them than that mission.

And even if their mutual favors weren't their immediate goal, they both wanted different things from their significant others. As much as she cared for Ben, she wasn't giving up her career for anyone, and he'd made it clear he'd expect noth-ing less from the woman who would share his life. She needed to keep that one essential fact in her mind.

And keep his body out of it.

When she eventually emerged from the bath-room, she found a note on the dresser.

"Coffee is waiting for you downstairs."

Moving quickly, she dressed in a navy blue floral romper, pulled her silk scarf off, spritzed her hair with a leave-in conditioner, and shook out her curls until they puffed up and floated to her shoulders.

And so it begins . . .

She took a deep breath and left the bedroom. The many windows on the upper floor allowed the bright sunlight in and provided a solar path she followed down the wide landing. It was a beautiful home, warm and welcoming despite its size. Her fingers skimmed along the banister as she descended the stairs, but the sound of laughter, like fingernails on a chalkboard, halted her midstep.

"Benji, you're exaggerating. We had some great times!"

Nic rolled her eyes. What was up with this "Benji" thing? He was a grown man, not a dog!

And she knew how much of a grown man he was.

What if I start with my hands? Gently cover your breasts, then press them hard against you, as your nipples pebble against my palms?

The pleasure from reading the texts blended with the feel of his hands on her this morning, resulting in a sensory overload. She placed her palms on her face and willed herself to calm down. To be believable as Ben's girlfriend was going to require showcasing some intimacy between them, more than she'd anticipated considering Tinsley's resistance to the idea. Nic couldn't be effective if she got flustered each time they touched each other.

Stopping on the split landing, she surveyed the scene below her.

Ben and Tinsley were the only ones in the great room. Ben leaned back against the kitchen counter, cradling a cup of coffee in his hands, a plain white T-shirt covering his glorious chest. Tinsley faced him—her back to Nic—wearing a short teal satin robe, her long pale legs bare.

"I never said we didn't." Ben scratched his cheek. "But toward the end, you made it clear they were few and far between."

"I was young. What did I know? But I've grown since then," Tinsley said, sliding a hand through her blond mane and pulling it forward over her shoulder.

Nice move, Nic begrudgingly allowed.

"Why did you make that comment to Nic last night?" Ben asked.

Nic's breath caught in her throat and her fingers clenched the railing. She didn't need him to get into the specifics of that statement. She'd handled it.

Tinsley huffed out a breath, fluttering a lock of her hair. "I don't want to talk about her."

"I don't give a shit. You couldn't stop talking last night."

Wow, he was angry. He hadn't moved from his position, but he'd narrowed his eyes and his voice had changed. Hardened. It was always startling to experience, since he rarely exhibited that emotion around her.

"Hello, all!" Bronwen strolled in, wearing cut-off jean shorts and a purple tank top, her dark hair pulled into a ponytail. "You're up early, Tinns. I can't recall the last time you emerged from your room before ten."

"That's what I said." Some of the tension seemed to escape Ben's posture. He took a sip of his coffee and Bronwen squeezed his shoulder as she passed him on her way to the coffee machine. "She used to always complain that I got up too early and disturbed her."

Tinsley pivoted away from Ben and mimicked his stance against the counter. "Why does everyone insist on bringing up stuff from the past?"

"I asked you about last night," Ben said.

"Yes, like I said. The past. Besides"—Tinsley shrugged one shoulder—"I only wanted to spend a little more time with you in bed."

Cuddling like Nic and Ben had this morning? More, probably.

Not wanting to get caught eavesdropping, and knowing she'd already pushed her luck, she pasted a smile on her lips. Time to get this show on the road.

"Good morning," she said brightly.

Ben straightened and set his cup down. He met her as she descended the last step. "You feeling better?"

Was he asking about her motion sickness or her massive freak-out from before? She stared up at him, struck by the masculine beauty of his face. Why had she ever thought him safe? With his tousled hair and lean, scruffy cheeks, he looked downright dangerous.

Mesmerized by him, she nodded.

He smiled. "Good."

Here we go . . .

She curved a hand around the nape of his neck and drew his head down to brush her lips against his. The kiss lasted only a moment, but it was long enough to do some serious damage to her composure. She pulled away and their eyes opened at the same time. They gazed at each other for one heart-stopping, world-erasing moment, before she released him, letting her arm fall to her side.

"Very good," she whispered. "That was really believable."

Ben blinked and his expression closed. "Thanks. Now, let's get you some coffee."

She preceded him into the kitchen where its two occupants were watching her with curiosity-tinged expressions from the opposite ends of the welcoming spectrum.

"How did you sleep?" Bronwen asked.

Nic slid a sidelong glance at Ben. "I don't know. How did I?"

Coming over behind her, he placed a hand on her hip and nuzzled her neck. "Very well," he murmured, in a tone that turned her insides to mush.

It's only pretend. It's only pretend. It's only pretend.

"I think I threw up a little in my mouth," Tinsley said, rolling her eyes.

"Oh hello, Tinsley. How are you?"

No matter how she personally felt about Tinsley, the only way to handle a woman like her was to act as if she wasn't bothered by her. Tinsley would feed off the misery she caused and see it as her way in with Ben.

"Just peachy. Ben and I got up early and spent some private time catching up."

Nic smiled blandly, not wanting to spend the entire day verbally sparring with the other woman. "I'm glad."

"I was thinking. Nic is so masculine. I'm going to call you Nicole. You don't mind, do you?"

Mind you disrespecting me by calling me something that isn't my preference?

So much for avoiding early conflict.

Nic waved an airy hand. "If you don't mind me calling you one of the many names that come to mind?"

Tinsley narrowed her eyes. "Nic it is."

"Would you like a cup of coffee?" Bronwen asked.

"I've got it, Bron. Thanks," Ben said.

"But we were in the middle of a conversation." Tinsley pouted.

He grabbed a mug and poured Nic a cup. "I can multitask."

"But it was private!"

Nic was surprised Tinsley didn't stomp her foot.

"Was it?" Nic asked.

Ben brought Nic a cup of coffee. "Just as I promised."

She almost went boneless. "Bless you." She blew away the steam and took a sip.

Ben resumed his stance at the counter and pulled Nic into the vee of his legs. He wrapped his arms loosely around her waist. "Never get in the way of Nic and her first cup of coffee. She values it more than Gollum treasured the ring."

Tinsley laughed loudly and tilted her head. "Benji, that's not a nice way to describe her. I mean, we all can't be beautiful early in the morning."

Nic paused in sipping her coffee and her hand tightened around the mug. Maybe she needed to rethink how she handled the other woman. Although acting this way wasn't a good look. Did Tinsley really think hiding her bitchery beneath a thin veil of joking was going to win her Ben back? Had she ever known Ben?

Did you?

Nic had known Ben only a few years. These guys had known him most of his life. Maybe Tinsley did know him better than Nic did. After all, she was the one who'd been engaged to him.

"Tinsley," Ben warned.

"It's okay," Nic said, leaning briefly into him. "She was just joking."

"Exactly. Chill out," Tinsley said, flipping her hair.

"And as we learned from last night, her jokes aren't funny."

Davis strolled into the kitchen yawning. "I'm going to allow it this morning, but once the partying commences, being up this early will be a sin."

"I heard about Sabine," Bronwen said, going over to Davis and giving him a hug.

Davis returned the embrace briefly, before pulling loose. "Did someone say coffee?"

"I'll get it," Bronwen said, pouring him a cup. "Guys, I'm sorry about last night. My plans were . . . Anyway, I thought we'd keep it easy today. Maybe just hang out at the beach? The chef will come in later to make us lunch and then we'll head into town for dinner."

A day at the beach.

Nic looked down at her outfit. "I think I'm a little overdressed."

Ben smiled and brushed a knuckle against her cheek. "Yeah, but you're always beautiful, no matter what you wear."

She admired his tall frame as she watched him walk over to Davis. He had a quiet, confident swagger she found extremely appealing and she suddenly understood why she'd worked so hard to keep him in the friend zone. Her mother was right: he was perfect.

Funny, smart, caring, and handsome.

And looking for a woman who wasn't a doctor, like his parents.

Turning to help herself to another cup of coffee, she caught Tinsley staring after him, a look of longing on her face. Nic would've almost felt bad for her. Almost.

Ah, who was she kidding? She'd never feel bad for the other woman.

It's too late. You tossed him aside and he's mine now.

Except he wasn't hers. And for the first time she found herself questioning the wisdom of that decision.

Chapter Thirteen

With his left hand, Ben tossed the volleyball high in the air, then leaned back with his right and made contact with the leather, sending the ball soaring over the net. On the other side Davis met his serve with a bump, hitting the ball straight upward. Bronwen ran forward and launched herself in the air, smacking the ball with the flat of her hand and spiking it back to their side.

Ben pointed to his teammate. "Palmer, that's you!"

Palmer dove, kicking up sand, but keeping the ball in play. Ben bumped it, setting it up for Palmer, who leaped in the air and spiked it over the net, where it landed on the sand in a sweet spot between Davis and Bronwen.

"Game!" Ben yelled, high-fiving Palmer. "You two want to go again?"

"With Davis? Hell no." Bronwen glared at her partner, who stood hunched over with his hands braced above his knees. "Next game, I get my husband back and you take Mr. Hangover!"

"I said 'a nice and easy game' of volleyball. How was I supposed to know you were expecting Olympic-caliber play?" Davis straightened. "I need a break."

Palmer looked at his watch. "And I need to make a quick phone call. I'll be right back." He slapped Bronwen playfully on the ass and jogged to where he'd left his belongings.

Ben grabbed a bottle of water out of the nearby cooler and drained it, his eyes searching for Nic. It didn't take long to spot her. Not only because of the red bikini that had actually given him heart palpitations when she'd come downstairs wearing it, but because they were the only six inhabitants in the area. In addition to the six acres on which it sat, the estate boasted over three hundred feet of private beachfront. Loungers, chairs, umbrellas, and coolers were all provided for a perfect day of fun.

He didn't go to her, needing a bit of distance. He wiped his face with a towel, resettled his shades on his nose, and dropped down onto a beach lounger. His eyes tracked Nic as she and Bronwen walked to the water's edge, the waves lapping their ankles and calves.

Lucky water.

She'd gathered her curls on top of her head and secured them with a scarf. The red bikini she wore wasn't the skimpiest, but it made the most of her curves. He honestly didn't know if he was being rewarded or tortured. That's why he'd been ready for a game of beach volleyball, hoping the physical exertion would tame his raging hormones. It had worked for a time.

Now they were back.

In truth, he'd been in a constant state of near arousal since he'd awakened this morning to find Nic's delectable ass grinding against his cock and the slight weight of her breast resting on his arm. At first he'd been sure he was dreaming, since being entwined with Nic in his bed had run on a constant loop in his fantasies all week. When he'd realized he was indeed awake, he couldn't believe his luck. But he'd needed to make sure she was cognizant, too.

She had been and the fantasy ended.

Which is why he'd been surprised when she'd kissed him on the stairs. It had been too brief, though it had stoked his desire for her, made him crave more.

"Very good. That was really believable."

She'd been acting. For Tinsley's sake.

He'd been disappointed but it was the reminder he needed. Nic was the whole package. Not only was she extremely intelligent and funny, she was so beautiful, she made his chest hurt. He could get caught up in believing this was all real when it wasn't. He was here to spend time with his friends and Nic's presence allowed him to enjoy himself without worrying about Tinsley. Something he'd do well to remember.

A shadow fell over him and he glanced up.

Tinsley stood beside him, dazzling in a shimmery turquoise bikini. "Good game out there. Congratulations."

"Thanks," he said.

"Sitting over here all by yourself?" she asked, her tongue pushed between her teeth.

Maybe wallowing in space hadn't been a good idea.

"Appears so." He watched as Nic threw her head back and laughed at something Bronwen said.

Tinsley lowered herself onto the end of his lounger and pushed her sunglasses up on her head. She stared at his shirtless chest. "You're looking great, Benji. Are you doing something different?"

"Not really."

Unease with her constant attempts to seek him out prickled his scalp. He would've been incredibly flattered, instead of annoyed, if he'd believed her attention had anything to do with him as a person and not her perceived belief in him changing because of what he'd acquired. He was the same person now as he was six years ago; it was his personal wealth and status outside of his family that was new. He moved back, increasing the space between them.

"Are you sure? I don't remember you being so . . ." She inhaled, then tilted her head down, her long blond tresses tumbling forward over her arm and her breasts. She glanced at him from beneath her lashes, as she reached over and began lightly stroking his thigh.

He sighed and put his hand over hers, trapping it flat and preventing her fingers from traveling any higher. "Stop."

"What?" She fluttered her lashes. "We're just talking."

He encircled her wrist and removed her hand from his leg. "I know what you're doing. I'm very familiar with your moves."

She bared her unbelievably white teeth. "You used to like my moves."

"I did. But that time has passed."

"We can bring it back," she said playfully.

"No, we can't."

Her expression hardened and she turned her head to look away from him. "Because of her?"

Remembering his purpose here, he answered, "Partly."

But what Tinsley didn't seem to understand was that even if Nic wasn't in the picture, he still wouldn't be with her. She'd left him when he'd needed the support of the person he loved and wanted to marry. Long after the affection disappeared, the betrayal remained.

He just wasn't interested in her anymore. He wished she would listen to what he was saying. He didn't want to have to hurt her feelings.

She tried again biting her glossed lower lip. "Is there anything I can do?"

Actually— "You can apologize to Nic."

Tinsley's head jerked back.

"For what?" she asked, all traces of her kittenish demeanor and coy remorse gone.

"For what you said last night."

"It was a joke!"

"Hennessey and Courvoisier. They sounded familiar but I didn't understand why you'd bring them up." Or why doing so had made Nic angry, though she'd denied it. "So I googled them and I'm pretty clear about your intent."

"Benji—"

"Nic is my guest and the way you acted, what you said, it wasn't cool."

"It's not that serious. If Nic was offended, she should've said something."

She was actually going to sit there and try to defend her behavior?

"She shouldn't have to! It's not her job to activate your morality. You shouldn't have said it. But you did and it was fucked-up. You owe her an apology."

She pressed her lips together and set her chin.

He removed his sunglasses, so she could see how serious he was. "What are you doing? The snide remarks, the rudeness, the lack of respect? Did I ever seem like the type of man who'd think that was okay? I mean, even if I were interested, and I'm not, do you think I'd find that behavior attractive?"

Her mouth trembled. "Why are you speaking to me this way? Is this something you picked up from your girlfriend?"

"No."

"I don't believe you."

Forget not being in love with her. At this moment, he didn't even like her. He couldn't believe he'd ever asked her to be his wife.

"That's not news. You never could accept that I knew my own mind."

Her eyes narrowed and her features tightened, but before she could respond, Nic ran up. The smile slid from her face and she glanced from one to the other. "Am I interrupting anything?"

He'd been expecting Tinsley to take issue with the intrusion, and was prepared to address it, so he was surprised when she said, "No, we're done."

Her response must've astounded Nic, too, because she didn't try to hide her incredulity. She cleared her throat and held out her hand to him. "Walk with me?"

"Absolutely. Excuse us."

Pushing to his feet, he took Nic's hand, his skin tingling at the contact, and headed down the beach. With the sun shining bright and the sounds—in stereo—of the waves crashing and seagulls cawing, Ben felt a serenity settle over him. He released Nic's hand and slung his arm around her shoulder, thrilled when she slid a corresponding arm around his waist and snuggled close.

"Is she watching us?" Nic asked.

The question disturbed his peace. "I don't know."

She bumped him with her hip. "Then look. But don't be so obvious about it."

"How am I supposed to do that?"

Nic exhaled audibly. "Oh my God, men can be

so useless! I bet if I asked Bronwen to do this, she'd know exactly what to do."

She stopped abruptly and turned to face him, raising her arms and clasping her hands behind his neck. He did what felt natural, grasping her around her waist. Though she stared up at him with eyes hidden behind a pair of oversized sunglasses, she said, "She's still watching us. Let's talk."

He felt ridiculous. "Isn't that what we're doing?"

"Then let's continue."

She laid her hand flat over his heart and it hammered inside his chest, beating wildly like it wanted to break free and touch her palm.

What this woman did to him!

He struggled to come up with some innocuous topic of discussion. "I can't wait until we go into town for dinner tonight."

Smooth, Ben. Real smooth.

"Me, too. I think my stomach is finally settled enough to eat. You must've worked up quite an appetite."

"Excuse me?" he said, certain he'd somehow given himself away.

"Volleyball." She motioned her head toward the net. "I didn't know you could move like that."

"What are you talking about? I've got lots of moves," he said.

"Oh really. Why haven't I seen them?"

Though uttered with levity, the question hung in the air between them, a hovering verbal grenade that could explode any minute.

She refused to meet his gaze. "Never mind."

"You should join us for the next game."

He noticed a lone curl nestled below her earlobe. He grabbed it between his fingers.

Her lips parted on an exhale.

He wanted to kiss those lips. And not like the fleeting peck from earlier. He wanted to capture her mouth with his, nibble at the fullness, tug it gently beneath his teeth before running his tongue along the seam of said lips and deepening the kiss.

His cock strained against his shorts.

She swallowed before responding. "No thanks."

"Why not? I remember you mentioning a game you played with your friends on your recent vacation."

"That's pool volleyball. Very different from beach volleyball."

He released the curl, then traced it flat with his finger against her skin. "How?"

Her pulse throbbed at the base of her neck. "The water. It's like a secret weapon, giving you extra athletic ability. I'm able to dive and jump in the pool in a way that would terrify me on the sand. Damn, she's persistent. She's still watching us."

Nic pulled away from him and jerkily touched her hair.

Thinking of his recent conversation with Tinsley he said, "I wouldn't worry about it. She'll get over it."

"Are you sure you want her to?"

He frowned. "What does that mean?"

"Just that Tabitha may be a lot of things, but she's not stupid."

"Tinsley," he corrected, more to play their little game than over any real concern that Nic got her name wrong.

"Whatever. If you were truly clear about your feelings, she'd stop. I have a hard time believing she'd chase someone she knew didn't want her."

"Whoa. *If*?" She didn't believe him? She thought he was lying or playing some game? "Do you think I've been vague about what I want?"

"She's responding to something."

"I don't know what she's responding to, but it's not any mixed messages from me. In fact, I told her as much before you walked over."

Her eyes widened. "You did?"

"I did," he said forcefully. He lowered his voice. "And I owe you an apology."

"No you don't."

"Yes, I do. I'm embarrassed I had to google it to figure it out, but I get the point of her comment last night and why it made you so angry. And I'm sorry."

She placed a hand on his arm. "That wasn't you. That was her."

He caressed her cheek. "I would never knowingly invite you anyplace where I thought you wouldn't be treated with the utmost respect. I'm sorry I didn't get what she said, not only because it was ugly and ignorant and you had to hear it, but because I couldn't have your back and you had to deal with it on your own. But no more. If she says something like that again, I want you to tell me."

She rolled her eyes. "You can't protect me twenty-four seven from all the intolerant bullshit I have to deal with."

Unfortunately. Though he'd gladly sign up to do it.

"I know." He cupped her shoulders. "But here, with these people, I can. Promise me, okay?"

Her tongue darted out to wet her lower lip and he almost groaned.

That's my job!

"Okay."

"Good. Now, can I propose something completely wacky?"

She eyed him suspiciously. "How wacky?"

"You graduate in a couple of weeks and a little after that you'll be gone and I'm . . . I'm going to miss you. We're here for three more days. Starting with tonight, let's just enjoy ourselves." He spread his arms wide. "It's our first vacation together. I know it can't possibly live up to a Ladies of the Fever vacation, but—"

"Ladies of *Le*fevre," she said, a grin lighting up her face.

He knew. He just liked looking at her when she laughed.

"And I'm going to miss you, too." She went into his arms, her soft curls tickling his chin.

This was it, all he could ever have with Nic. Friendship. She'd made it clear she wasn't interested in pursuing anything more between them and he had to respect that. Any outward affection she showed him was for Tinsley's benefit.

His theory was proved moments later when Nic lifted her head. "Hey! You were right. She's finally gone."

She moved away, leaving him unsettled and oddly bereft.

Chapter Fourteen

𝒩ic glanced at the clock on her phone, then shielded her eyes and stared at the guys laughing and throwing a football on the beach.

"Leave them," Bronwen said, her ponytail swaying as she shook her head. "They'll be out here for another hour."

"I thought you said our reservation was in ninety minutes?"

Their lack of concern about the time was making Nic anxious and turning her into Caila, something she did *not* appreciate.

"It is. But, if history is any indication, they'll saunter in, take a shower, throw on some clothes, and still be the most gorgeous things there." Bronwen wrinkled her pert nose. "Sickening."

Nic laughed. She could see that. All three men, though completely different in looks, possessed a handsomeness and an easy elegance that elevated anything they wore. She'd once seen Ben attired in a wrinkled shirt with a pair of jeans and hadn't been sure if he'd grabbed it off the floor of his closet, or if the designer had intended it that way.

Ben caught the ball on the run and tucked it close to his body, raising one triumphant arm in the air. The early evening light added dimension to his dark strands and she bit her lip. Damn, but she enjoyed watching him. When he caught her staring, one corner of his mouth lifted in a confident grin . . . just before Palmer crashed into him and they fell in a tangle of limbs. Davis scooped up a mound of sand and chucked it on them, over their laughing protests.

Nic snorted. "What are they, twelve?"

"When all three of them get together? Yeah."

Nic watched Ben execute a move that brought Davis down. Even as she winced, leery of the broken bones that could carelessly occur, she admired the easy camaraderie born from knowing each other for years.

"You're going to love this restaurant," Bronwen said. "It's a Vineyard institution and the food is spectacular. We haven't been there in years, but Palmer introduced me to it when he brought me here for the first time."

Nic mentally ran through the clothes she'd packed. "Is it dressy?"

"Not really. I wouldn't go like this," Bronwen said, pointing to her bikini top and cut-off shorts, "but a simple sundress is fine."

"Sounds good. I'm looking forward to it."

Leaving the men behind, they climbed the

wooden steps and crossed the walking bridge. They closed the gate behind them and descended the steps to the manicured back lawn.

"Hey, before we go in . . ." Bronwen stopped Nic with a hand on her arm. "I want to apologize for Tinsley."

Nic resisted rolling her eyes. Not only was she tired of talking about this woman, Nic was annoyed that through Tinsley's actions, she'd been turned into some sort of a victim.

"Don't worry about it."

"She can be a lot of fun, but how she's acting is inexcusable. I didn't object when she invited herself along because the guys can be a handful when they get together and I thought having another woman here would be nice. But if I'd known about you and Benji . . ." She massaged her temple with her fingers. "It's a mess and I'm sorry."

Nic tried to imagine herself in Bronwen's shoes. She'd thought she was going to spend a few days with some close friends before heading halfway across the world to selflessly help others for three years. Instead, she was having to deal with a real-life soap opera. And Bronwen had been nothing but friendly and welcoming toward her, despite the truth that Nic *was* crashing their party. She could cut the other woman all of the slack.

Nic reached out and squeezed Bronwen's hand. "I appreciate that, but it's all good. I can handle Tinsley."

Bronwen's expression softened and her lips

pressed into a wobbly smile. "I'm glad to hear that because . . . Ben looks great."

Nic recalled him shirtless on the beach, the muscles in his back rippling when he served the volleyball.

"That he does," she murmured.

Bronwen's bark of laughter surprised them both. "I didn't mean it that way, although . . . uh, yeah. But, the two of you together, you look happy."

Nic thought of her relationship with Ben, not just here, but over the past three years. "We are."

"If anyone deserves a little happiness, it's Ben. If you breathe a word of this to anyone, I'll deny it to my dying day, but with Palmer, it was love at first sight. That doesn't mean I didn't make him work for it," she said impishly, "but I knew he was the one. It didn't take long before he introduced me to Ben and Davis. Those boys are his brothers as much as Pete is. And now, *my* brothers. I worry about them. With Davis, his issues are obvious."

Nic pictured the tall man with his jet-black hair and light blue eyes and nodded. "You can read that book from a mile away."

"Oh my God, right?" They shared a look before Bronwen continued. "But with Benji, most people don't dig beneath the surface. They assume his life is perfect, but . . ."

"It's not," she finished.

Nic had been one of those people. She'd heard his last name, saw his easygoing manner, and couldn't imagine his life being anything but charmed. The more she'd gotten to know him, the more she'd been treated to the reality of the true man who was smart, generous, and funny. But also, really lonely.

"Anyway, it seems like I didn't need to worry. You obviously make him happy. Thanks for hearing me out." Bronwen started walking. "I already know what I'm going to order. Did I mention the restaurant is Italian? Their osso buco is to die for."

Carbs. Just what she needed. It amped up her anticipation for the evening. But Nic needed to do something first. "You go ahead. I'll be up in a second."

"Okay." She waved then continued up to the house.

Nic sat down on one of the white Adirondack chairs and pulled her knees up to her chest. She tapped the screen of her cell phone with her thumb and waited for the call to connect.

"Hey you," Ava said, her beautiful face breaking into a smile.

Nic grinned. "Your Honor. I hope I'm not disturbing you."

"My trial ended early and I'm finishing up some paperwork."

Behind Ava, her credenza and hutch were filled with books, knickknacks, and framed pictures of her family and the four friends during their vacation to see the giant redwoods in California.

Ava didn't wait for Nic to respond. "Your girl's

a trip. I guess I shouldn't be surprised. She'd mate with a spreadsheet if she could. She needs help."

The words, though harsh, were spoken with obvious affection. Nic used the context clues skills she'd honed in the third grade. Caila. "What did she do?"

Ava raised two perfectly sculpted brows. "Her email? About shopping for her wedding?"

Nic hadn't checked her email in a couple of days. "I haven't seen it. What did she say?"

"She wants to coordinate our dress fittings so we could all Skype in." Ava frowned and waved a hand. "If you didn't call about her email, what's up?"

Nic recoiled in horror. Skype their dress fittings?

"Can you imagine being in the store and having to ask the clerk to hold our phones while we conferenced?" Nic pinched the bridge of her nose. "Not going to happen."

"We can talk about it *after* you read the email. But don't change the subject. What's going on? Is it work?"

"Kind of."

She hadn't told her friends what happened, probably because admitting it to them would be akin to accepting it was a done deal. She planned to rectify the situation and get her fellowship back. Her friends would never have to know.

"You only have a few weeks left. How could you get in—" Ava broke off as the sound of a seagull's cawing bellowed nearby. She narrowed her eyes and her face suddenly filled the screen. "That doesn't look like Baltimore to me. Where are you?"

Nic sighed. "Martha's Vineyard."

"Martha's Vin— What in the hell are you doing there?"

"It's a long story."

"You can give me the abridged version while I finish this paperwork." Ava placed her phone on a stand and her image widened to incorporate more of the shelves behind her. "It'll be like listening to a podcast."

The short version. How about she'd awakened in the arms of the man she'd come to consider as one of her best friends and now couldn't stop craving those arms around her again?

"You remember Ben, right?"

"Sure. He's the guy you rent from?"

This would all be much easier if that's all he was.

"A couple of his friends are going out of the country for a few years and they're gathering over the long weekend to celebrate. Like a fancy bon voyage party. He invited me."

"That was nice of him." Ava wrote something on the paper in front of her then glanced up at Nic. "How did you manage to get the time off for a long weekend?"

"I had some time coming to me."

Nic didn't miss the suspicion in Ava's tone. She should've known the other woman couldn't be diverted from a topic of interest unless she wanted to be. It was part of what made her an amazing legal mind. Nic would reveal it all to Ava . . . one day. Right now, she needed help with another problem.

She cleared her throat and took a deep breath. "I think I might like him. Like, *like* him, like him."

"Oh sweetie." Ava's dark brown eyes softened and she put down her pen. "I know we just saw each other, but I'd be happy to fly you out for a few days. I can rearrange my schedule a little and we can hang out . . ."

Nic was confused. Her confession was important and she'd wanted Ava's input, but her response didn't seem . . . proportionate. What she'd admitted to didn't rise to a level one DEFCON emergency, the kind that would make any of the Ladies of Lefevre drop what they were doing and immediately fly to the aid of another. The way Ava had for Caila during that whole work debacle last year.

"Why would I fly out—"

"You've been working so hard and you probably take no time to relax and get out to meet people. When you do have time off, you spend it in the house with Ben. This was bound to happen. But you know it won't work, right?"

Despite her own similar thinking, Nic bristled at Ava's frank statement. "Why not?"

Ava's glossed lips fell open. "Because he's gay!"

Nic couldn't help herself. She burst out laughing. "You're laughing at him?" Ava wrinkled her nose. "You can be harsh, but that seems cruel, even for you and it's not a good look."

Nic blew out a stabilizing breath and attempted to speak. Failed, then tried again. "I'm not laughing at *him*. I'm laughing at *you*! Ben isn't gay!"

"He's not?"

"Fuck no! Why would you think that?"

Ava had actually met Ben last year when she'd visited Nic after spending some time with Caila in Chicago. It had been only in passing; he'd come in just as they were leaving.

But still.

"Because he's gorgeous, rich, and, according to you, a real sweetheart and until this point, you've never expressed any interest in him at all!"

Not one of her brightest moments. How had she gone all of this time not seeing what was right in front of her? It was like learning the secret behind a magician's trick. She couldn't imagine how she'd never known.

"Well, I'm an idiot. And trust me, he's not gay."

I won't take it into my mouth until you're moaning loudly & your hot body is writhing against me.

She shivered.

"And you haven't jumped on that?"

"He was my friend! But now, 'jumping on that' is all I can think about. And I'm scared."

"Because you don't want to ruin the friendship." It was a statement, not a question.

Ava understood. True friendship was extremely important to Nic. It was the reason she treasured Ava, Caila, and Lacey as much as she did. She'd found a really good friend in Ben. Was she willing to risk that for sex?

"When's the last time you got laid?"

"Six months."

It had been on her mind a lot lately. It's why she'd tried to reach out to Carlos last week. It's why she was in this situation!

I'll swirl my tongue around them, savoring their feel & taste.

"Damn."

"I know." Nic had always had a healthy sexual appetite. But recently, she hadn't wanted to expend the minimal effort required with her usual lovers. She enjoyed spending her free time with Ben. And she had a drawer full of toys when the ache had gotten to be too much.

"Maybe it's not Ben," Ava offered helpfully. "Maybe you're just horny and any old dick would do?"

Nic stared across the yard to the spot where they'd stood yesterday. Before Davis had appeared, she'd wanted to climb Ben the way he'd described scaling that grand oak as a teen.

"No. It's definitely Ben."

"Then you win the group's award for self-discipline. I don't know any of us who could've lived with a man like that for three years without adding a little bonus to the rent," Ava said, adding a sassy shimmy of her shoulders.

"But what do I do?"

Ava sighed. "What do you want to do?"

That was easy. "Him. I want to do him."

"Does he feel the same way?"

God, my skin is tingling & I'm so wet.

Can I feel?

Nic licked her lips. "Yeah."

"Then what's holding you back?"

Frustration tightened her stomach as a confusing brew of conflicting thoughts whirled through her mind.

"Let me ask you this," Ava said. "If you fuck and it's . . . not good, do you think he'd be an ass about it?"

She couldn't imagine either scenario being true. "No."

"Then this is the perfect time to explore your attraction. If it doesn't work out, he'll still be your friend. And if you can't go back to being friends, you're leaving soon. There's nothing he can do to negatively affect you."

Except not ask his parents to talk to the head of the Duke fellowship on her behalf.

Nic dismissed that thought as soon as it entered her mind. That wasn't the kind of man Ben was. It may have been better for her if he was. It would give her an easy excuse to keep him in the friend zone.

"I have to go," she finally said, unfolding from the chair. "We're leaving for dinner soon and I need to get dressed."

Ava nodded. "Have fun. And we'll deal with this Caila thing later."

"Sure."

Despite what Ava said, Nic knew they would all end up doing exactly what Caila wanted.

"Oh! Don't forget Lacey's out here for her audition. We're all on call in case she needs us."

Nic pinched her lips together. She *had* forgotten. "Thanks for the reminder."

"You call or text if *you* need *me*."

"I will."

"And Nic? Listen to your gut. Whatever you decide is what will happen."

"How do you know that?"

A soft, loving smile tilted the corners of Ava's mouth. "Because you're the most determined woman I know."

"I thought that was Caila?"

"No, Caila is driven. Some may say obsessed. You are determined. When you set a goal for yourself, you let nothing stand in your way and I've always admired that about you. Just . . . consider the repercussions. Make sure you truly want it, all of it, before you decide to go after him."

Chapter Fifteen

Ben knocked on the closed en suite bathroom door. "Are you almost done?"

"Stop rushing me!" Nic called back.

Rushing her? She'd been up here at least an hour before him. In fact, when he'd gotten back to the room, he'd had to grab his stuff and get dressed in Davis's room because she'd been in the bathroom. The only reason he knew she hadn't been in there the entire time he'd been gone was the missing dress that had lain on the bed.

"You have ten minutes and then we're leaving, with or without you!"

"Like I'd ever believe that, Van Mont!"

She knew him well.

Still— "You don't have to believe it, but you better listen," he called back, before sliding open the patio door and stepping out onto the balcony.

"They never listen."

Ben froze, recalling the words he'd thought he'd heard and the disturbing mixture of resignation, anger, and disappointment that had poured off

Quentin Miller. He knew that pain, that sense that you were screaming for something as loud as you could and no one seemed to hear.

Let alone care.

And he hadn't been any better. He'd leaped to conclusions about Quentin's life, having the man broke and retired before he'd even played his first professional game.

Before he could talk himself out of it, he pulled out his phone and accessed the player's files. Finding Quentin's number, he placed the call.

"Quentin?"

"Yeah?"

There was music and the sound of people talking in the background. Shit!

"This is Ben Van Mont from Reed Financial Services." He spoke loudly to be heard over the commotion. "Do you have a moment?"

"Make it fast. I'm having dinner with my family."

Ben could hear the impatience in Quentin's voice. He was grateful the man had even taken the call, considering the way their initial encounter had ended.

"When we met in my office you said, 'They never listen.' If you don't mind me asking, who were you referring to?"

"People like you. The money people. Usually white."

"And what don't we listen to?"

Quentin sighed the sigh of someone exhausted

by dealing with people who didn't understand him. "To me. To why those names were on the forms. To why I need to take care of them."

"All of them?" He didn't bother hiding his skepticism.

"You and I may have gone to the same high school but we come from different worlds," Quentin said. "I lived in a rough neighborhood only a few miles from your office, if you can believe it. Football was my way out of there, for me and my family. Some of the people on that list made sure I got to school safely. Some of them ran interference, kept the bad element off me. Some of them gave me a place to crash when things weren't great at home. Yeah, it was my talent on the field, but I wouldn't have made it without *them*."

Ben admired the fortitude Quentin had to have possessed to triumph in the face of those odds. He understood why the player would want to share his success with those who helped him. But—

"I've seen these relationships. They never work out. People get resentful."

"I don't need a father figure. I had one. I just need a financial manager to take care of my paper and advise me when it comes to getting more. I'll make the final decision on how to spend it."

Ben nodded, though the other man couldn't see him. "I understand. Thank you for taking the time to speak with me."

They disconnected the call. Ben placed the phone in his pocket and headed back into the bedroom. He thought he'd made a decision about

Quentin but now he was questioning himself. He really liked the player, but if Ben took him on as a client, he might be stretching his business beyond his solo practitioner capabilities. He'd had no interest in doing that before.

Had that changed?

"Who's out there with you?" Nic asked through the door.

He frowned. "Nobody."

"I thought I heard you talking to someone?"

Oh. "I made a phone call to a potential client."

"Another app creator?"

"No. This one's in sports. Quentin Jackson."

She paused for a lengthy moment then asked, "Q-ball?"

He jerked his head back. "How do you know him? You hate football."

"Yeah, but I watch ESPN and I know sports. He's really good. He'd be a great catch for your firm." She chuckled. "'Catch'? See what I did there?"

His lips twitched. "It appears Tinsley isn't the only one with bad jokes."

He couldn't hear her response, but he was certain it contained a curse word or four.

He gave in to the grin. "We *would* be fortunate to get Quentin but taking him on would increase my workload beyond what I can realistically manage on my own."

"Then hire help."

The same solution Ezra had given. Neither of them seemed to get it.

Ben exhaled and leaned against the wall. "I've always wanted Reed Financial Services to remain small."

Her reply was immediate. "But you're too good for that. Are you afraid of success?"

He set his jaw. "The firm is successful *now*. If I take on more clients and employees, running the business will become my life."

"And then you won't have time for the type of family you want." Nic's sigh was audible through the door. "Ben, you don't know what the future holds. You have the chance to do more of what you love. Why limit yourself?"

"There's nothing wrong with placing a higher value on the 'life' option in the work/life balance."

"You know that's a privilege not everyone can claim, right?"

"What is?"

"Turning down the opportunity to make more money so you can be available for this fictitious family you're planning." A clatter, the sound of an aerosol spray, and then, "There, I'm done."

A moment later, the bathroom door opened and she emerged in a mouthwatering cloud of fragrance.

"Cuteness takes time," she said, smoothing a hand down the pretty green dress she wore.

His heart skidded to a stop, then began to pound for all it was worth. She'd left her hair free, though the curls seemed more pronounced, more . . . defined. Her lashes looked fuller, her lips redder and poutier.

He couldn't stop staring at her. His eyes finally left her face and dropped to her body. The top of the dress cupped her breasts, showcasing her pert cleavage, and molded to her torso. The flowy skirt swirled around her legs and the thigh-high slit teased him with the occasional tantalizing peek of skin.

And what the color did to her eyes . . .

He swallowed. "You look . . . incredible."

"Thank you. I hope it was worth the wait," she said with a soft—flirtatious?—smile.

"It was."

"Good." She walked over to her suitcase and pulled out a pair of strappy silver shoes. "I had fun this afternoon. Your friends are great."

He watched her slide into her shoes and suddenly understood how foot fetishes could become a thing. Was there anything about this woman that didn't turn him on? "That's nice of you to say."

"It's true. They're all outgoing and interesting, for the most part."

Except for one. "I'm sorry about Tinsley."

After she'd left them on the beach, he hadn't seen Tinsley for the rest of the day. He still didn't know if she was joining them for dinner.

Nic paused in the act of putting on silver hoop earrings. "Jesus Christ! I wish everyone would stop apologizing to me for her. She's not your responsibility. She's a grown woman."

"She's not acting like it."

"Your other friends have been lovely. Especially

since I'm sure my presence has thrown off the dynamic."

"No it hasn't."

She gave him a knowing look. "One year, Lacey invited a woman she'd met dancing in a master class to join us."

That was news to him. "You allow guests to come on your vacations?"

"Not anymore," Nic said, her eyes wide. "It's taken years to work out how we like to do things. A lot of trial and error. And the woman, as nice as she was, wouldn't make an effort. She didn't want to spend any time with us and kept sneaking off on her own when we weren't looking. She even brought some rando dude back to the house where we were staying. By the end of the vacation, the rule was no more invitations."

"Ouch."

She winced. "I know. That sounds horrible. We're not some cliquish group, I promise. We all have other friends—"

"Clearly," he said.

She smiled. He loved her smile.

"—but our annual trip is our time. To catch up, reminisce, celebrate our accomplishments, mourn our failures. It's like an annual rejuvenation. And it requires trust and privacy."

He knew of her trips; she'd gone on one each of the three years she'd lived with him. But he'd thought of them as simple vacations. The way she spoke made them seem almost spiritual.

"I understand your friends' concerns," she said.

"And they've been wonderful. As for your ex, I can handle her. That's my job while I'm here, right?"

Right. As far as Nic was concerned, it was the main reason she was here.

So get your lust in check, Van Mont, and enjoy this time with your friends.

THEY ENDED UP at a casual Italian restaurant in town. Tinsley hadn't joined them, telling Bronwen she'd made other plans. She hadn't been missed. They'd eaten, laughed, and shared a lot of memories. Recalling what Nic had mentioned about the extra guest on her vacay, he made sure to check in with her often. But she appeared to be enjoying herself, talking to Bronwen, occasionally joining in on their ribbing, but mostly, watching them—him—with an indulgent smile curving her lips. At one point during dinner, he'd reached for her hand. With their fingers entwined together, it had felt natural to raise them and kiss her knuckles.

Tinsley wasn't present. There had been no need to pretend. But he'd done it for no other reason than he'd wanted to.

Nic had turned her bright vivid gaze on him and in that moment, everyone else faded away, leaving just the two of them.

You know my nipples are supersensitive. I can come just from you pulling & sucking on them.

Then that's what I'll do . . .

"Do you need us to leave?" Davis had asked, a smirk on his face.

Ben blinked as reality came crashing back.

"Don't offer if you don't mean it," Nic said.

Everyone laughed, sweeping away that moment of tension. But when he'd shot a quick glance at Nic, it was to find her heated gaze on him. He waited for her to look away.

She didn't. She'd held his gaze, then tilted her head to the side, as if issuing him a challenge.

What was going on here?

"This has been fun," Palmer now said. "The place hasn't changed one bit. I think that's the same jukebox we used to play in high school."

"Is it? I don't think I noticed it when we came the last time," Bronwen said, accepting a glass of wine from the server with a smile. "It may look like the same facade, but jukeboxes are digital now. And there are newer songs."

An idea occurred to Ben and he stood. "Will you excuse me for a second?"

"Dude, see if they have Green Day," Davis called out.

Ben waved him off and walked over to the machine. Bronwen was right. The outside was the same: rounded top, rectangular bottom, with plastic tubes that lit up in a rainbow of different colors. However, instead of the usual letter-number button combo, there was a large touch screen. He scrolled through the selections, stopping when a particular song caught his eye. Checking the queue, he saw his choice would come after the song currently playing.

"What's coming?" Davis asked when he returned to the table. "Did they have 'Holiday'? Or are you yearning for the nostalgia of the aughts? Some Evanescence, perhaps?"

"I wouldn't do that," Ben said. "We barely made it through Palmer's Amy Lee fascination the first time around."

"Can you blame me?" Palmer asked. "She was the perfect combination of beauty and toughness."

"It's clear you have a type," Nic said.

They all looked at Bronwen before bursting out laughing. As their merriment died down, the familiar strains of the song he'd chosen filled the area.

"Wise men say, only fools rush in . . ."

He watched Nic, waiting for her to—

She gasped and glanced at him. "No fair, Van Mont!"

He stood and held his hand out. "Dance with me?"

She glanced around. "No one else is dancing."

He didn't care. He wanted to hold her, to be close to her. To confirm the signals she was tossing in his direction.

His skin burned to touch hers.

"Then we'll be the first."

NIC STARED UP at Ben, warmed by the heated longing radiating from his beautiful eyes. As Bronwen had predicted, he and his friends had transformed from sandy beach bums with little effort. More than one appreciative eye had followed them as they'd walked from their parked cars to the restaurant. Ben's dark hair gleamed and he looked casually chic in a pair of army green chinos and a blue-and-white-striped collarless shirt. She'd never gotten off on the Ivy League, New England prep style before, but damn if Ben didn't make it look good.

Placing her hand in his, she was no longer surprised at the tingle jolting up her arm with the skin-on-skin contact. She allowed him to pull her to her feet and lead her closer to the jukebox where there was a small space next to a darkened hallway that led to the bathrooms. When he stopped, she went into his arms and, with his hands clasped at her lower back, began swaying to the music.

They'd hugged before but, with the song playing in the background, everything felt a bit more intimate than in the past. The notes flowed over her and her body relaxed into his. She laid her head against his chest and heard the deep, steady thrum of his heart. So solid. So strong. Just like Ben.

"But I can't help, falling in love with you . . ."

"I'm glad you're here with me," he said, his fingers massaging her hips. "Thank you for coming."

Sensation arrowed through her and she swallowed. "You're welcome. It's the least I can do, considering."

"One isn't conditioned on the other," he said softly, their conversation for their ears only. "No matter how this turns out, I'm going to make sure no one interferes with your fellowship."

She knew that. It was another weight tipping the scale in favor of opening up and giving them a chance.

Because that's what she'd decided to do.

"I love Haley's version of this song," she said instead, drawing a pattern on his bicep.

"I know." His breath tickled the curls at her temple.

"Just like I know you prefer the original Elvis version."

"I do."

"I can't believe I'd never heard it before it was used in a gum commercial. Now it's in heavy rotation on my favorite playlist."

"And since you're not shy about sharing your music . . ."

She laughed. "Sharing" was a nice way to put it. She had a tendency to play her music loudly when in certain moods.

"Oh, like a river flows, surely to the sea, darlin' so it goes, some things are meant to be . . ."

He squeezed her close as they continued swaying to the haunting, romantic melody. His thighs were strong as they brushed against hers and the muscles in his back flexed against her palms. Her fingers roamed over the square footage, with a latitude and abandon she'd never before felt free to indulge.

She took a deep breath and admitted, "And that's what scares me."

He stiffened. "You've lost me."

"The song. Us. Other than my mom and my

girlfriends, you're the person closest to me. I don't even know how that happened."

"I said something similar to Davis and Palmer."

She looked up at him then. It was time to be honest. To put it all out in the open. No more flirty signals. "We haven't done anything irrevocable yet. We can go back."

His eyes glittered down at her. "Can we?"

"If we pursue this . . . attraction, we could risk our friendship. I don't want to lose that."

But the compulsion to be with him was getting harder and harder to resist.

"I don't, either. I haven't."

She frowned. "What does that mean?"

"Do you think this is the first time I've thought about you in that way?"

Wait, what? "It wasn't?"

"No. But I can't ignore it anymore. I don't want to lose you but I can't get those texts or the picture you sent out of my mind. Can you?"

"Oh, for I, I can't help, falling in love with you."

She shook her head and a curl flew into her face. He smoothed it back, his fingers lingering on her cheek.

"Hey guys," Davis called out. "The song is ove— Hey! Where are you going?"

"Davis, be quiet," she heard Bronwen say as Ben led her down the darkened hallway and past the restrooms to another door she hadn't noticed.

"I want to finish our conversation," he said, pushing open the door and leading her out to a

Chapter Sixteen

Ben opened her door and helped her out of the car, but made no move to enter the house. After dinner, Davis had lobbied to hit a nightclub one town over in Oak Bluffs, but Nic had been so worked up from their foreplay that she was practically vibrating.

They'd declined the invitation.

Standing in the driveway, the moonlight casting shadows over his features, he asked, "Are you sure you still want to do this?"

Disappointment tightened her chest. Had he changed his mind? "Yes. Don't you?"

"Oh yeah." He pushed her back against the vehicle and captured her lips in a hot openmouthed kiss.

There was no tentativeness, no testing of the waters with sweet, soft pecks that gradually heated into something more. Ben took her mouth like a person claiming what was rightfully theirs. She shivered in delight at the confident display and allowed the possession.

His tongue swept into her mouth and rasped

exquisitely against hers. Butterflies performed aerobatics in her belly like they were auditioning for the Blue Angels. Wanting to be closer to him, Nic clutched his shirt in her fingers and stood on her toes to deepen the kiss. He grabbed her ass and lifted her against the solid ridge in his pants. The bulge that'd had her mouth watering since she'd felt it half an hour before.

She'd kissed a fair number of men and there had been some skillful kissers in that group. Sometimes the kisses led to more, sometimes they didn't. While technique was everything in an operating room, when it came to fucking, passion was paramount. Ben didn't have perfect technique, but he made up for it with an intensity she'd take over precision any day. Ben was overflowing with passion, making him far and away the best kisser she'd ever had. He kissed her with an erotic longing and desperation that sent moisture to her pussy, drenching her panties.

I want you, his kisses seemed to say. *Don't hold back. Give me everything.*

And she did.

As his mouth devoured hers, she ravaged his, letting her hands sift through the soft strands at the nape of his neck, flitter across his broad shoulders, and clutch his wide, muscled back. She couldn't get enough of him, his taste, his smell, his touch. Their loud, ragged breaths acted as an audible aphrodisiac, turning her on even more. Only when the warning signs of lack of oxygen began blaring, did she pull away from him and drag in deep mouthfuls of air.

Eyes wide, she stared at him. Holy fuck. Their first real kiss and it had been . . . extraordinary.

Is this what she'd been missing?

He watched her, his eyes glittering, his chest rising and falling swiftly. "You're so beautiful."

Her heart leaped in her chest at his quiet, reverent words.

She'd always wanted to be judged for her intellect, not her aesthetic. But Ben was her friend. He knew her strengths and her weaknesses. Knew her capabilities and her deficiencies. She didn't have to prove herself to him and that made her want to be attractive for him.

Lifting her in his arms, he placed a brief kiss on her neck, turned, and headed inside.

So strong. She wrapped her legs around his waist and held on. "Where are you going?"

"To our room."

"No." She squeezed his hips with her thighs to get his attention. "Let's go over there."

He turned his head to see where she'd pointed. "To the hammock?"

"Uh-huh." She laved his earlobe with her tongue before taking the fleshy part between her teeth.

He moaned and dipped his head toward her. "You're not worried about people seeing us?"

What people?

"No one's here. But even if they were, it'd just add a little excitement."

He growled. "Damn, you're perfect."

He crossed the expanse of the manicured lawn, alert and careful. She used the short trip to kiss every part of him she could. His cheeks, his neck, his jaw, his mouth. And still it wasn't enough. She wanted to consume him and the intensity of her desire almost frightened her.

Almost.

When they reached the hammock, he released her and her body slid down his, every part of her sparking with pleasure at the contact, until her feet touched the soft grass.

He cupped her cheeks. "Do you know how long I've wanted to do this?"

His voice was a verbal abrasion against all of her sensitive parts.

She shook her head, unable to speak, mesmerized by the inferno blazing in his eyes.

"From the first moment I saw you."

He'd wanted her back then? She didn't have time to process his words or what they meant before he was lowering his head. This time when they kissed, it was slow and languid and carnal and she'd been oh so wrong about his technique. Or lack thereof. He knew how to work his tongue, so that it sensually explored her mouth. Long, bold strokes that stole her breath and her soul and made her a part of his. He cradled her face and nibbled along her lower lip, feasting upon her until her bones were molten and all she could do was grip his hips and hold on for the ride.

He broke their kiss and stroked his thumb across the wetness he'd left behind.

"Have you fucked on a hammock before?" he asked, his parted lips so close to hers that she tasted his words more than heard them.

Her nipples hardened. "No."

"Then I get to be your first."

He sat on the hammock and shifted his body, swinging his legs up and over until he straddled the netted fabric. Then he grabbed her by the waist, and lifted her until she was settled on his lap, facing him. He'd handled the entire maneuver with an ease and an aplomb she found incredibly sexy and led her to wonder . . .

"Will I be *your* first?" she asked slyly.

He stared at her with a fevered longing that made her shiver. "The first to make me go out of my mind with wanting her? Absolutely."

His hands settled on her waist, their size underscoring her petiteness. Beneath her, his thighs were hard, his cock an impressive bulge pushing against her core. Her mouth watered.

"You made a lot of statements the last time we talked about this," he said, the tip of his tongue peeking between parted lips.

Sliding a finger beneath the strap of her dress, he eased it down her shoulder. Goose bumps arose from her skin at his touch.

She lifted her arm free and bit back a moan as he repeated the gesture on the other side. "The last time?"

He slid the fabric down her chest. "When you texted me."

Oh. Right. She tried to respond, only to gasp and throw her head back as the material abraded her sensitive nipples and pooled around her waist.

"That picture you sent has been engraved on my brain for a week. I've dreamed about these beauties, stroked myself to completion thinking about them. Now, let's see how often we can make you come."

Who was this man? Where was her easygoing roommate and friend?

His words were more potent than any drug or spirit, lulling her into a hazy reality where he—and the sensations he aroused in her—was her sole focus.

He had morphed into the sexual partner of her deepest fantasies.

And she was here for it.

He pressed a hand into her midback, arcing her forward until her nipple hovered in front of his mouth. She inhaled when his lips puckered and he blew a stream of cool air against the nub. Her gasp morphed into a moan when he devoured it with his tongue. She clutched his shoulders in desperation as electricity shot through her and molten heat oozed to her core.

"Oh God, Ben. Please. Don't stop."

Sex was something she controlled. Something she enjoyed when the urge moved her. But she'd never been this wanton, this consumed by the feelings tearing through her. She was a leaf, swept up and blown along by a tornado of desire that was *uncontrollable*. Out of her hands.

Ben transferred his attentions to her other nipple, but continued to pluck the wet one he'd left behind. Nic's fingers clasped his skull and she gripped his head close to her. All sensations were centered on her breasts and it started to overwhelm her. As if they couldn't be contained in one place. The feelings had to spill out, move somewhere else before she exploded. She began undulating her hips against his stiff cock and when that wasn't enough, she tilted her hips until her clit was rubbing against his fabric-covered hardness.

"Damn, Nic. You're so fucking hot. You're driving me crazy."

The friction was unbelievable. Indescribable. Between that and what his magical tongue was doing to her nipples, she was one throbbing mass of unthinking, pure feeling pleasure.

His breath was the perfect backdrop to her feelings. Hearing how it increased, seemed heavier, hotter, thicker . . . He breathed with exertion, like a man possessed. Crazed. By her.

She expected it to take a while. It usually did. Her clit wasn't "easy." So she was surprised when, minutes in, she began to feel the stirring low in her belly followed by the familiar whole-body shivers. She wanted it to last, but trying to prolong the feeling was like walking across a gossamer thin tightrope. In stilettos.

Impossible . . .

She screamed as the orgasm bloomed from her core and ripped through her.

"Fuck yeah, baby," Ben moaned. "Come for me."

He reached a hand between them, pushed her panties aside, and slid two fingers into her drenched heat.

"Ben!"

The intrusion prolonged her climax. She clenched around the digits and bucked against him, trying to draw out every last drop.

"That's it, baby. That's it," he said, his other hand plucking her stiff, so sensitive it ached, nipple. "You're so goddamned beautiful and wet . . ."

When the last wave receded, leaving her spent, she rested her forehead against his and tried to breathe in as much air as possible.

Wow.

Just . . . wow.

Thank God she was a doctor and understood the medical logistics behind what had just happened. Because it could've been misinterpreted as something holy. Divine. *Had* that just happened? Had Ben given her one of the best orgasms of her life? She also needed to thank her mother for that talk. Because if Nic ever believed that what she'd just experienced was tied only to this man, she'd never want to leave him.

Ben brushed the curls off her forehead and they kissed, their tongues tangling in a sensual dance. He lifted her off him—the ease with which he continued to do so was sexy as hell!—and laid began to build until, once again, she was carried away on the crashing waves of pleasure.

She struggled to catch her breath and when she opened her eyes it was to find Ben watching her, with a heated intensity she wanted to remember for the rest of her life. His mouth was moist with her juices and she scrambled up and straddled him, licking his lips, his chin, anywhere she'd marked him. He squeezed her bare ass beneath her dress as they kissed, their combined tastes turning her on.

She wanted him. So much she thought she would pass out from the need.

"Next time I get to sample you," she said, her fingers trembling as she unbuttoned his pants.

"I can't wait." His voice was barely more than a growl.

And then his cock was in her hand and she was stroking its veiny thick length, reveling in the smoothness of the skin over the steely hardness beneath.

"Beautiful," she whispered.

Cum pearled on the meaty cap and she spread it with her fingers.

Fuck.

"Now *I* can't wait. Just one taste."

She leaned forward and swirled her tongue around the head. Ben hissed out a breath and threw his head back, his fingers clenching her curls. She chuckled and glided her tongue along the seam on the underside of his cock, inhaling his musky masculine scent. When she reached his sac she pressed her tongue into the space between his balls, drawing one into her mouth. He groaned, tilting his pelvis toward her and she alternated between the sensitive glands encased in the soft, delicate skin.

She wanted to do more—how would he feel about a little ass play?—but her own impatience prevented her from savoring him as she would in the future.

Next time.

She moved up his body and braced herself above him, staring down into eyes as fevered as her own.

"Condom?"

Realization pierced the lustful fog. "Shit! No. I didn't think to bring them. Davis or Palmer probably have some."

They both looked back at the house.

So far away . . .

"Dammit!" Ben wrapped his arms around her waist and she rested her chin on his hair. Both were breathing heavily.

"Go get one."

He pulled away and stared up at her. "Now?"

"Now." She leaned back against the hammock and stuck two fingers in her mouth. Keeping her eyes glued to his, her tongue laved the digits, getting them wet. She spread her legs. "I can occupy myself while you're gone."

His Adam's apple worked as he swallowed. "Don't come until I get back," he ordered.

"You'd better hurry, then."

Hopping off the hammock, and getting briefly tangled in the ropes, which made her laugh, he buttoned his pants and took off for the house.

She bent an arm behind her, rested her head on her elbow, and slid her fingers down between her wet folds. She couldn't believe she was about to have sex with Ben. Images of him flowed through her mind.

Making sure she ate on her rare days off when she was chained to her desk working on research or studying for rotations.

Taking care of her when she was super exhausted or not feeling well.

Laughing next to her on the couch while they watched a show or a movie.

The things he said echoed in her head like a playlist on repeat.

"What if I start with my hands? Gently cover those breasts, then press them hard against you, as your nipples pebble against my palms?"

"You know where else I want to put my mouth? On your pussy. I've dreamed of spreading your thighs and tasting your sweetness on my tongue."

"I've dreamed about these beauties, stroked myself to completion thinking about them. Now, let's see how often we can make you come."

She arched her back and cried out silently as the sensations poured through her. Again.

"Damn, Nic," he breathed.

She looked up to find him standing over her,

his hands at his sides, a condom packet clenched in his fist. His cock was at eye level and close to ripping through his shorts.

She turned her head and licked her lips. "I need one more taste."

He pulled it out and, gripping the dick at the base, slid it into her open mouth.

He sighed. She moaned.

She swirled her tongue around his shaft as she played with her pussy. Out in the open with the air against her heated flesh and the sounds of the waves and nature, she could've spent another hour in that exact position. But Ben's tortured "Fuck!" and withdrawal and the tear of the condom packet prevented that.

He slid the condom on his engorged length and gingerly settled onto the hammock. He crooked his finger. "Come here."

She straddled him and then with one lingering kiss, lowered herself onto his shaft.

They both groaned at the melding.

She enjoyed that brief moment of connection until urgency had her moving up and down on his steely length. He reached up and took a nipple in his mouth and she grabbed the edges of the hammock and braced herself, enjoying all of the sensations crashing within her.

"Do you like that?"

She nodded, unable to verbalize her approval. Bracing her hand on his calf behind her, she leaned back and began playing with her clit.

"I'll never get enough of watching you touch

yourself," he said, seeming to push the words between clenched teeth.

His admiration warmed her. She loved how her pleasure seemed to bring him pleasure. She rotated her hips and clenched her pussy against his shaft.

"Fuck me," he moaned.

"I am."

Her breathing hitched and tension coiled low in her belly.

"Ben!" She screamed as she came, unable to believe her body had another one in it, overwhelmed by the sensation that ripped through her. Her pussy pulsed against his cock, its hardness a brace that prolonged the rapture as it ricocheted from pleasure point to pleasure point. She sobbed when the last swell departed, leaving her an awed, satiated husk.

His fingers gripped her hips and he took control, pistoning his hips upward and driving into her welcoming flesh. Over and over.

"Fuck. Oh fuck. I'm coming, Nic! I'm coming, baby!" he bellowed, his face tight, the tendons in his neck on display, when his own release burst through him.

"Well, damn," he said later, when they'd regained their breath and the ability to speak. "I thought we were friends."

"What?" She planted a hand on his chest and lifted herself on wobbly arms to stare at him. "Of course we're friends."

"I don't know," he said with a grimace and a

shake of his head. "Real friends can't wait to share their good experiences and you've been keeping this to yourself for three years."

She laughed. He was incorrigible!

She rubbed her nose against his. "If you can maintain that stamina, I promise to make up for lost time."

Chapter Seventeen

Watching Nic's ass sway as she climbed the short but steep stairway inside the Edgartown Lighthouse, Ben resisted the urge to grab her hips, pull those peachy cheeks back toward him and take a bite out of the firm flesh.

But just barely.

His willpower was given a hefty boost by the fact that they weren't alone. Though the tourist attraction wasn't busy, there were several other people, including a family with three small children, taking advantage of the mild morning weather. He was pretty sure Nic wouldn't appreciate a picture of them, with his face smashed into her rear, going viral on Instagram.

He wouldn't mind. Being with her last night had rocked his world. It was more than an itch he'd needed to scratch. He'd realized he'd barely grazed the tip of the iceberg. There was so much more he wanted to do to her. Wanted to experience with her. Wanted to have her do to him. This trip wouldn't provide enough time. In fact, he didn't know how much time he'd need.

"My quads are cursing up a storm. After the workout they had on the hammock last night, and again this morning, they are not enjoying these steps."

Nic winked at him over her shoulder and his knees buckled. He'd told Davis he knew the sex between him and Nic would be good. He'd highly underestimated that. It had been superb. Unreal. Out of this world.

After their ride in the hammock, they'd sneaked up to their room like mischievous teenagers and he'd attempted the gargantuan task of trying to slake his desire for her. Between her slim thighs, staring down into her flushed face, he honestly didn't know if it would ever be possible.

Being with her had also brought out his selfish side. He'd wanted to memorialize the occasion alone, just the two of them. Not dealing with Davis's comments or Tinsley's wounded quietness. So he'd awakened her in the wee hours and lifted her leg onto his hip. He'd slid into her from behind, pulling on her taut nipples, capturing her moans and sighs with his tongue until her pussy gripped his cock with her orgasm and he'd buried his face in her shoulder and given in to his own release. After sharing a shower, punctuated with laughter and kisses, he'd driven her into town to have breakfast at a little cafe, followed by a walk, and a visit to the lighthouse.

He'd just had undeniably great sex with his friend. What was better than that?

Could anything ever be better than that?

But a tiny part of him wished it had been bad. It would've made the eventual ending of their arrangement easier.

When they reached the top of the stairs, Nic pointed to the large red light that sat on a metal platform in the middle of the glassed-in space.

"What's that?"

"It's the beacon that would aid boats and ships by directing them to their destinations. Back in the early 1800s, the original Edgartown Lighthouse was built to safely guide in large whaling vessels. It's no longer needed to help with navigation, but it's a part of the town's history and was restored in the '80s."

Placing a hand on the small of her back—he couldn't stop touching her!—he led her out of the light room onto the gallery deck that rimmed the top of the lighthouse.

"Wow." Nic pressed her hands to her cheeks and stepped over to the railing to stare out at the breathtaking view before them. "This is so peaceful and serene."

Thin wispy clouds twisted in the sunny sky like stretched cotton balls. Sailboats dotted the glistening harbor water and fishermen lined the sandy shore, rods outstretched, patiently waiting for their next catch.

"Absolutely beautiful," she murmured.

A slight breeze lifted her loose curls and blew them across her face. They concealed portions of her profile, though nothing could take away from its exquisiteness. "Yeah, it is."

She looked at him then rolled her eyes. "That was so corny. Even for you."

"Maybe, but it doesn't make it any less true."

She surprised him by letting it go. "You know a lot about this lighthouse."

"When we'd come to the Vineyard on vacation, this was always one of my first stops."

"With your parents?"

"No. I came by myself."

Even when he was a kid, his parents didn't seem to care when he'd get on his bike and ride off for hours at a time. Didn't care or didn't notice. After he met Davis and Palmer, he spent most of his time with them.

He leaned over and braced his forearms on the railing. "The support and unconditional love you get from your mother? You shouldn't take it for granted."

"I know you don't always get along, but they have to be proud of you, considering what you've accomplished."

"They're not. My mother even stopped by my office last week to offer me a job back at Van Mont Industries."

She frowned. "That's a shitty thing to do. You already have a job."

"But it's not good enough for them. It never will be."

He briefly recapped his conversation with Fallon.

"Damn. No wonder you rarely talk about your parents or growing up. Was it always that bad?"

He clenched his jaw. He didn't want to talk

about his childhood. Not after last night. He'd finally experienced being with Nic in the way he'd never thought possible and it had been better than he could've dreamed. He didn't want to taint their encounter by dredging up his issues with his family.

"I had all of the material things a kid could ever want. I made good grades in school and I had a lot of friends."

"Yeah. Sounds like torture."

Was it? Her skepticism didn't anger him. After all, did he really have the right to complain?

"Maybe not, but I didn't have my parents."

"What does that mean?"

"It means I had parental surrogates. House-keepers, nannies, tennis pros."

But he'd have given it all up to actually spend time with his mother and father.

He sighed. "Look, no one wants to hear someone who had my advantages in life complain. I'd sound like a whiny prick."

"I asked you. I do want to hear about it." She placed her hand against his back.

Every molecule in his body raced to that heated spot. "Though both of my parents came from wealth, they weren't raised to assume they were entitled to it. The money meant they wouldn't have to limit themselves; that all of life's resources were available to them. But they still had to be productive. They worked hard, but they also lived incredible lives. They didn't believe being parents required that to change. So it didn't."

Which wouldn't have been a problem if they'd just included him.

But that wasn't part of the plan. For them, having a child completed the familial picture. It showed they'd done their duty in passing on the Van Mont name.

"Oh Ben." She wrapped her arm around his back and pressed her face against his shoulder. "I'm sorry."

He'd been so lonely growing up. Sure, he was surrounded by kids during the day, but when the bell rang, it was home to a big empty house. Not that anyone pitied him his existence. His school friends used to tell him he was lucky not to have brothers and sisters. Who wanted to share toys and clothes or compete for their parents' attention?

But it wasn't the parents-as-best-friends, birthdays-as-holidays fantasy they'd imagined. He wasn't the special sole recipient of his parents' time and focus. Just the single unifying cause of their reluctance to spend time together as a family.

It was why he wanted a big family. So his children would have siblings to love, brothers and/or sisters with shared experiences of growing up together. And not just the fun ones, but the ordeals that had seemed unpleasant in the moment, but that would later provide a knowing chuckle. He wanted them to have people they could count on. Friends might come and go, but siblings would always be there. Would always have each other's backs.

And Ben wouldn't put his children through what he went through. He wouldn't leave them to be raised by others.

"I'm not looking to emulate an old fifties-style school sitcom," he said. "My wife and I would do it together. I want both of us to be there for our kids. To attend their plays, their recitals, their science fairs."

She straightened away from him, her brows high on her forehead. "All three? You must plan on having some high-achieving children."

He glanced at her as his brain formulated a sudden thought. *Our kids would be brilliant.*

He exhaled slowly. "Yeah. But it's not all about recognizing their accomplishments. I want us to go on family vacations, to spend time with them and get to know them as people. I want to read them stories and tuck them into bed at night." He spread his hands wide, palms open upward. "Is that unreasonable?"

"No, Ben, it's not," she said softly.

She faced forward and they stood side by side staring out at the horizon.

After several more minutes of silence, she said, "We should probably talk about last night. And this morning."

Shit. That was a conversation he'd hoped to delay for as long as possible, if not outright avoid. "Okay."

She licked her lips. "It was great."

His gaze dropped to her mouth. Pink, full, glistening. Perfect. "Oh I know."

She bumped his shoulder. "You're an arrogant bastard! How come I never knew that before?"

"There's a lot of things we didn't know about each other before last night," he said.

"Like the way you enjoy watching when you're receiving head?" she asked, sliding him a sidelong glance and lowering her voice when a man walked past.

Oh, so that's what we're doing?

"Exactly. And like the way you make this little sound in the back of your throat when you're close to coming," he said.

Heat dotted her cheekbones, but she didn't look away from him. His cock hardened, ready for round four. Being with her had surpassed any expectations he'd had. And the best part was how easy it had been, the layer of fun that had coexisted alongside the intense passion.

Nic reached over and covered his hand with hers. "Your friendship means everything to me."

That statement could've been a mood killer. No guy wanted to hear that the woman they'd just slept with considered them a friend. But this situation was different. Everything about him and Nic was different. He knew exactly how she felt. Because he felt the same way.

"Not wanting to ruin what we have was one of the main reasons I never pursued you," he confessed.

Her green eyes widened. "Hold up. You mentioned wanting me, but I never knew you considered dating me."

"From the moment I saw you."

Nic stroked her fingers over the back of his hand. "I'm kind of glad this happened now."

"Why?"

"If I still have my fellowship—"

His jaw tightened. "You will."

"Yes, well, I'll be leaving in a few weeks."

Extreme sadness threatened to pull him under and never let him emerge. For three years he'd seen or talked to her almost every day. He knew the day of her departure loomed, but the idea of her not being there hit him with the force of a Mack truck and left him scrambling.

"And that makes you happy?" he asked, testily.

"Of course not! What I'm saying is if we'd done this sooner it would've made things more difficult."

She was right. One day and the sweetness of her body had already imprinted itself on his. The taste of her saturated his tongue. The smell of her infiltrated the very air he breathed. How much harder would it have been after three months? Six months? Three years?

He'd been naive to believe they could sleep together, he'd excise her from his system and they could go back to being friends without the crazy tension between them. Being with her hadn't abated his desire. If anything, it had made it stronger.

"We've always been straight with each other, right?"

She nodded. "Yes. That's one of the things I appreciate about us. No games."

He took a deep breath. *Here we go . . .* "I want you."

She inhaled sharply and her lips parted.

He turned his hand over and captured her fingers. "Last night was amazing. It was the perfect combination of being with the sexiest person in the world who also happened to be my friend. I want more."

With a blindingly single-minded, laser-focused passion that left him shook.

Her lashes fell and she dipped her head, concealing her thoughts. Uncertainty chilled him. Maybe she didn't feel the same way.

"Don't shut me out, Nic."

Finally she said, "I'm afraid."

"Of what?"

"Of this." She looked up and the heat in her gaze seared through him, blasting away the coldness of his doubts. "Because I feel the same way. And I shouldn't."

Pleasure sent him soaring, but those last three words brought him crashing back to earth. "What's wrong with us enjoying this time together?"

"We can't get used to it. I'll have to go. And being with you makes me want to stay." Her face tightened and she shook her head. "I came here to help you with your ex because you offered to talk to your parents on my behalf."

He stiffened. "*You* linked the two, made one conditioned on the other. I didn't. You're my friend and I want to help you. I would've done it whether you came here or not. Whether we did what we did last night or not."

"I know."

"I don't even care about the Tinsley situation anymore."

He didn't. The once-significant importance of convincing Tinsley of his disinterest paled in comparison to the magnitude of convincing Nic not to prematurely end their time together.

A mission he *needed* to achieve.

"Can we really do this?"

Hope sparked to life in his chest. "We like and trust each other, and we have a good time."

One corner of her mouth lifted. "Last night proved how good of a time we could have."

"This morning, too. I do some of my best work before dawn."

"Good to know." She slid her arms around his neck. "Ben, this can't go any further than the next few weeks together."

Which meant it wasn't over! Euphoria turned his insides to goo. He settled his hands on her hips and began nuzzling the soft skin of her neck. "Uh-huh."

"I'm serious," she said, even as she angled her head to allow him further access. "I'm going to finish my fellowship and concentrate on my career. There's no room for a relationship in that equation."

"You smell amazing."

She smacked his shoulder. "Ben!"

He inhaled her delectable scent one last time before lifting his head and moving away from her. "Busy doctoring, no time for relationship. Got it."

"And even if there were . . . I'm not the type of woman you want long-term."

He swallowed and shoved clenched fists into his pockets. "That's right."

Though that's not what you were thinking last night when you were balls deep in her body.

They were both quiet for several moments before she spoke again. "I need you to promise me something."

"Anything."

"When this is over and it's time for me to move, promise me we'll still be friends. That what we do here won't come between us. I don't want to lose you from my life."

It should be an easy promise to make, for all the reasons she'd just stated and everything he knew about his childhood. He wanted a big family; she'd be focused on her career.

Just like his parents.

Anything beyond friendship wasn't in the cards for them. And he didn't dare consider the possibility of not having her in his life.

He brushed a stray curl from her cheek. "I promise."

He hoped like hell it was a vow he could keep.

Chapter Eighteen

After their morning in town, they'd come home to find the house empty and a note that the others were down on the beach. Ben had made slow, amazing love to her and they'd drifted off to sleep. When she'd awakened, it was to find herself alone in bed.

She smiled and flung herself back on the bed, limbs spread in the classic starfish pose. She'd had sex with one of her best friends and it had been incredible! Hell, she'd endure another six-month drought if it meant she'd experience another night like last night. Thankfully, she didn't have to. They had several more days here and another week when they got home. She looked forward to making the most of their time together before she left for Durham.

IF she left for Durham.

No, she wouldn't allow herself to think that way. She trusted Ben. He was going to talk to his parents on her behalf. She wouldn't lose her fellowship. And in the meantime, they could enjoy each other's company free from the specter of his ex.

Fifteen minutes later she conceded that latter directive was easier said than done.

From the secluded spot on the beach, created by the wooden walking bridge and a sandy dune covered with grass, Nic possessed the perfect vantage point to see everyone without being seen. They were the picture of health, wealth, and entitlement, with Ben, Davis, and Palmer tossing a neon green frisbee back and forth, while Bronwen lay out on a towel, sunning herself. These people didn't have to concern themselves about the roofs over their heads or where their next meal would come from. They were free to fully enjoy themselves, a luxury that Nic silently envied.

And speaking of envy—

Tinsley stood near them, resplendent in a skimpy white string bikini, cheering on Ben each time he caught the frisbee. In the few minutes Nic had been watching, Tinsley called out to him twice, one time handing him a bottle of water. He wasn't encouraging her attentions, but he wasn't exactly telling her to stop, either.

She knew that he never would. Because it wasn't his personality.

But it damn sure was hers.

Nic left her secluded nook, the sand warm beneath her bare feet, and headed over to the group. Ben was poetry in motion, his leanly muscled body golden and glistening as he played with his friends. Shirtless and in a pair of navy blue shorts, he looked like a professional lifeguard who called the beach his second home and not a financial planner who spent many hours of the day in an office, behind a desk.

She cupped her hands around her mouth. "Hey, Van Mont!"

He caught the frisbee then turned to look at her, a smile brightening his face. Shoveling a hand through his thick breeze-tousled strands, he flicked his wrist and sent the plastic disc sailing in Palmer's direction before jogging over to her.

Nic's nipples hardened against her bathing suit and a corresponding moisture bloomed between her thighs. She wanted to lick every inch of his body. From the hard line of his shoulder blade, across his well-defined pec, down the rippling ridges of his abs, and even farther. Hell, she still needed more time with his cock in her mouth. Whenever she had her fist wrapped around him, ready to slob on the knob like the corn on the cob, she'd only get several minutes in before he was hauling her up his body, flipping her on her back, and slamming into her with an agonized moan.

Not that she was complaining. That long, thick shaft was her third favorite organ on his body, behind his brain and his heart. But depending on the occasion, she reserved the right to reorganize her order of preference.

As soon as he reached her, he slid an arm around her waist and brought her close. The smell of his heat-baked skin, the salty tinge of sweat and his own unique scent combined to make her exquisitely dizzy. A sensation that intensified when he covered her mouth with his own. His kiss was intense, wet, and ravenous; its potency filled with the promise of long, deep strokes that hit her spot over and over and had her calling out his name. She finally understood Beyoncé singing about being drunk in love; knew that as long as Ben continued twirling his tongue with hers and cupping her ass as if he couldn't get enough, he could convince her to do whatever he wanted.

When he raised his head, his dark eyes glittered down at her. "Hey, sleepyhead."

"Hey, you." Unable to resist, she stood on tiptoe to briefly press her lips against his and get more of his laced kisses. Delicious. She brushed her palm against the scruff shadowing his jaw. "I think I've slept more in the past couple of days than I have in years."

"You needed to catch up."

She laughed at the common misconception. "That's not how sleep works."

"Tell your body that."

"My body would prefer to hear it from you. And I know just the opening where you can start!"

He growled and nuzzled her neck. She grasped his shoulders and angled her head back, allowing him full access as the sun warmed her skin. She felt carefree and wanted. She couldn't remember ever feeling this . . . happy.

"Can I get you anything?" he asked, brushing

a curl off her cheek. "We've got water, Gatorade, and beer in the coolers."

"No thanks," she said, her reason for calling him over finally pushing its way through the intoxicated haze he'd created. "But I'm worried about you."

Furrows of concern creased his brows. "Why?"

"Did you apply sunscreen earlier?"

He flicked a glance at the sky. "It's cloudy."

"Clouds block the sun, not harmful UV rays." She bit her lower lip and gazed up at him beneath the thick curtain of her lashes. "I think you might need a little . . . coverage."

He arched a brow. "Is that right?"

She nodded and moved into his personal space, caressing his lower back.

His hands settled lightly on her hips. "I'm willing to take whatever you've got."

"I'm so glad you feel that way."

Peering around his body she was pleased to see everyone's attention was momentarily diverted. Nic took his hand and quickly led him to the secluded spot and setup she had waiting. A quick glance back confirmed that Tinsley was still talking to Bronwen and the guys had continued their game. No one appeared to have seen them leave.

She gestured to the yellow-and-white wide-striped beach towel she'd lain beneath the bluff. "Have a seat."

He did, pulling his legs into his body and wrapping his arms around his knees.

She dropped to her knees behind him and grabbed the bottle from the sand. Pouring some sunscreen out into her palm, she rubbed her hands together and transferred the cream to his strong back. The muscles in his shoulders bunched as her hands glided over his warm, smooth skin. In their secluded hideaway, the sounds of the beach were muted, allowing her to enjoy his heavy breathing and pleasure-filled moans.

She let her fingertips travel up the back of his neck and tangle in the crisp hairs located at his nape. He leaned into her touch, so open and trusting and she couldn't resist nibbling on his earlobe. He straightened his legs and a hand came up to bury itself in her curls, holding her tight to him.

The hardened buds of her nipples pressed into his back as she whispered, "Lean back."

He complied, the muscles in his torso contracting and then releasing as he stretched out on the oversized towel. She shifted her position to kneel next to him and her mouth watered at the sight. Forget the fine grains of the sandy beach, the crystal clear aqua blue waters, and the vastness of the overcast sky; she was privy to the more impressive view. She trailed her fingers along his body, mournful when she had to break contact and reach for more lotion.

"Am I good?" he asked, his eyes closed, a flush settled high on his cheeks.

She spread sunscreen across his chest, down his sides, and along his flat belly, allowing her fingers to dip beneath the waistband of his shorts. "Oh yeah. You were last night. And this morning. And again about two hours ago."

His lids lifted and his heated gaze melted her insides. "I was talking about the lotion."

"I know," she said, her heart pounding in her chest, as if it, too, wanted to break free to be near him. "But I wasn't."

Looking around and confirming they were still alone, she straddled him, settling herself on the hard ridge of his cock.

He hissed and gripped her hips, pressing up against her. "Then I'll do my best to keep the streak going tonight."

She tossed her curls back and moaned at the friction against her clit. "I can't wait."

Did she have to? It would be so simple to ease aside the fabric of her bathing suit, slide down his hot length, and ride him until they were both out of—

"There you are," Davis said, his voice shattering the mood, like a dirty finger popping a bubblegum bubble.

Nic froze, her hands braced on Ben's chest.

"I must've missed the notice that christened me as your official cock-blocker." Davis laughed and waved his hand. "Come on. Palmer's designed a sandcastle town and we've been drafted to help build it. It's all hands on deck."

"Dammit, Davis," Ben muttered.

"You'll thank me later. Nothing screams unsexy like getting sand in all your sensitive nooks and crannies. Talk about chafing."

He shuddered and grimaced before hurrying back to the others.

Ben exhaled audibly then scrambled to his feet. He took her outstretched hand and pulled her up next to him. "You're coming, right?"

She'd planned to.

God, why did everything he say make her think of sex?

"I'll be there. Just give me a minute to wipe my hands."

"Hurry," he said, pressing a hard kiss to her mouth.

An unfamiliar but refreshing giddiness took hold of her as she stared after him and she pressed the only clear spot on the back of her hand against her tingling lips. If she had only three more days of this—of him in this way—then she planned to wring pleasure from every second of it. And that included showing all of them how to make a stellar sandcastle. Nic strode over to the lounge chair, grabbed the towel draped over its back, and hurriedly wiped the surplus lotion off her hands and the bottle.

"You're good," Tinsley said, the tone of her voice making it clear that the words weren't intended as a compliment.

Behind her sunglasses, Nic rolled her eyes. It must've been too much to hope the other woman would keep her distance. Especially after her earlier display. "Excuse me?"

"You've got that whole exotic"—Tinsley gestured at Nic's face and hair—"damsel-in-distress thing going on. Ben never could resist helping someone in need."

Exotic? *Damsel in distress?*

It was obvious Tinsley had always been allowed to spout off at the mouth without retribution. Only someone who'd never experienced the imminent danger of having their ass kicked would feel free to be such a rude bitch to another person's face. Tinsley had already done it twice . . .

Nic's hands curled around the towel she held. She needed to walk away. She had no reason to engage with Tinsley. She absolutely believed Ben when he said he wasn't interested in his ex. That he wanted to spend the remainder of their days on the Vineyard enjoying what had developed between them. But something about Tinsley irritated her. Like a mosquito bite she knew she should ignore but had to scratch.

Nic pursed her lips and tilted her head. "What do you want?"

"Isn't it obvious? I want Ben," Tinsley said, shifting her weight onto one foot and cocking her hip to the side in a stance meant to intimidate as it showed off her gorgeous figure and legs that seemed to be as long as Nic was tall.

The sorority where her mother worked. The girls at UVA. In that moment, the recognizable feeling of being different, of not belonging, seeped its way between them, swirling around Nic's ankles, like an ominous fog threatening to overwhelm her.

Then her inner Caila stepped in to prop her up.

Snap out of it, Nicole! You're not that little girl anymore. You've worked hard to make a name for yourself. You're an orthopedic surgeon! You do belong! And you will not *let this woman get the better of you.*

Reinforcing her resolve—and her spine—Nic scoffed and discarded the towel on the chair. "You would've had a better chance asking for world peace."

Tinsley's eyes narrowed. "You think you're so funny and clever. It's clear Ben finds you amusing. But it won't last. He'll tire of you and come back to me, where he belongs."

Nic shook her head. She refused to participate in a reenactment of some tawdry scene that could be found on every nighttime soap from *Dynasty* to *Melrose Place* to *Empire*. Although if there was ever someone begging for a bitch slap . . .

"You need some new material," she said, spinning to go join Ben and the others.

"*You're* new. There's something to be said about a shared history. Ben and I have that."

Don't respond. Don't respond.

Nic turned around. "Because your relationship is in the past! You broke up with him."

Tinsley waved a long-nailed, manicured hand. "A mistake. I plan to get back what's mine."

Her proprietary attitude grated. Amazing sex aside, Ben was her friend. And he was a good man. She might not have a say in who he eventually dated after her—the thought caused a lance of pain to spear her chest—but he couldn't end up with Tinsley.

"Ben's a person, not a possession." A thought occurred to her. "You don't think much of him. Why do you want him back?"

"Because he's a Van Mont! His family is very important and influential. I thought he'd lost sight of that."

Uh-huh. Nothing like striking out on your own and being mentioned in *Kiplinger's, Bloomberg Businessweek* and *Forbes* to suddenly make someone take a second look in your direction.

"Ben and I come from the same world. What's the point in growing more attached to him, only to be devastated when he breaks up with you after realizing you'll never fit in?"

"So, you're doing this for me?"

"Exactly." Tinsley's bright smile was malicious. "I'm a philanthropist. I often give back to charity."

Strike three.

Nic took a step toward the other woman and let the pleasant veneer she often wore slip from her face to reveal the outrage and resentment that had fueled a young girl to fight her way past low expectations and institutional and structural barriers to take her place in a very formidable profession.

"You've been skating by with these little racist taunts of yours. You might be surrounded by people who tolerate it and think it's cute, but I don't."

At "racist," Tinsley opened her mouth, probably to refute the label being applied to her and to argue about Nic bringing race into things. A common technique.

"What did I say?"

"I never used that word!"

"Why are you so sensitive? Can't you take a joke?"

Not today.

Nic allowed her intent to infuse her expression as she eyed Tinsley from the top of her wind-blown hair to the tips of her polished toes. "So you can keep trying me if you want to. I promise, you're not going to like my response."

Tinsley flinched, a visible sign that the message had hit home. Then she swallowed, threw her shoulders back, and flipped her hair. "Do you think you're special? You're not. Ben thinks he wants a nice, regular woman who'll fit into his cookie-cutter idea of what a family should look like. He's wrong. He needs someone who understands our world. Someone who knows all the right people and all of the best connections and can push him to the top."

"Shouldn't he decide what he wants?"

"Oh please," Tinsley said, one corner of her mouth curling in distaste. "Men don't know what they want. They're easily confused by 'grass is always greener' syndrome. They can never make up their mind. That's where we step in. They want what *we* tell them to want."

Damn. Nic pitied the person who ended up with her. Although . . .

Hadn't she thought the same thing? Not about telling men what they wanted, but about the type of women Ben dated? Hadn't she wondered why he seemed to pick women who seemed nice but were . . . unchallenging? Especially for someone as smart, funny, driven, and dynamic as he was?

What was she doing? Why was she even lending credence to this claim? Especially when this fight didn't technically involve her. She and Ben weren't a real couple. They were only pretending.

Not anymore.

True, but their sexual relationship would soon end and they'd go back to being friends. It wasn't her business and she wouldn't like it, but if Ben decided he wanted to be with Tinsley—

Yeah, the sour, palate-obliterating taste in her mouth wouldn't let her brain complete that thought.

"Look, if Ben wanted you, he'd be with you. But he's not. He's here with me. Which reminds me that I have better things to do than to stay here in this conversation."

Without a further word, she left Tinsley and started down the beach toward the spot the others had set up for their sandcastle showdown.

Tinsley's final taunt chased after her. "That history you laughed at? It matters. I know Benji's soft spots and I know what makes him tick. I *will* get him back."

Chapter Nineteen

Nic snuggled next to Ben on the loveseat, enjoying this new dimension to their friendship. They'd never shied away from exhibiting their affection for one another, a brief squeeze of a hand, a hug when needed. But now that their relationship was more intimate, she felt a freedom to do more. Like lean over and give him a kiss if she wanted.

And she wanted. So she did.

Outside, a steady rain was falling, prompting them to stay indoors. After a chef-prepared meal of *barramundi en papillote*, mussels in white wine sauce and linguine with grilled shrimp and peppers, they'd retired to the great room to relax.

Except relaxing wasn't on Bronwen's agenda. In that way, she reminded Nic a lot of Caila.

"Let's play a game where we get to know each other. Kind of like an ice breaker and a way for Nic to get to know us."

Tinsley looked up from her phone. "Is this trip about spending time with you or making newbies feel welcome?"

Their conversation on the beach had finally convinced Tinsley to keep her distance. She'd ceased her racist comments and blatant come-ons, but it hadn't stopped her from uttering smart-ass remarks on a continuous loop. But Nic ignored her because Ben did. She was pleased to see he had eyes only for her. And hands and lips. They both seemed to be all in on spending this time together, separate from their ruse to dissuade Tinsley.

"For someone who invited herself at the last minute, you certainly have a lot of opinions," Davis said, an ever-present tumbler of some dark liquid in his hand.

Tinsley flipped him off.

Nic eyed the two of them. Their constant bickering almost had her thinking they were fighting off some sort of sexual attraction, except their utter dislike for each other was as deep and consistent as the ocean waves that crashed onto the beach.

Bronwen glared at them. "As I was saying, this should be fun. If all else fails, we have a fully stocked bar. Nic, can you help me?"

"Sure." Nic stood, laughing as Ben reluctantly released the back of her shirt.

Bronwen handed her a stack of legal pads and a fistful of pens. "Hand these out to everyone."

Nic did as she was asked, and mentally patted herself on the back for not responding to Tinsley's smirk.

"I've put everyone's name in this bowl and some numbers in this one," Bronwen explained, holding up two glass basins. "When it's your turn, you'll pick a name and a number. Each number corresponds to a question on this list. You'll ask the question to the name of the person you pick. That person will write their answer on the pad. When they're done, you'll try to guess their response to the question. If your answers match you win a point. The person with the most points at the end wins."

"I've seen complex engineering drawings that were less confusing," Palmer said.

"That's not funny," Bronwen pouted.

"But it's true."

"What do we win?" Ben asked.

"Choice of which movie we'll watch later," Bronwen said with a flourish, as if offering a prize on par with the Publishers Clearing House Sweepstakes.

"Yes!" Davis pumped his fist. "Which will I choose: *Terminator* or *Billy Madison*?"

Nic sat down next to Ben and shot him a look. *You'll be on your own, buddy.* She wouldn't allow the collateral damage to her brain cells from watching something so silly. He threw his arm along the back of the sofa and tickled her shoulder with the tips of his fingers.

"Over my dead body," Tinsley said.

Nic frowned. Had she missed the arrival of the four horsemen of the apocalypse or some other sign of impending doom? Clearly, the world was coming to an end if she and Tinsley actually agreed on something?

"I appreciate you offering me more motivation, Tinns," Davis said, an ugly twist to his lips.

Ben's quad muscle stiffened beneath her palm. "Knock it off, Davis."

Nic's brows rose in surprise. Ben rarely used that hard tone. Was it wrong that him doing so now sent desire spiraling between her thighs? She wondered what scenario they could role-play later where he could use that tone of voice on *her* . . .

Davis clenched his jaw but he didn't say another word.

"Thanks, Benji," Tinsley said, her blue eyes soft and luminous.

Irritation threatened to burn through her desire but Nic forced herself to remain calm. Ben's speaking up didn't have anything to do with Tinsley and everything to do with the type of man Ben was.

An uncomfortable silence settled in the room, filling all the air and space around them with the heaviness of an insulation-like foam. Bronwen bit her lip and turned a furrowed brow on her husband.

The secret spousal signal worked.

Palmer stood and reached into one of the bowls. "I'll go first. Davis. Number six. What's your dream car?"

Davis straightened and immediately started scribbling on his legal pad. "Done!"

Palmer adjusted the frames of his glasses. "That's too easy. He just bought it. The Lamborghini Aventador SVJ."

Davis whooped and lifted his sheet to show his answer. "Lambo, baby!"

Tinsley rolled her eyes. "Isn't that the stupid car you've wanted ever since you guys have been in college?"

"It's not a car, it's an experience," Davis said with reverence. "It has a 760 horsepower V12 engine and goes from zero to sixty in two point seven seconds. They only made nine hundred of those babies and I got one."

Cars weren't Nic's thing, but she knew Lamborghinis had to be expensive. She wondered how much a car like that would cost but knew asking would be extremely gauche. Grabbing her phone off the side table, she did a quick google search and almost choked on her silent gasp. Base price started at over half a million dollars! And she had the distinct feeling Davis wasn't the type of man who bought "base" anything.

Ben pinched the bridge of his nose. "I can't believe you got it. What did I tell you? You're just wasting money. The car depreciated the moment you drove it off the lot. If you had to have one, you should've bought used."

"If practicality was my main concern, what's the point of buying it? I've wanted a Lamborghini for a long time. I plan to enjoy it."

Where Nic had grown up, people couldn't afford to buy a house for a quarter of that amount. Hell, it would have to feed her, massage her, give her incredible orgasms, and cuddle her to sleep before she'd even consider the possibility of spending even a fifth of that price on a car.

"Alright, Davis, you're up," Bronwen said.

Davis reached into the bowl and then rolled his eyes. "Tinsley. Talk about going from high points to low . . ."

"Davis!" Ben sighed.

"Sorry," he muttered. "Habit."

Brackets appeared on either side of Tinsley's mouth. "I never agreed to participate in this game."

Bronwen shrugged. "Your presence implied your consent."

Davis pulled a slip of paper from the other bowl. "Number three. What is your pet peeve?"

Tinsley looked down for a moment, tucked a lock of hair behind her ear, then wrote something on the pad.

Davis tapped his index finger against his chin. "Let me see. Decency? No. Hard work? No . . ."

Ben tensed beside her.

Davis snapped his fingers. "I've got it. When she makes brunch reservations at Hotel du Mode and they seat her next to the restroom instead of at the chef's table."

They laughed and Ben's posture eased.

Seriously? Nic glared at him from the corner of her eye. Tinsley was a big girl. She didn't need his protection.

"That's true," Tinsley admitted. "If I wanted to smell shit while eating my eggs Benedict, I'd go to a chain restaurant."

When it was Tinsley's turn, she was unable to hide her pleasure. "Benji."

She didn't seem to mind participating *now*.

Ben sat up straight. "I'm ready."

"What's the one country you'd like to visit? Oh, I know this. It's—"

Bronwen held out a hand in protest. "You have to wait for him to write it down."

Tinsley held back several seconds longer. "We'd been dating a year when Ben took me to Paris. We had an amazing time, but we didn't really get a chance to do as much sightseeing as we'd anticipated."

Tinsley's implication was clear from her tone.

Nic pressed her lips together to keep from responding. This woman was trying her. She knew that Tinsley was no longer relevant to what was going on between her and Ben, but she didn't know how much longer she was going to be able to keep from speaking her piece.

"As we were flying home," she continued, "he said the one thing he regretted was not visiting the French Riviera. He'd always wanted to go."

Ben's brows rose. "That's right. I had wanted to go during that trip. I'd totally forgotten about that."

"That's not what you wrote down," Nic pointed out, annoyed at him. She tapped her finger on the pad. "This says Indonesia."

Tinsley curled her lip. "Indonesia? Why would anyone want to go there?"

Ben shrugged. "There are so many islands to explore. I think it would be fun."

"Whatever. But you said I was right," Tinsley said. She turned to Bronwen. "I should get a point for that."

"That's not how you play the game," Nic pointed out.

"How would you know?"

"Because Bronwen told us the rules before we started!"

"Her answer was correct, too," Ben said, in full mediator mode. "She can get the point."

Suddenly he and Tinsley were rule-busting co-conspirators? Were they playing a game or taking a stroll down memory lane? The former suggested there'd be a winner and a loser and Nic damn sure didn't play to lose.

"Relax. It's not a big deal," Ben whispered in her ear. He kissed her cheek then stood and reached into the bowl. He picked Bronwen. "What's your perfect meal?"

When Ben laughingly protested there was no use in him guessing because he had no clue, Bronwen held up her pad showing: *My nanny's spaghetti Bolognese.*

"It was my favorite growing up. She was from Modena in northern Italy and she'd cook the sauce for hours." Bronwen's eyes flickered. "Heaven."

Bronwen picked Palmer. "That wouldn't be fair. Nic, you come choose."

"Gladly." She hopped up, overcome with a craving to win this game. "Number ten. What sports team would you love to own?"

Looking at Palmer she guessed he might like football or baseball. It was a fifty-fifty shot. And he was from New York, so— "The Giants?"

Palmer grinned. "Ooh, close. The Cowboys."

"Does she need to repeat the question?" Davis asked. "You hate Dallas."

"I do. I really do. But she didn't ask about my favorite team—the Yankees, by the way—she asked which team I'd love to own. And the Dallas Cowboys are the most profitable sports franchise in the world."

"Boo!" Davis said, lobbing a pillow at Palmer.

Nic threw up her hands. "At least I got the sport right. I almost went with baseball. Since the rules of this game are so flexible, can I get half a point for that?"

She waited a beat.

"Just kidding," she said, poking her tongue between her teeth.

Not really.

She bumped Davis's outstretched fist with her own and ignored the look Ben gave her when she sat back down.

After several more questions, where the memories, laughter, and drinks flowed freely and lightened the mood considerably, there was one last slip of paper in each bowl.

Since Nic had just answered a question about the scariest movie she'd ever seen, it was her turn. "Ben. Number one. Your favorite childhood memory?"

Tinsley, whose entitlement had mixed with too many vodka martinis, said, "I know the answer."

"You're not a part of this," Davis said. "This is between Nic and Ben."

"But she's not going to know it. It's that time when you guys sneaked to Boston to see U2 in concert and you got to go backstage and meet the band! Ben flipped out because he got to shake The Edge's hand. Technically you were teenagers, but it counts, right?"

"Jesus, Tinsley." Palmer slouched back in his chair.

Bronwen rolled her gaze skyward and exhaled audibly.

"What? I was just helping Nic."

Ben had met U2. Though she wouldn't call herself a fan, she knew who they were and liked a few of their songs. Who didn't? And having the opportunity to meet them would be epic, fan or not. What kind of life would a person have to lead where meeting a member of a world-famous rock band wouldn't rate as one of their top moments? Probably like the lives they'd all led, with their Lamborghinis and Italian nannies and trips to the French Riviera.

Tinsley's response made sense. But Nic's gut screamed another answer, beseeching her to remember an evening of heartfelt confessions after a particularly strained visit with his parents.

She only hoped this wasn't another answer that he'd "totally forgotten about."

"When Ben was eight, his appendix almost burst and he needed to have an emergency appendectomy. His parents took a week off of work and stayed with him."

They'd watched movies, read books, did puzzles, and brain teasers. He'd told her he'd felt like they were a real family.

Ben stared up at her, his dark eyes wide. "I told you about that?"

It seemed he *had* forgotten.

"A couple of years ago. We were discussing common pediatric surgeries and you mentioned yours. It was a throwaway comment but it stuck with me because it was clear that it was really important to you."

He held up his pad showing his answer: *My parents took off work to be with me after my surgery.*

Warmth suffused her body and she smiled slowly. She'd gotten it right. Yes, she could own her pettiness over one-upping Tinsley. But mainly, her pleasure came from showing Ben that he mattered to her.

He licked his lips and an intense expression stole over his face.

She knew that look.

Her nipples tightened beneath her bra. Her body knew that look.

"That's an interesting topic," Bronwen said, gathering the slips of paper and putting them back in one of the bowls. "Not many people would go around discussing surgeries for children."

"I have a habit of bringing my work home with me," Nic said absently, her gaze still focused on Ben and his wicked tongue. That man played her pussy like nobody's business.

"Wait!" Tinsley slammed her palm down on the counter. "Your work home with you? You're a doctor?"

Nic became aware of the sudden shift in mood. She bit her bottom lip and glanced around. "Yes."

"And you knew this?" Tinsley asked Ben.

Ben's jaw tightened. "Yes. Nic is a surgeon. In orthopedics. She's brilliant."

The words were perfect, but his tone left a lot to be desired. She wasn't the only one who noticed. Tinsley's eyes appeared to gleam and a nasty smirk curved her lips.

"I find that fascinating, considering how much you hate doctors."

Nic shot a look at Ben. He hated doctors?

She knew he didn't regard the profession with the same reverence most people did, probably because he'd grown up around them. The public saw doctors as the living embodiment of gods. Unfortunately, a lot of doctors saw themselves that same way. It didn't always make for humble, likeable beings.

But *hate* them? Hate who she was? Hate how she'd worked hard to define herself?

"Why does everyone insist on that interpretation?" Ben asked, throwing his hands up. "I don't *hate* doctors."

"Uh-huh," Bronwen said, eyeing Nic with a frown.

"I guess you really have changed, Benji," Tinsley said.

Ben crossed his arms over his chest. "Not really."

"You must have," Tinsley persisted. "When we were engaged, you were adamant that I make our family my top priority. Correct me if I'm wrong, but surgeon isn't a nine to five profession."

"It's not," Ben said, his jaw set, "but we'll make it work."

"Oh." Tinsley turned to Nic, a sculpted brow lifted. "So you're willing to make compromises in your career?"

Compromise her career? The phrase didn't compute. She wasn't giving up her career. And she definitely wasn't going to make decisions to the detriment of her professional growth just to fulfill some patriarchal notion of familial structure.

But how did she answer? If she was playing the role she'd originally agreed to play, she'd smile and answer in the affirmative. However, she and Ben had decided that they were going to explore what was between them, irrespective of Tinsley. And if she were honest and she was asked if she would make concessions in her work, the answer would be simple.

"No."

Chapter Twenty

ℬen closed the bedroom door behind him while Nic strode over to the windows on the far wall. Her displeasure was evident in her stiff stance and crossed arms, even if he hadn't been able to see her tight expression reflected in the glass.

Well, tough!

She wasn't the only one upset with the turn of events. After their talk at the lighthouse, he'd felt closer than ever to her. When they'd returned home, he'd let his body express his appreciation. Then she'd shown up on the beach, declaring he needed to wear sunscreen and managing to be very creative in how she applied the lotion. Thorough, too. By the time she was done, his cock had made a tent so large in his trunks they could've camped out beneath it. He'd wanted to kill Davis when his friend had interrupted them before he'd had the pleasure of returning the favor . . .

He couldn't remember enjoying a day more. The rain had finally driven them inside, but it hadn't dampened their teasing foreplay. There was an electricity between them, charged and hot. It was in the way he'd catch her staring at him, the heat in her gaze that was dampened only by the lowering of her lashes. The constant touches that lit his skin on fire. The way she'd lick or bite her lips whenever he spoke to her. It had all driven him out of his mind.

When she'd remembered his favorite childhood memory, she'd blown him away. She was beautiful, sexy, smart as hell, and funny, but her compassion, especially for those she cared about, often went unnoticed. He hadn't made a big deal about that memory of his parents. In fact, he barely mentioned it because there were times when he'd convinced himself it had been a dream. That it hadn't ever really happened. But he'd told Nic and she'd remembered. It had made him want her all the more. He'd pictured their night ending with his head between her thighs and her pulling his hair while she screamed his name.

Her response to Tinsley's question had altered the mood of the room . . . and the evening. Davis and Palmer had already known about Nic's profession. But once Bronwen and Tinsley knew, they'd wanted to make it an issue for discussion. Ben's feelings on the subject of his future wife were too well known for his friends not to question the sustainability of their relationship.

But their concerns weren't his priority. He needed to talk to Nic.

Ben shoved his hands into the pockets of his shorts. "Really? Just a flat-out no? That was your answer?"

It was an effort to keep his tone measured and calm when his insides churned like ocean storm surges during a hurricane.

Nic didn't turn around. In the glass her expression hardened further, if that was even possible. "Did you expect me to lie?"

No. And that was the frustrating part. He didn't want her to lie. He wanted her to actually feel that way. To care enough to consider making concessions if it meant they could be together.

"That answer didn't do anything to dissuade Tinsley."

"I don't give a fuck about her. I thought we'd decided to make these last few days about us?"

She was right, but he wasn't in the mood to receive it. He'd experienced a bevy of emotions toward Nic. Tenderness, curiosity, amusement, jealousy, frustration, desire.

But anger?

At her and not on her behalf?

That was a new one.

"Can you turn around? I don't want to have this conversation with your back."

Exhaling audibly, she turned and faced him, her head tilted with a disconnected look on her face. "Better?"

"Why can't you make compromises? Why does it have to be your way or the highway?"

"This is who I am. If you don't like it, we can end it right now. That's probably what you want anyway."

"What does that mean?"

"You're not a stupid man. Don't pretend that you are!"

He clenched his jaw. "I know how smart I am. If you actually made sense, I'm pretty sure I'd grasp your meaning."

"Then let me be clear." She pointed a finger at him. "You're sending mixed signals. You're leading her on!"

"Don't be ridiculous," he laughed, though he knew doing so would annoy her. He was right.

"Really?" She narrowed her eyes and jammed her hands on her hips. "Does Tatiana seem weak and helpless to you?"

His lips quirked, but he resisted. "No."

"But you certainly enjoyed riding to her rescue."

"I didn't ride to—"

"She and Davis don't get along. That has nothing to do with you, yet you felt the need to jump into their dispute and defend her. Why?"

"He was being an asshole."

And if left unchecked, Ben knew their comments would get more malicious, leading to an argument none of them wanted to witness. The ugliness would poison the remainder of the trip and affect their time together.

"So was she. And she can handle herself. She's proved that numerous times this week. But what you did showed her you care."

"I *do* care. That didn't change because I'm no longer in love with her."

"Oh, she knows you care. She's unable to keep

her comments to herself, but at least she was leaving you alone. Now she's back to acting like she has a claim on you."

He waved a hand. "That's just Tinsley being Tinsley."

She arched a brow. "Cooing, batting her lashes, and flipping her hair is Tinsley being Tinsley?"

"It's practically her second language!"

Nic pursed her lips. "Then why doesn't she act that way around Palmer and Davis?"

"We have a different history."

Nic's green eyes flashed and she shook her head. "'History.' Yeah, tell yourself whatever you want. But she wants you back and what you did tonight doesn't do a damn thing to dissuade her. Which is fine. It's your life. But if you're going to flip the script, let me in on it!"

"Why do you keep bringing up Tinsley? I'm standing here telling you I'm not interested in her."

"It's none of my business. But I want to be clear. I did my part. I held up my end of the bargain. I expect you to do the same."

Astonished, he staggered back a step. "You think this is about our arrangement?"

For a brief second, her defenses were down and he saw regret color her features. But then she mended the breach. "It is for me."

"When I told you I wanted to be with you, it had nothing to do with convincing my ex of my disinterest. It was because I wanted you so fucking much I could barely breathe. And neither one of those things played a part in my offering to help you. How many times do I have to say it? I suggested speaking with my parents on your behalf because you were my friend."

Although nothing about her was being particularly friendly at the moment. He needed to get out of there before he said something he regretted.

"I'll be back."

"Where are you going?"

"I need to get some fresh air."

"Of course. Make sure you tell Tinsley I said good-night."

"It'll be my pleasure," he said, slamming the door behind him, but not before he saw her eyes widen and her chin tremble with hurt.

Goddamn it!

He shoved both hands through his hair, yanking on the strands and reveling in the pinch of pain. He obviously didn't mean it. He'd told her Tinsley wasn't an issue. He wanted to be with Nic. He had no interest in getting back together with his ex. He'd thought last night and their conversation this morning had cemented that fact for her. But she was so fucking stubborn. She acted as if it was easier for her to accept the sex between them than to believe in the affection he offered along with it.

When he descended the stairs everyone, except Tinsley, was still in the great room. They immediately ceased their conversation when they saw him.

"Everything okay?" Davis asked from behind the bar, pausing in the act of pouring a drink.

Uh-huh, their studied nonchalance was real convincing.

"Not really," he said.

Palmer swiveled on the kitchen counter bar stool to face him. "We're here if you want to talk about it."

He clenched his jaw. "I don't."

Bronwen walked to the base of the staircase. "What were you thin—"

He raised a hand to stem the incoming tide of her questions. "Not now, Bron."

"Well when?" she asked, crossing her arms.

"Honey," Palmer said, "give him some space."

"I'm not done with you," she said, pointing a finger at her husband. "You knew and you didn't tell me."

"A rare occurrence," Davis muttered.

"Screw you," Bronwen told him. She turned back to Ben. "What is going on? Anyone can see how much you care for Nic, but a doctor? After everything you've said? Shouldn't we—"

"No we shouldn't," he erupted, his harsh breath burning his chest. "I said I didn't want to talk about it! If I was looking to debrief, I would've said so. If I wanted your opinions, I would've fucking asked!"

Their stunned expressions would've been comical had he been in a more accommodating mood. He understood their surprise; he rarely raised his voice and he never spoke to his friends in that manner. But his argument with Nic, their biggest, had untethered him, leaving him without his usual filter. Like taking the restrictor plates off a race car. He was hot, agitated, and in self-preservation mode, uncaring of protecting anyone's feelings in that moment save his own.

Unfortunately, knowing his friends, it wouldn't be long before the shock of his outburst wore off and they'd proceed to bombard him with questions he didn't want to answer and comments he didn't want to hear. Instead of making the great room his final destination, as he'd initially planned, he continued out to the deck.

The afternoon rains had passed breaking some of the humidity and leaving the air relatively cool. He sank down onto a patio chair and hunched forward, bracing his elbows on his thighs. Like a magnet, his gaze was immediately drawn to the hammock.

Nic lying before him, her thighs spread, her pussy glistening with her desire.

Nic taking his cock in her mouth, her fingers deftly bringing her pleasure.

Nic astride him, her hands braced on his shoulders, her pebbled nipples so close to his waiting tongue.

Fuck! Maybe this wasn't the best place to be, either.

He scrubbed his face with the palms of both hands and leaned back against the cushioned frame. In twenty-four hours he'd experienced the highest of highs and was now dangling around on the low end. What in the hell had happened?

He heard the door open.

He pushed out an audible breath. "Can I have a few minutes by myself?"

"Of course," Tinsley said, her voice cool. "I just thought you'd need a drink."

Oh.

He dropped his arms and sat up. Tinsley stood next to his chair, a tumbler of amber liquid in her outstretched hand.

There was no denying she was beautiful. Tall and slender with long blond hair and deep blue eyes, she was polished, cultured, and well-thought of by many in their social circle. And as a young man, he'd ascribed traits to her based on that presentation. Clearly, that had been a mistake. Had she ever been the caring, gracious, generous person he'd thought she was? Or had he imagined it, wowed as he'd been by her face and her assertions that they shared the same values and wanted the same things out of life?

He took the glass. "Thanks."

"You're welcome," she said, her expression soft. She turned to leave then hesitated. "Benji?"

"Yeah?"

"Thank *you*."

He frowned. "For what?"

"Earlier. For sticking up for me against Davis."

"She and Davis don't get along. That has nothing to do with you, yet you felt the need to jump into their dispute and defend her . . ."

"She can handle herself. She's proved that numerous times this week . . ."

Nic had been right. Tinsley could hold her own. So why had he felt the need to step in?

"Don't worry about it."

"No, really." Her eyes widened. "He can be such a jerk sometimes."

He'd said something similar to Nic. Tinsley and Davis rubbed each other the wrong way. They always had. But before, when he and Tinsley had been in a relationship, he'd felt obligated to step in when he thought Davis was being offensive, though Tinsley could give as good as she got.

Now, it wasn't his place.

He tried to imagine how he'd feel if the roles had been reversed. If Nic had unnecessarily stood up for an ex when he'd been sitting right there. If the glass he'd been holding had been made of sugar—like in the movies—instead of Baccarat crystal, it would've shattered in his hand.

". . . game was fun though," Tinsley was saying. "It brought back memories."

He exhaled. He needed to apologize to Nic.

"Especially our trip to France. We had so much fun," Tinsley continued.

He didn't want to be rude, but he really hoped she was leaving.

"Nic won't make you happy, Benji," she suddenly said, her voice fierce. "Not like I can."

And there it was. Hadn't he brought Nic to prevent this very scenario from happening?

He sat the untouched glass of bourbon on the round teak side table. "Tinsley, we're over. We've been over for five years. That was the decision *you* made."

"When you worked at Van Mont Industries, I thought our lives were perfect. And then you started talking about opening your own business and I got scared. I expected to live a certain way and after you left the company, I didn't think we could." She circled the chair to crouch down in front of him and place a hand on his knee. "But I was wrong. I see that now. I should've had more faith in you."

That was nice for her personal growth but it had nothing to do with him.

"There was a time when I would've given anything to hear that." He covered her hand with his as a nostalgic sadness touched him. "But that time has passed. And we're better off for it. I've moved on. I'm with Nic now."

The placid, pleading lines of her face hardened. "Oh please. There's a thrill in trying something different. Trust me, I get it. But you can't be serious about her."

Ben clenched his jaw. What the fuck? He spoke English, he didn't whisper, and he didn't stutter. Why did everyone insist on acting as if they didn't understand him, as if he didn't mean what he said?

Granted, being the loudest in the room had never been that important to him. He was secure enough in himself that he didn't feel the need to bluster or put anyone else down to make himself feel more esteemed. If others in his orbit wanted the spotlight, more power to them. He was happy to share it or relinquish his claim on it altogether. But apparently, people had mistaken his even-temperedness for weakness.

He stood. "I'm very serious about her. But even if I weren't, it wouldn't change my feelings about us. We're over. Done. And I have no interest in being with you ever again."

His tone was harsh but necessary. He knew mincing his words or softening the delivery would lead only to more willful ignorance about what he wanted. He needed his intentions and desires to be clear.

She scrambled to her feet. "Okay, Benji, I'm sorry. I went too far. But you can't possibly mean—"

"I can and I do. This weekend was supposed to be about our friends and you hijacked it, making it all about you. Showing up here to do what? Dupe me into getting back together with you? It was juvenile and an embarrassment to us both. And once here, your behavior toward Nic was insulting and your racist comments unforgivable. There's nothing you can say or do that will make me change my mind."

She stiffened and an ugly expression suffused her features. "No last name is worth all of this. Not even Van Mont."

She whirled around and stalked into the house.

Ben lifted a brow. So much for worrying about her feelings. He followed her inside, in time to see Bronwen hurrying in the direction of Tinsley's bedroom.

"I don't know what you did, but I'm guessing it was unpleasant," Palmer said.

"I told her I wasn't interested in resuming a relationship with her."

"Bravo!" Davis made a show of clapping his hands. "And long overdue. I didn't think you had it in you."

"Fuck off," Ben said, heading for the staircase.

Something was going on with his oldest friend and they needed to have it out. But it could wait. Right now, there was only one person he wanted to talk to.

Chapter Twenty-One

The door slammed behind Ben and Nic finally allowed her shoulders to relax and sag forward. That had been a shit show. She'd meant it when she said he was a smart man. How could he not see what Tinsley was doing? The fact that he wasn't meant he didn't want to see it. Which meant a part of him enjoyed it.

And she wasn't about to play a role in that game.

Her cell phone rang and vibrated against the glass-topped side table. Grabbing it, she saw Lacey's picture on the screen.

Friendship duty calls.

She grabbed a sweatshirt and stepped out on the terrace. The rain had finally moved on, leaving behind a cool, gentle breeze. She slipped into the warm garment and took the call. "Hey! What's up?"

Lacey's fine-boned features were tight with worry. "Thank God you answered. I'm freaking out!"

"Why?"

"Because I'm nervous about this weekend."

Lacey had flown to LA to audition for a spot as a featured dancer on the international tour of one of the most popular musicians in the world. It was an incredible opportunity. According to Lacey, thousands had tried out and only twenty had made it to this callback. Except Lacey didn't look as if it were good news. She kept biting her fingernail and scraping a hand through the end of her long thick honey blond ponytail.

"You know you got this, right?"

"Thanks, except I'm having a hard time rehearsing because I want to throw up every five minutes."

"You're going to be amazing. You were co-captain of the UVA dance team and a member of the Virginia Dance Company. You spent four years with the DCC and you've been in several Broadway shows. You're brilliant and they'd be lucky to have you."

"Thanks, Nic. I feel much better."

"Good. Now, once you make the tour, if any of your fellow dancers get hurt, pass along my information, would you?"

Lacey's gorgeous face broke with laughter. "There we go. You looked like one of my best friends, but I was starting to wonder if aliens had invaded your body. Too much niceness without snark is definitely not you. How are you doing?"

She had no intention of burdening her friend on the eve of the most important audition of her career. "I'm good."

"Bitch, you lie like an expensive Persian rug! I can hear it in your voice. You're not yourself."

Busted. "I've been better."

"Things not going well in Martha's Vineyard?"

"How did you know?"

"Ava texted me, of course," Lacey said in her "duh" tone. "I wanted to go to Martha's Vineyard for vacay one year, but I was outvoted."

"Our bad. It's beautiful here. Peaceful, tranquil."

At least it was when she wasn't being a bitch.

"What's going on?"

"Ben and I got into a fight."

"No offense, but that can't be a novel occurrence. You tend to be very opinionated and forthright."

"Believe it or not, Ben and I never fight. We may disagree, but we don't have raised-voice arguments."

"Then what's different now?"

Their pretense of being involved turning into reality?

"Let's just say he offered to do me a favor and I questioned the intent behind it."

Questioning Ben's integrity was a dick move. He'd never given her any reason to doubt his honor.

"Ouch. Why?"

If she were honest with herself . . . "I was jealous."

Lacey laughed out loud. "Seriously? I never imagined you being jealous of anyone. You're always so sure of yourself. Why do you think you're the one I call when I get nervous? I feed off your poise and energy. It's like a confidence transfusion."

"It doesn't happen often, but sometimes, when I feel like I'm out of my depths . . ."

"Oh, Nic." Lacey's expression softened. "If I could, I'd reach through this phone and give you a hug. You don't have any reason to be jealous of anyone."

Says the woman who grew up in this world Nic was only visiting.

"Thanks, Lace."

"I mean it. You're smart, talented, insanely beautiful, and cool enough to have me as a friend."

Nic laughed. Just hearing Lacey's voice and seeing her face grounded Nic. Reminded her of who she was, where she came from, and what she'd overcome to be here. In this moment.

"Make sure you tell Tinsley I said good-night."

Her amusement faded.

Shit.

Correctly guessing at Nic's silence Lacey said, "It'll be okay. You've always said Ben was a good guy. Explain and he'll understand."

She didn't know if she *could* explain it to him. Or, if she even wanted to. What had she been thinking? Ben had been willing to do her a favor and when she'd wanted to help him, she'd ended up making the situation worse.

And then she'd blamed him for it.

Behind her, she heard the terrace door open. Glancing over her shoulder she saw Ben standing in the doorway, a calmer expression on his face than when she'd last seen him.

Without breaking eye contact with him she said, "I've got to go, Lacey."

"Call me later if you want to talk."

She glanced back at her phone. "Thanks for the offer, but I want you to focus on your audition. I'll be fine. You go be spectacular."

Lacey blew her a kiss and signed off. Nic stood silently and watched as Ben came to stand beside her. Nothing in his demeanor exhibited anger or irritation. Though he had every right to be.

"Is the coast clear?"

She shoved her hands in the pocket of her sweatshirt and closed her eyes. "Ben, I'm so sorry."

"We've never argued like that," he said, repeating what she'd told Lacey.

His words were quiet but his anguish was evident and she received it like a punch to the gut. She didn't want to hurt him. He didn't deserve it. They were friends who'd become temporary lovers. Who cared what his ex thought of her? After this week she'd never see her again.

She could've said yes.

"You've always said Ben was a good guy. Explain and he'll understand."

Lacey's words.

She needed Ben to know it wasn't him. That it was Tinsley who pushed her buttons.

And why.

"Do you remember when I told you my mother worked as a housekeeper for a college sorority?"

"Yeah. You were making fun of one of my girl-friends who belonged to one."

Nic rolled her eyes to the side. "She was way too excited about being a chapter advisor. She'd been out of college for over ten years. She needed to let it go."

"I guess Tinsley's not the only one who isn't shy about sharing her opinion."

The rebuke of her behavior stung.

"About that. I owe you an explanation." She took a deep breath. "You know I didn't grow up with a lot of money."

"C'mon, Nic! Let's not make this about—"

"Please. Let me finish."

His jaw tightened, but he nodded.

"My father left us when I was ten and my mother had to work several jobs to take care of us. She got the job at the sorority when I was around fourteen."

Remembering that time, her stomach clenched. Her mother had been so excited about that opportunity.

"It was more money, which meant she'd only need to work one job. But it was two hours away. She was gone before I woke and often got home long after I'd gone to bed."

Even when her mother worked several jobs, Nic had seen her more often.

"It sounds crazy when I say it out loud now, but I became jealous of her job." The shame burned her stomach like she'd swallowed acid.

Ben's hand was warm and comforting on her

shoulder. "You were a kid. Trust me, I understand. I'm not a stranger to wishing my parents were around."

"I should've been better. Instead I ruined the time we had together acting like a class-A brat." She smiled ruefully. "Sound familiar?"

"I assume this is going somewhere? What happened?"

"I was determined to see what they had that I didn't. Why my mother gave them all of her time. So I skipped school one day and took the bus to the campus. When I got there I couldn't believe my eyes. It was a mansion, easily the biggest house I'd ever seen in real life. The grass was so green it looked like a carpet."

It had seemed worlds away from the concrete and steel of their four-story walk-up.

How was she supposed to compete with this? Why would her mother ever want to come home with her when she could live here in luxury? Anger and betrayal had warred within her and she'd marched up the steps and into the door.

"I can see you, all pissed off and indignant, curls probably shaking."

"Pretty much. I'd already reached my full height," she said ruefully, gesturing to her height. "As for the curls . . . It was the last time I wore my hair natural for a while."

He frowned and turned to her. "What do you mean?"

"I straightened my hair for years after that."

"Why?"

She shrugged. "I don't know."

She did. She just didn't want to talk about it.

He looked upset. He reached out to grab a curl and fingered it, as if the thought of it not being in existence hurt him. "What happened next?"

"There were dozens of beautiful young girls hanging around in the living room and going up and down the stairs." They were varied ages and different races, but they still seemed interchangeable: straight hair, pearls, and a spectrum of Southern ladylike looks. "One of the girls stopped me. Told me I couldn't be there. That I didn't belong."

Even now, over eighteen years later, she could still feel that mixture of anger and humiliation. Could see the contempt in the girl's eyes, the curl of her pink lips, the toss of her chunky highlighted hair. Nic curled her fingers into her fists.

"I'm not blaming her, but Tinsley reminds me of those girls. Gatekeepers of appropriateness, telling me that I don't belong. Here . . . or with you."

"Nic." He cupped her cheeks in his hands. "You belong anyplace you want to be. Because of who you are. You command every room you walk into. As for the other issue, the only people who matter in the discussion of whether we belong together are you and me."

Ordinarily, she knew that. She believed that. Hell, she'd stand up to anyone who said different. But the mixture of her burgeoning feelings for Ben and the specter of Tinsley had coalesced into her self-esteem's kryptonite.

"But she wants you back. You have history and you're from the same world." She lowered her lashes. "Why won't you consider it?"

She hated the insecure tone in her voice. What was wrong with her? She wasn't some high school girl needing reassurance from her boyfriend. Still, she held her breath, afraid of the answer, but yearning to know. She wasn't brave enough to examine why.

"Because we've always wanted different things out of life. That hasn't changed, even if we've grown older."

It wasn't the clear declaration she was looking for, but it was enough. For now.

"And I meant what I said earlier. In fact, I'd already called my father about your fellowship. He promised to look into it."

"Why didn't you tell me?"

"I was waiting for it to be a done deal before I told you."

"Thank you." She slid into his arms and pressed her cheek to his chest, reveling in his strong and even heartbeat. Safe. He made her feel safe. "And I didn't mean what I said about this only being about our arrangement."

He kissed the top of her head. "I know."

"I hope you'll let me make it up to you," she said, withdrawing from his embrace and locking her fingers with his. Tingles bloomed where their skin touched and moisture gathered between her thighs.

She wanted him.

Now.

She glanced from their joined hands up to his face where the heat in his gaze scorched her and broadcasted his interest. Slowly, she pulled him back into the room and maneuvered him over to their bed. She pushed him until he sat on the edge of the mattress. She braced her hands on his thighs, then spread them while simultaneously dropping to her knees.

He inhaled sharply and she smiled, her belly clenching in anticipation. Finally, she could spend some quality time with his gorgeous cock in her mouth. She slid her hands through the crisp hairs feathering his skin toward the thickening bulge in his shorts. She fondled him through the fabric, teasing both of them until she slipped her fingers inside and pulled out his dick.

Yes, please.

She stroked him slowly but ardently, not relenting even when his hips lifted to meet her pumps.

"Fuck, Nic," he groaned.

She squirmed, receiving the words like loving pats against her throbbing pussy. She glanced up at him through her lashes and stilled at the torrent of hunger cascading down on her. She shivered.

This man undid her.

"Lie back and relax, Van Mont. I got you," she murmured, before lowering her head and sliding her tongue along his hard, thick shaft.

Chapter Twenty-Two

"What about this?" Nic held up a black velvet sleeping mask with the word "Snoozing" written on the strap. "This is so Ava. Of all of us, she's the one who treasures her sleep the most. She travels with a Do Not Disturb aura."

Ben frowned and scratched his cheek. "You can get a sleep mask anywhere. Don't you want to get her, all of your friends, something specific to the Vineyard?"

Nic pursed her glossed lips. "Hmmm, you mean like a tie-dye sweatshirt or a rainbow beach towel with 'Martha's Vineyard' scrawled across it?"

"Yes."

"No. We're not twelve years old and visiting Myrtle Beach." She leaned over and kissed him gently on the lips. "But thank you for caring."

The hum of attraction skimmed along his skin making him extra aware of her. Of how she looked, moved, smelled. Their argument yesterday bothered him because they never fought. He'd gotten used to being the one she turned to when she was upset. To be the one on the other side didn't sit well with him.

She held up a Ruth Bader Ginsberg cross-stitch kit then a framed print that read "Put the Seat Down, You Fucker," as if weighing her options, then sighed. "I may be a while. You don't have to wait in here for me. Is there anything you'd rather be doing?"

He moved close to her and whispered in her ear. "Yes, but I need you to do it and I'd rather not do it here, although . . . I'm not opposed to a little PDA."

She laughed. "Let me rephrase. Is there any sightseeing or shopping you'd like to do on your own?"

"In that case, no." He pulled his phone out of his pocket. "I'll be sitting outside at one of the cafe tables next door. Take your time."

It was a lovely day on their coastal island, the sun shining bright, the weather temperate. Couples strolled the beautiful old historic streets, peeping in boutiques and art galleries while families sat at many of the outdoor eating venues talking and laughing. He settled onto a metal-and-wood chair and began confirming their travel arrangements for tomorrow.

Just as he'd promised, he'd booked them on a flight back to avoid a repeat occurrence of Nic's seasickness. With those plans confirmed, he checked his email to see if any issues had arisen at work. He and Ezra talked once a day, usually in the morning, to handle any questions or situations that came up the preceding day.

He was just replying to the email his assistant had forwarded him confirming some meetings next week when a voice calling his name caused his fingers to freeze midair.

"Benjamin! I thought that was you."

His mother stood in front of him, polished in white pants and a pink blouse, a triumphant smile on her face.

A sudden ache throbbed in the back of his throat. He stood and kissed her on the cheek. "What are you doing here?"

"Where else would we be?"

Anywhere I'm not.

Fortunately, her question was rhetorical. Fallon continued, "You called your father with a cryptic request and I remembered when I visited you last week you asked me about the same person. We wanted to get to the bottom of this little mystery."

That was unexpected. It had been years since they'd taken the time to seek the reason behind anything he asked.

"I thought you were in New York."

"I am. That's why it was so easy to hop up here on a quick weekend jaunt. Now"—she sat down, crossing one leg over the other—"what's so important about this James Newman at Duke?"

He clenched his teeth, unsure of how to respond. This personal interest in something he was doing was new.

"What the hell? I got them all. I even threw in that jute fabric tote with 'Martha's Vineyard' written on it. Happy?" Nic asked, peering into the plastic bag in her hand. She looked up and her brows rose. "Oh, I'm sorry. I didn't mean to intrude."

Ben rose again. "You're not. Nic, this is my mother, Dr. Fallon Rothschild Van Mont. Mother, this is my friend, Nic."

Nic's smile illuminated her entire face. "Doctor Van Mont. It's an honor to meet you. I enjoyed your paper on the impact of new technology on cardiothoracic surgical practices."

Fallon shook Nic's hand, expertly scanning her from the top of her curly hair, down to her "Started from the Bottom" T-shirt, past her cut-off Levi's and the black Converses covering her feet. "You read my paper?"

Nic gave a brisk nod. "I did. It's an interest of mine. Emerging technology impacts orthopedics, too, whether it's the next great implant or a new care delivery model. It represents an opportunity to improve quality and access to care for our patients."

"Orthopedics?" Fallon shifted her gaze back to Ben.

"Surgery. I just finished my residency at Johns Hopkins. I'm supposed to start a fellowship in sports medicine surgery at Duke."

"Ah," Fallon said. "You're the reason behind Benjamin's curious inquiry."

Shit. "Sorry. Yes, this is Dr. Nicole Allen."

Nic's smile dimmed a fraction. "He was doing me a favor."

"And I appreciate the two of you doing *me* that favor." Ben looked around. "Is Father here with you?"

"No. It's just me. There's a charming little book-store with a great coffeeshop attached not too far from here. Would you care to join me for a cup?"

"We'd love to," Nic said.

The last thing he wanted was for Nic to spend time with him and his mother. "Can you give us a moment?"

Fallon adjusted the printed scarf wrapped around the handle of her purse. "A brief one, Benjamin."

Placing his hand on the small of Nic's back, he escorted her to the side. "You don't have to do this. Take the car and head back to the house."

"Are you kidding me?" Her eyes shone with the light of fanaticism usually seen in the recently converted. "Dr. Fallon Rothschild Van Mont invited me to have coffee with her. She's a genius. Plus, she's my best chance to save my fellowship. There's no way I'm turning down this opportunity."

Fuck! He knew that worshipful look. "I understand, but you don't know her like I do."

She lifted a shoulder. "She was perfectly pleasant."

"You've spoken to her for five minutes. I've had over thirty years. Trust me that I know her better than you do," he said, shoving a hand through his hair. "I will talk to her and close this deal, I promise."

Nic set her jaw and advanced into his personal space. "I appreciate your help, Ben. But the best person to advocate for me is me."

This wasn't a good idea but he recognized that firm tilt to her chin. Nic was determined to go; she wouldn't back down. He'd do his best to try to keep everyone on topic.

They found the cafe on Main Street. It was a hidden garden oasis where thick foliage-lined trellis fencing offered privacy while sail awnings and string lights lent the space an inviting, secluded feel. They got their coffees and grabbed one of the few remaining tables.

"Have you been to the Vineyard before?" Fallon asked Nic.

"No. This is my first time."

"We've been coming here for years, since before Benjamin was born. We have a house here but he chose not to stay there."

"I didn't know that but you don't have to worry. Palmer's house is gorgeous."

"You're staying with Palmer, too?" Fallon took a sip of coffee and eyed Ben over the rim.

Damn. When he'd left the message for his father, Ben hadn't gone into detail about the nature and closeness of his relationship with Nic. He didn't think his parents would give his request enough thought for it to matter. But now with his mother subjecting them to the same scrutiny as her surgeries, he wished he'd come up with a better cover story.

"We're all there," he said.

"I know. You mentioned that the last time we talked." Fallon shifted back in her chair, crossed her legs and asked Nic, "Have you enjoyed your time here?"

"I have." Nic must have sensed the undercurrents because she glanced at him, a frown sullying her features before continuing, "It's a beautiful place."

"That it is," Fallon murmured.

Ben couldn't tell what his mother was thinking and that bothered him.

"Tell me about yourself, Nicole."

"I went to college and med school at the University of Virginia and, as I mentioned, I just completed my residency at Johns Hopkins."

Nic's earlier excitement had vanished along with his hope to shelter her from witnessing his family dynamic. The tension present when he interacted with his parents could smother joy and suck the air out of any room they occupied.

He also noted that she didn't respond with information about her hobbies, what she liked or disliked. She'd gone straight to her profession.

That was Nic in a nutshell.

"I assume that's how you know Benjamin?"

"Yes," he said, heeding the instinct to protect their nascent relationship.

Nic must've gotten the message because she didn't elaborate.

Fallon's pursed lips showed her annoyance, but she continued, "And your family? Where are you from?"

"Tennessee. A small town north of Memphis. As for family, it's just me and my mom."

"Did your father pass away?"

Nic's expression tightened. "I don't know."

And her tone made it clear that she wasn't interested in continuing that line of conversation.

He stepped into the verbal void, a role he was so comfortable in, he did it unconsciously. "Nic's a brilliant doctor. She didn't just finish her residency, she was actually chief resident."

He wanted to draw the attention away from Nic's family and put it back on her work where he knew she wanted it to be. His parents weren't the most evolved people and he worried that his mother would make a comment that betrayed her lack of empathy.

The tactic worked.

"Chief resident? That's an impressive achievement. You must be really good at what you do to receive that accolade."

"Thank you," Nic said, appearing pleased by the compliment.

"I wish Benjamin had your same work ethic. Who knows how far he could've gone."

Now *that* was the type of comment he expected

from his mother. Ben narrowed his eyes, but he held his tongue.

This isn't about you. You can endure anything if it means helping Nic.

"Why did you need us to speak to Dr. Newman at Duke?"

Nic answered before he could. "I was accepted into his fellowship program, but the parent of an intern I disciplined threatened to smear my name."

"I abhor the way politics interfere in the practice of medicine. If you were already accepted into the fellowship by your merits, you shouldn't be denied what you achieved because of someone's hurt feelings." Fallon set her cup down. "I'd be happy to make a call on your behalf."

Nic laid a hand over her heart. "You don't know what this means to me, Dr. Van Mont. Thank you so much."

"Yes, Mother. Thank you." That had gone better than he'd anticipated. "If you could call as soon as possible, that would be great. Nic starts in a few weeks. I'll text you a reminder—"

"I'm one of the top surgeons in the country," Fallon said. "I'm quite capable of remembering what I'll need to do, Benjamin."

Your father and I are very important people, Benjamin! Our patients need us. Are your wants more important than theirs? Isn't that a bit selfish? Sacrifices must be made.

Heat singed his cheeks but he refused to look at Nic. He hated that she was seeing this.

Beneath the table Nic's hand landed on his thigh and squeezed. That show of support warmed him more than she could ever know.

She cleared her throat. "Ben mentioned you were in New York for a research project. What are you working on?"

Fallon brightened. "I'm working with the Thoracic Oncology Research Laboratory. They're interested in the biology of non-small cell lung cancer and aggressive malignant tumors of the chest lining."

"Mesothelioma," Nic said, nodding.

"Yes. They're actively investigating complementary aspects of lung cancer biology at the single-cell level while also looking at the critical cell signaling networks contributing to the development of the disease."

Nic leaned forward. "How fascinating. A breakthrough there could help develop more effective patient-specific therapies."

"Exactly . . ."

Watching Nic and his mother's discussion, he couldn't help but notice their identical absorbed expressions. He knew Nic's work was important to her, but this was the first time he'd seen her interacting with a peer.

It was eerily familiar.

"I need to be going. It was a pleasure meeting you, Nicole. It's so nice to be able to discuss my work in such pleasant surroundings. Benjamin never shows the least bit of interest."

Death by a thousand paper cuts.

"I thought I was doing us both a favor," he said, lightly. They'd almost made it through the encounter. He didn't want to do anything to jeopardize the feat they'd accomplished. "You don't want to hear about my work, either."

"Come now. Your father and I save lives. What you do isn't comparable."

Fuck.

He'd been clenching his jaw so often, he'd probably worn down the top layer of enamel on his molars. Resentment curdled in his stomach. How many times did he need to hear proof of his parents' disrespect for him and what he did before it stopped hurting?

Nicole glanced at him, her expression full of sympathy and concern.

Which made him feel worse.

"You know, Nicole, Benjamin had a bright future. Of course, we were devastated when he decided not to go to medical school, but there were plenty of opportunities for him at Van Mont Industries. He was doing so well and then he just abandoned them. The family has worked so hard to build an important, successful business for the next generation. Why he'd want to leave it to start up some fly-by-night back alley boiler room is something his father and I will never understand."

Nic offered a little laugh. "I don't think it's fair to compare Reed Financial Services to a boiler room. He's been recognized several times by the city and in his industry."

Fallon arched a brow. "That's nice but he could've been chief financial officer of a multibillion-dollar company."

"That's not what I wanted," he said flatly. He didn't know why he even bothered. "I wanted to help people."

Fallon waved off his response with her usual disdain. "Van Mont Industries is a multinational biopharmaceutical company. They help people all of the time."

"From a distance. I wanted to be more involved. It's the difference between teaching in medical school or practicing in the ER."

"Don't be ridiculous. You had the chance to help people on a global scale and you chose not to. It's as simple as that."

Nic stiffened next to him and narrowed her eyes. This time he grabbed her thigh beneath the table and squeezed.

Don't do it.

She ignored his mental plea.

"Dr. Van Mont, I find your comments about Ben and his work peculiar."

"Really?"

"Yes. He's a good man. He's hardworking and his firm is doing well. He may not be a doctor, but he does provide an important service to people who need it. But even if none of that were true, as his mother, you should be proud of him anyway."

What was she doing? This was not in her best interests and it would not end well. He needed to intervene.

"It's okay, Nic. She's entitled to her opinion." Fallon should love hearing that. She reminded him of it often enough. "Mother, it was good to see you. Please give Father my—"

"You're offering me unsolicited parenting advice?" Fallon arched a sculpted brow at Nic. "Do you have children?"

Nic frowned. "No."

"Then why do you presume to know my son better than I do?"

This was *not* good.

"Because I see him more than you do. I spend more time with him than you do. And from personal experience I can tell you that it takes more to parent a child than contributing DNA. Their presence, care, and consideration are also required. It seems you've been lacking on the latter three qualities."

The silence between them was deafening. Suddenly, as if she'd just emerged from a trance, Nic's mouth dropped open and horror seeped over her features with the realization of what she'd done.

She stood abruptly, her hip jostling the table. "Um, please excuse me."

She turned and hurried down the street.

He leaped from his seat. "Nic, wait!"

"Let her go," Fallon said, staring after Nic, her lips firmly downturned.

"She was upset on my behalf. Make the call. You said you would."

He rushed after her. She moved fast for one so

small. It took a block before he caught sight of her curly hair.

"Hey! Nic! Stop!"

She finally did, but so abruptly that several people quickly sidestepped her to avoid causing a pedestrian pileup.

The blood had drained from her face and her eyes were too wide and too bright. "What the fuck was I thinking? I just reprimanded Fallon Rothschild Van Mont!"

He was glad she wasn't focused on him. She'd be pissed if she saw the smile he couldn't suppress. "It was a novel experience."

"I was so excited to meet her. Then she started being awful to you and saying the worst things and I remembered what you told me about your childhood. How could a mother not be proud of *you*?" She looked off into the distance, hugging herself while she absently stroked her upper arm with the opposite hand. "She's never going to call Duke on my behalf."

Probably not.

But there was a chance for *another* miracle. Because something extraordinary had already happened.

He pulled her into his arms. "No one's ever done that for me before. You stood up to my mother. For me."

Instead of melting into his embrace she pushed away from him. "Why didn't you?"

Was Nic mad at him? "Why didn't I what?"

"Stand up for yourself?" she said, her body rigid. "Why do you let her speak to you that way?"

He shrugged. "That's who she is. I don't let it bother me."

"Oh my God! Do you always have to be so reasonable? With your mother putting you down. Your friends calling you Benji. Maybe you *should* let it bother you."

"What do you expect me to do?"

"Get mad! Tell them off! Don't just sit there and take it."

He clenched his jaw. "Isn't that what got you in this situation in the first place?"

"I'm not going to apologize for refusing to let people walk all over me."

Is that what she thought he did?

"My mother's angry because I'm not living my life the way she wants me to. How will yelling at her change that?"

"Maybe it won't. But someone had to do something. Unlike you I couldn't sit there and take it in silence. Clearly, I should have. If I'd kept my mouth shut, I wouldn't have just fucked up my life."

"You didn't fuck up your life."

"Just—" She took a step back and lifted her hands to ward him off. "I need some space. I'll see you back at the house."

"Nic—"

She shook her head then turned and walked away.

Great!

When he returned to the cafe to get Nic's forgotten purchases, he was surprised to see his mother still sitting there.

"How close are you and Dr. Allen?"

He collapsed into a chair. "Why?"

"You implied you were asking this as a favor for an acquaintance, but it's clear you know each other well. She seems to believe she knows you better than I do."

"She does." He raked a hand through his hair. "She's one of my best friends."

"And more, by the looks of it."

From her hard eyes and tight expression he could tell Fallon was displeased. Dammit.

"I told you she was angry on my behalf. Don't hold that against her."

Fallon's nostrils flared. "Why did she think you needed protection from me?"

Fuck, he was making it worse!

He braced his elbows on the table and dropped his forehead into his palms. He knew how much that fellowship meant to Nic, had witnessed firsthand her dedication and drive to meet her goals over the past three years. He'd promised to fix this for her and they'd been so close. The thought that he'd ruined her chances broke his heart. Her happiness, her success was as important to him as it was to her.

Because you love her.

Euphoria surged through him and he raised his head. He loved her. He loved Nic! He didn't care about her job or whether she ticked the boxes on some imaginary wife checklist. She was funny, smart, beautiful, clever, caring . . . everything he could ever want in a woman.

He leaned forward, his heart acting as a paddle ball against his rib cage. "Mother, this was my fault."

"Benjamin—"

"Nic is an exceptional doctor and a hard worker. She deserves that fellowship!"

Fallon shrugged. "Not if Duke wants to revoke their offer."

He couldn't let Nic lose this opportunity. He'd give anything he had to make it right. But what could he do? He had nothing his parents wanted—

A memory blossomed. "I'll do it."

Fallon paused, the cup of coffee midway to her mouth. "Excuse me?"

His gaze was direct and determined. "If you call Dr. Newman on Nic's behalf and ensure that she keeps her fellowship, I'll come back to Van Mont Industries and run the foundation."

Chapter Twenty-Three

What in the hell had she been thinking?

Nic swung back and forth in the hammock, ruminating on her visit with Ben and his mother. She couldn't get past what she'd done. Dr. Van Mont had agreed to make the call on her behalf. Nic's problem had been solved and in less than ten minutes, she'd blown it. All because she'd been unable to keep her opinions to herself.

But was she supposed to sit there and remain quiet in the face of her disrespectful comments? Anyone listening in would think Ben was some spoiled dilettante who'd blown his trust fund on frivolous and superficial interests. Nothing could be further from the truth. He was hardworking, generous, smart, and caring. Quite simply, he was the best man she'd ever known.

I hope so. Because it'd be shame if you ruined your chances for the fellowship because of some basic dude.

Fuck. That.

She'd earned that fellowship fair and square. And if they aimed to take it away from her, they'd better have a damn good reason. One that would stand up to public opinion or a judicial challenge. It was time to come clean to her friends. She would talk to Ava about her legal rights and get ideas from Caila about framing her story for the public. She couldn't allow this to stand. She wouldn't!

It took several seconds for the vibration against her hip to penetrate her righteous indignation. Pulling her phone from her pocket, she checked the caller ID.

Duke Med School, Durham, NC.

Shit.

They were persistent. This was the third time they'd called since the incident with Whitaker. Probably to officially confirm they'd revoked her acceptance. She didn't know because they never left a message. She wasn't avoiding them, per se. She'd wanted to wait until after the Van Monts had spoken to them, a part of her hoping a return call from her wouldn't be necessary. But since she'd fucked *that* up . . .

Bracing a hand behind her, she did her best to sit up. It wasn't easy. Damn hammock.

She took a deep breath and answered the phone. "Hello?"

"Dr. Allen?" A crisp, male voice.

"Yes."

"I'm glad to finally talk to you. This is Dr. Newman from Duke's Sports Medicine Surgery Fellowship."

Her hand gripped the device tightly. "Yes, sir."

"I wanted to touch base with you regarding

your spot. This isn't something I wanted to leave on a voice mail. Which is why it was important to me that we actually speak."

Her chest felt compressed, making it difficult to breathe. Her heart beat out of control against her flattened palm. Tears burned the back of her eyes, but she refused to let them form and fall. No matter what this man told her, it wasn't over.

"I wanted to personally assure you that your spot in this program is secure."

Nic couldn't contain her gasp and she covered her mouth with her free hand.

Dr. Newman continued. "I received a call from a Vincent Whitaker a couple of weeks ago. The specifics aren't necessary but I made it clear that while I know how other programs work, I don't make decisions based on outside influences."

Her fingers trembled against her cheek and she closed her eyes in relief, letting those tears seep from beneath her lashes. Was this really happening?

"Although I have to say, getting a call from Dr. Fallon Van Mont is quite the outside influence and an unusual occurrence."

"Dr. Van Mont called you?"

"She did. About an hour ago. Told me you were bright and hardworking and would be an asset to our program."

Shock at that declaration almost curbed the swell of exultation sweeping through her.

"But I already knew that. From the moment I first received your application, I was impressed with your impeccable credentials and your phe-nomenal work record. And my opinion hasn't changed."

Yes! Yes! Yes! Her enthusiastic triple fist pump disturbed her precarious balance, causing her to fall back in the hammock, but she didn't care. She still had her fellowship.

"Thank you so much, Dr. Newman."

"No, thank you, Dr. Allen. I've been head of this program for twenty years. It's been a while since I've been this energized by a fellowship class. I can't tell you how excited I am to work with you. I look forward to seeing you in six weeks."

"Yes, sir. See you then."

She ended the call and swung forward in the hammock. When her feet touched the ground, she took off running across the lawn, up to the back patio, and through the French doors into the house.

She found Bronwen sitting on Palmer's lap in the living room, both watching the same iPad screen.

"Is everything okay, Nic?" Bronwen asked, straightening.

"Have you seen Ben?"

Bronwen frowned. "I thought he was with you?"

Nic hadn't seen Ben since she'd left him stand-ing on the sidewalk after their argument. She'd wandered around until she'd seen a local bus. She hadn't realized the Vineyard had public transportation. The bus didn't drop her off in front of Palmer's house, but it was close enough that she could walk the rest of the way.

"Not now," Palmer whispered to Bronwen. He looked at Nic and jerked his thumb over his shoulder. "He went up to your room to pack."

"Thanks. And everything's wonderful," she said, hurrying up the stairs.

She burst into their room and Ben looked up from where he was placing a stack of clothes into his opened suitcase.

She threw her arms wide. "I still have it!"

He made a face. "No one ever said you lacked confidence."

She rolled her eyes. "Now's not the time for witty wordplay. I'm talking about my fellowship! I. Still. Have it!"

She launched herself into his arms and he caught her and swung her around. She clutched his shoulders and threw her head back and laughed. The relief, the spinning, the euphoria, all combined to make her giddy . . . and dizzy.

"That's wonderful! When did you find out?" he asked, setting her down.

She held on to his forearms, attempting to regain her balance. "Just now. Dr. Newman called."

"I'm so happy for you," he said, trailing a finger down her cheek.

"Guess what?" She was practically bouncing on her toes, she was so excited.

"Dr. Newman admitted you're so awesome you don't even need to complete the fellowship? He'll give you the accreditation anyway?"

"No!" She popped his chest with the back of her fingers. "Your mother still called him, like she said she would, only it wasn't necessary."

He frowned. "What do you mean?"

"He said it's what he wanted to tell me when he called last week. He said my spot in the program had never been in jeopardy. He had no intention of revoking my fellowship."

He squeezed his eyes shut and the bottom dropped out of her stomach.

Was he annoyed with her? He'd gone to his parents for help and had endured a difficult encounter with his mother and a tongue-lashing—not the fun kind!—from her and none of it would've been necessary if she'd just taken Newman's earlier calls.

But then Ben shook his head and when his lashes lifted, he smiled. "Turns out, you didn't need my help. You saved yourself." He cupped her cheek. "Like you always do."

She gazed into his dark soulful—yes, she could finally admit they were soulful!—eyes and her heart fluttered before tumbling over and over, like it was falling down a flight of stairs.

She stepped into his personal space and brought her lips close to his. "You are a good man, Benjamin Reed Van Mont."

Then she kissed him.

Desire spiraled in her belly as he pressed his hot, hard body against hers. She didn't think she'd ever tire of his kisses. Strange but true. She reached for the hem of his shirt and pulled it off, exposing his yummy, tanned chest. She kissed the exposed skin, and began moving forward, pushing him backward until he fell back onto the bed. Staring down at him, with his flushed cheeks, his erection straining against his shorts, she realized the one negative in all of this was losing Ben.

And she didn't want to. Couldn't imagine him not being in her life.

She straddled his thighs. "You know, once I start my fellowship, I'll be pretty busy."

His hands slid beneath her shirt and up to cup her breasts. "I know."

She arched into him. "But my schedule will be much better than it has been the past few years."

His fingers pulled on her taut nipples just the way she liked. "Really?"

"Hmmmm," she murmured, unbuttoning his shorts. "I might be able to manage monthly trips to Baltimore."

"Could you now?"

"Then we wouldn't have to stop doing this." She slid her hand into his shorts and sighed when her palm met his hard length. She stroked him.

"Please, don't stop doing that."

She bent over him and kissed the pulse in his neck.

He moaned. "If you're willing to do all of that, I guess I could also make monthly trips down to Durham."

"Hmmm, then we could see each other every couple of weeks?"

His low chuckle stirred heat between her thighs. He grabbed her hips and pressed her against his hardness. "That would change the rules."

"I know. I just don't want this to end."

"Me neither." His eyes glittered, the flecks of amber glowing.

"Too long to drive, but it's what? Probably an hour flight?"

"That's doable."

She smiled. "So are you." She glanced over and spied his open suitcase on the bed. Yeah, that was going over the side. "I hate to mess up your neat packing, but what I want to do to you requires a lot of room. I promise I'll redo it for you before we leave tomorrow."

He exhaled. "Yeah, about that. Unfortunately, I have to fly to New York tonight for a couple of days. But don't worry, you're still confirmed for your flight home."

She jerked her head up from where she'd been running her tongue along the side of his neck. "Is everything okay?"

"Yeah, yeah. Of course. It's nothing for you to worry about. Although, I guess I should tell you since you'll find out sooner or later." He took a deep breath. "I've accepted the offer to head up the new Van Mont Industries charitable foundation."

Stunned, she sat back, and the motion caused her to fall off him and tumble to the mattress. "What?"

He shrugged. "It's not a big deal. I'm taking the

position. I'll be able to help a lot of people. Make a difference."

What was he *saying*?

"A few days ago you were adamant about not doing this. Why would you suddenly change your mind?" It came to her in a flash and she gasped. "Is that why your mother called Dr. Newman? Because you agreed to go back to Van Mont Industries?"

He couldn't do this. He loved his job and he was good at it. More importantly, it gave him independence from his parents and allowed him to have the type of life he wanted. If he went back to the company, he'd be miserable. Why would he give up the business he'd created, his peace of mind, his future family . . . for her?

"Ben? Why would you do that?"

He flipped her until she was lying beneath him, his hips cradled by her thighs. A loose smile tilted the corners of his lips. "Because you sacrifice what you have to for the people you love."

Pain sliced through her. "No."

"Yes. I love you."

She shook her head wildly. "No."

He laughed. "You're not in charge of the whole world, Nic. You can't tell me how I feel."

Though she usually loved the weight of him on top of her, he was suddenly too heavy, taking up her space, making it hard for her to breathe. She pushed against his chest but he didn't budge. Damn, was he made of stone?

"How many times did I tell you? I'm not interested in that. Especially not in the way you mean it."

His expression darkened. "What does that mean?"

"Call your mother and tell her the deal is off."

He frowned and rolled off her. "No."

She scrambled off the bed and pointed her finger at him. "Yes! And if you don't, I will. You can't do this to me. I'm not going to be one of those women who gives up everything they've worked to achieve for a man."

"I don't remember asking you to do that."

"But it's coming, right?"

Of course it was. He hadn't made this grand gesture for nothing. He said he loved her and wanted to be with her. She knew what he required from the woman he loved.

He rose up on his elbows. "You're smart, driven, and want your own life. That's one of the things I love about you."

"Stop saying that!"

"Why? It's true."

"Because I don't want to hear it. And since when did you want a woman who wanted her own life? You think Jennifer-the-elementary-school-teacher or Gabby-the-Pilates-instructor were going to continue teaching and Pilate-ing after they married you?"

"I don't know. But it doesn't matter. I didn't want to be with them. I want to be with you. And I'll do whatever it takes to make that work."

She waved a dismissive hand. "That's your cock talking. You hate doctors. You don't want to be involved with one."

And after meeting his mother, she could see the oedipal cave that had crawled from.

"Nic! People make a lot of grand pronouncements when they think they know something. I was an idiot. I thought I knew all the traits the woman I would love needed to have. What I didn't know, couldn't understand, is the woman is all that matters. You're who I want. I can adjust to everything else."

"No." She covered her ears with her hands. She knew it was childish, but she didn't care. His words were ripping her apart.

He stood and approached her, grabbing her wrists and pulling them down. "I support you. I would never ask you to give up your fellowship. And it's only a year. We were just talking about visiting each other during that time. Then, when it's over, we can decide—"

"There you go. 'We can decide.' *We* don't decide. *I* decide."

He held his hands up. "Of course. But I don't see the harm in trying to find a job in Baltimore. Hell, between Baltimore and DC, you'd have access to all the opportunities you'd ever want. World-class hospitals, colleges with competitive sports teams, professional teams for every sport imaginable."

He sounded so reasonable and his argument

was so cogent. Is that how men did it? How they convinced women to give up everything? Until it was too late and they were left with nothing?

Is that what her father had done to her mother?

"Maybe I don't want a job in Baltimore. Maybe I'll find a better job elsewhere."

"I'm just asking you to look." Ben frowned and shook his head. "But you're not even willing to do that, are you? To meet me halfway? Like I did for you?"

"Ahhh . . . here it comes." She wasn't going along on his guilt trip. Not when she didn't ask him to talk to his parents; he'd offered. And she never would've agreed with him taking that position with Van Mont Industries.

What about his own company? All of his clients? She refused to be held responsible for him giving up his dreams. Especially when she would never give up hers.

"I'm not limiting my options."

"Who's trying to limit you? If anything, I'm expanding your options. You could end up anywhere, Arizona, Colorado, Texas. I'm just adding Baltimore to the mix."

She shook her head.

His features hardened. "So, you can make compromises when it comes to fucking me, but if I want more, you can't be bothered?"

She winced. She hated the way that sounded but she had to do what was right for her. She had to protect her future.

"I'm not asking you to change your life. I'm

just asking you, begging you, to consider making room in it for me."

She squeezed her eyes shut to block out his tortured expression.

She wanted to. Wanted to throw caution to the wind and be carried away on a tide of emotion and trust. But wasn't that true for every woman who found themselves in this situation? And when it eventually fell apart, wouldn't they all want the chance to go back and make the correct decision? The decision before her right now?

"I'm not your father," he said sadly. "And you're not your mother."

Her breath caught in the back of her throat. How dare he bring that up? Anger swept away any lingering threads of doubt.

"I know. Because I won't make the same mistake she did."

Chapter Twenty-Four

The sun was setting as Ben braked his car to a stop and pushed the ignition button to cut the engine. He scrubbed a hand over the tightness in his chest, akin to a boa constrictor grabbing hold of his heart. When would his pain at Nic's rejection end? He wished he were home, by himself in the darkness where he could tend to his wounds in private. More than likely, he'd relive every moment on the Vineyard between them to see where it had all gone wrong and wish like hell he could go back in time and fix it.

Instead, he'd voluntarily come to the last place on earth he wanted to be. Sighing, he got out of his car and walked up the stone pavers to the large double front doors of the Van Mont family manor. Almost twice the size of Palmer's, the house sat on over fourteen acres of prime waterfront real estate in a well-established neighborhood.

Deciding not to announce his presence—visits only happened when they involved the element of surprise—he eschewed ringing the bell or knocking on the door. He walked directly into a foyer the size of the main floor in his home back in Baltimore. Going to the right, he entered a sun-splashed living room with wooden beams and soaring cathedral ceilings.

Directly across from him, wall-to-wall windows showcased a stunning ocean vista. The house had been renovated several years ago, so the interior wasn't as he remembered, but he'd never forget that view. He'd spent hours throwing rocks in the water on the private shoreline it showcased, either by himself or with his cousins and then later alongside Davis and Palmer.

Fallon sat on an upholstered wingback chair near the fireplace, reading from an iPad. Since she still wore her outfit from earlier, he assumed she didn't have plans for an evening out.

Her head flew up and her eyes widened behind a pair of stylish frames. "Benjamin! I wasn't expecting you."

"Mother."

She closed the cover of the iPad, took off her glasses, and placed them both on a side table next to a half-empty glass of water. "Sit down. Would you like Edith to bring you something to drink?"

Edith had been the family's house manager for years. Although he wanted to leave as quickly as possible, he made a note to stop in the kitchen and say hi to her before he left.

"No, thank you. This won't take long." He slid his hands in his pockets. "You called Dr. Newman."

She tilted her head back and stared up at him, her gaze steady. "I told you I would."

That was it. No comments about wasting her valuable time making phone calls. No obvious elation at getting him to come back to Van Mont Industries. Her energy, always contained and watchful, was calmer than usual. Less displeased and more . . . cautious?

"He's an interesting man," Fallon said, when Ben remained silent. "He runs one of the top sports medicine programs in the country and he had nothing but wonderful things to say about your Dr. Allen."

His heart twisted at her words. *His* Dr. Allen? Not anymore. If she ever was.

"He thanked me for calling, but said it wasn't necessary. Her spot had never been in jeopardy. He let it slip that Vincent Whitaker was the one who was trying to get her fellowship revoked." Fallon curled her lip. "I dislike that man intensely. But hospitals need donors to fund research and to continue providing affordable quality care to everyone who needs it. To do good, you sometimes have to deal with horrible people."

Truer words had never been spoken. Hence his reason for being here.

"Thank you for reaching out to him," he said. "And even though in the end, Nic didn't need the help, I still plan to honor our deal. I just need time to wrap up my business."

He'd have to legally dissolve the corporation, resolve any financial obligations, take care of Ezra and find two or three other planners to refer his clients to. Or, instead of terminating his business, he could sell it. He'd been approached before, but three years ago, he couldn't conceive of ever wanting to hand his business over to someone else to run. Today the company was an even better asset. The records were in order, there was a stable revenue base and, as Ezra and Nic had pointed out, the potential for growth was enormous.

And he'd failed to take advantage of it.

Perfect time for that realization, Van Mont!

Fallon reached for her glass and took a sip of her drink. "No."

No?

No!

Like a torrent of whitewater, anger sprang forth and ran roughshod over his usual temperate and accepting nature. It raced past his resentment toward his parents, his annoyance with Davis, and his hurt and heartbreak over Nic, gaining strength and momentum at each emotional checkpoint. In his pockets, his hands curled into fists.

"Do you wonder why I rarely ask you or Father for anything?" He didn't wait for her response. It wasn't necessary. "Because I don't expect you to do it! How fucked-up is that? I should be able to come to you. You're supposed to be the ones I can always count on. Instead there are at least ten people I'd call first if I was ever in a jam."

The color leached from her face. "Benjamin, I . . . I didn't know."

"Why would you? That would require you to know me. And that comes from spending time with me. Something else you can't be bothered to do."

As quickly and hotly as his rage flared, it flamed out, leaving him shaken and exhausted. He shoveled all ten fingers through his hair then dropped his head and sank onto the sofa on the other side of the fireplace.

"Why wasn't I enough for you?"

He regretted the words as soon as they caught air.

Why couldn't he have held on to his anger a little longer? It had been his armor, had protected him . . . and would've prevented him from asking the question that left him exposed. Vulnerable. He didn't want her to see his weakness, to know that a part of him was still that little boy seeking his parents' approval.

He straightened and pinched the inner corners of his eyes, ending the plans of any renegade tears. "Until I've properly closed my business, I will not be starting at Van Mont Industries. I'm fully prepared to oversee the creation and management of the new charitable foundation, but I have more pressing obligations. If you can't accept that, I'm sure the other members of the board—"

"Benjamin," she interrupted, her voice no less firm for its uncharacteristic softness, "when I said no, I didn't mean that we weren't willing to wait.

I meant that I wasn't expecting you to uphold your end of the bargain."

Wait, what? "I don't understand."

"That appears to be true for the both of us." She moved from the chair to sit next to him on the sofa. "When your father told me about your request I knew there was more to the story."

He was having difficulty comprehending the shift in the conversation. "You did?"

"Like you said, you rarely ask us for anything. I told him to hold off on making the call and I started asking around. I learned Nicole's a well-respected doctor. Everyone I talked to at Hopkins agrees she's going to have a brilliant career." Fallon shrugged. "There didn't appear to be a downside to doing what you'd asked."

"But you didn't?"

"Not right away, no. I wanted to talk to you first. Find out why it was so important to you. As soon as I could get away, I came here. The moment I saw you with Nicole I understood. And it hurt me." She shook her head. "She mattered to you and we knew nothing about her. I could suddenly see ten years into the future. You'd be married, maybe with children of your own, and your father and I wouldn't be a part of it."

The idea that his parents would care about being a part of *his* future family left him dumbfounded.

"But Nic stood up for me and that made you angry."

"It did. No mother wants to hear the things she said to me, even if they were true. I had no intention of ever making that call. But you came back to the coffeeshop and made that deal with me. And I should've been happy because getting you back to Van Mont Industries has been my goal since you left. Only it wasn't what you wanted. You were doing it for her."

"Why should that matter to you? You'd won. I was finally doing what you'd always demanded."

But instead of answering she said, "I never told you what I went through to become a doctor. It was harder than I'd anticipated. It was the late 70s and although the number of female physicians had increased, it was still woefully low. Even less were surgeons. And cardiothoracic specialists? Minuscule. I was constantly having to prove myself. The men always treated me as if I was only there temporarily, often remarking I'd leave after I had children. Once I was established and had earned the respect of my peers, I couldn't imagine giving it up, especially for the very reason I'd been shamed and mocked. It made me a first-class surgeon but, I realize now, a piss-poor mother."

He'd never considered the difficulty his mother may have endured in becoming a doctor. He'd only seen her actions, or lack thereof, from his perspective. Was her story supposed to excuse how they'd treated him? How they'd been absent most of his childhood and when they were around, barely present? It was something he'd have to think about later, but—

"What does that have to do with whether or not I come back to Van Mont Industries?"

"I'm getting there," she said, casting her gaze downward, away from his face. "I've done a lot of reflecting in a short amount of time and I'm trying to explain why I eventually decided to intervene on Nicole's behalf. Becoming a doctor isn't easy. And as a woman of color, without any family resources? The obstacles and attitudes were probably ten times worse. Despite that, she made it. She earned her spot in the rarest of airs and I couldn't stand the thought that it would be derailed by some snot-nosed entitled kid who didn't have a quarter of her talent. I had to do it, separate from my deal with you."

So not because he'd asked, but because Nic deserved it? Great, but . . . Was it wrong of him to be jealous of his mother's obvious respect for the woman he loved? A regard he'd never been able to claim for himself?

He sighed and rose to his feet. "Whatever the reason, you did your part and I'll—"

"Wait." She grabbed his forearm. "You don't understand. By the time I'd come to that decision, any joy I'd felt at bringing you back into the fold had curdled. The reason does matter. Your father and I lived our dreams, Nicole would be living hers. Why would I want less than that for you?"

Sitting down again, he crossed his arms over his chest and eyed her skeptically. "I find that hard to believe since you constantly and consistently disparage my choices."

The brackets curving her mouth deepened. "Your father and I raised you the way we were raised. Children were meant to carry on the family legacy. Their achievements, and their failures, were seen as a reflection of the family. We thought we knew what was best in terms of your happiness and we didn't handle it well when our visions didn't align. I'm not trying to excuse our behavior. We've made a lot of mistakes though . . . you turned out wonderfully, so we can't be all bad, right?"

Was she serious?

When he didn't react, she cleared her expression. "What I'm trying to say is . . . we love you and we want you to be happy. And that means following your own path, not ours."

Oh.

They loved him and wanted him to be happy? He was numb. He'd heard her words, understood them even, but could he allow himself to believe her after all of these years when he'd thought the exact opposite?

"I'm not sure how to respond. I've waited a long time to hear you say that."

"I'm sorry. And I should say, we're not going to always get it right. We'll stumble and make mistakes. But the intent is there. To do better. Now," she said, blinking rapidly—was she crying?—"I want to hear all about you and Nicole."

Thrown from the emotional frying pan into the fire. The boa constrictor coiled more of its body around Ben's heart and slowly squeezed.

Fallon cupped his shoulder. "What happened?"

"It's over. I told her I loved her and she doesn't feel the same way."

She waved a hand. "I don't believe that for a second. She stood up to me for you, despite what it could cost her. You don't do that for someone you don't love."

"She thinks I'll want her to give up her career."

"That's ridiculous." She frowned. "Why would she think that?"

Ben winced. "Because the entire time we've known each other, I may have said that I would . . . uh . . . never get involved with a doctor."

Dark sculpted brows reached for the heavens. "Benjamin! We can unpack that another time. And there will be another time."

Was that a promise or a threat?

"Does she know what you offered to do on her behalf?"

He nodded.

"Then she can't truly believe you would stand in her way."

"Maybe not. But it's what she's telling herself. And she won't compromise."

"Nicole is very smart. She'll figure this out. What you have to decide is if you can give her time to do that. Is she worth the wait?"

His best friend and the most beautiful woman, inside and out, he'd ever known?

"Absolutely."

His mother patted his knee. "You have the biggest heart of anyone I know. You always have. I'm ashamed to say I used to think of it as a weakness. Now I can't express enough how grateful I am for it."

By the time he'd returned to Palmer's later that night, his head was spinning from all he'd experienced. When he'd awakened this morning, if anyone had told him that he'd tell Nic he loved her, they'd break up, and he'd come to better understand his mother, he'd have suggested they contact a competent mental health professional. Before he'd left Fallon, she'd held out her arms for a hug and after an awkward moment, he'd gone into them. He couldn't remember the last time they'd embraced, though the smell of her Chanel No. 5 was familiar and unexpectedly comforting.

Entering the house, he stopped short at the sight of Davis sitting alone at the kitchen bar, a drink in his hand, pendant lights illuminating his stooped posture.

"Where is everyone?"

"Palmer and Bron went for a walk on the beach and I haven't seen Tinsley since she stormed out of here after your fight last night." Davis raised his glass then took a sip. "Thanks for that, by the way."

Ben could tell Davis was itching for a fight, but he'd have to look elsewhere. Ben was dealing with his own shit. He wasn't in the mood.

He headed to the stairs. "Whatever, dude."

"I gotta hand it to you, champ, you are *killing* it with the ladies."

He spun around to face Davis. "What's your problem?"

Davis shrugged. "I don't know what you're talking about. I'm fine. Just offering a little commentary."

"You've been doing that a lot these last few days." He walked over and took the tumbler from Davis. "Spurred on by this. You've been meaner than usual and no fun to be around."

Davis stood, his brow lowered, his jaw tight. "Who are you, my father? I can take care of myself."

"And this is how you do it? By being a drunk asshole on the last weekend we'll see our friends for three years?"

Adrenaline coursed through Ben's body and ratcheted up his breathing. He rarely rose to Davis's bait, but if Davis was stupid, or drunk, enough to start something, Ben would make sure to finish it.

They stared at each other for several long, tense moments before Davis averted his gaze. "Fuck. Sorry, man."

Davis hadn't started out being this obnoxious. Ben thought back to when he'd noticed the shift in his friend's behavior. "Is this about Sabine? You've been irritable since you found out she wasn't coming."

"She was going to come until we got into a fight."

Ben frowned. "I thought you said it was work."

Davis swiped at the air. "She accused me of being selfish. Said I always want everything on my terms."

"Do you?"

"Wouldn't you? It certainly makes things easier."

Ben rolled his eyes. "If you're interested in something more, something serious, you need to talk to her. Honestly. Without the charm and bullshit. Can you do that?"

Davis flicked his gaze upward and exhaled. "Yeah."

"And you can start by putting that glass down. I'm pretty sure she's not hanging out at the bottom of that bottle."

"You're right. Thanks, man. And I'm sorry. I haven't been very helpful to you this weekend."

"No, you haven't," he laughed. "But it's okay."

Nic hadn't left because of anything Davis had done.

Davis held out his hand and Ben clasped it, allowing the other man to pull him in for a hug. His second one in an hour. Did he have one of those middle school handwritten signs on his back, exhorting everyone he came in contact with to embrace him?

"Do you guys need more time? We could come back." Bronwen's cool, amused voice broke the silence.

"You good?" Ben asked Davis quietly. When Davis nodded, he stepped back and slapped his friend's shoulder before looking at Bronwen. "We're good."

Bronwen and Palmer stood with their arms around one another, looking calm, serene, and happily in love. He wanted that with Nic, but it might never be possible.

"I'm so sorry. I know this isn't what you guys pictured when you suggested this getaway."

"We got to spend time with you, which is what we wanted. If anything, I should apologize to you. About Tinsley. That was totally my bad." Bron reached out and squeezed his arm. "I know we just met Nic but I really like her. I hope you can work it out."

"I do, too," he said, kissing her cheek.

"As for you," Palmer said, pointing at Davis, who had the sense to look embarrassed, "I hope you've figured your shit out. Because if we get back in three years and you're still doing this same—"

"I know, I know," Davis said, rubbing the nape of his neck. "And for what it's worth, I'm sorry, too."

Ben looked at his friends. They'd sustained him and had been more like his family than his blood relations. He was really lucky to have them in his life. "Now, how about one last dinner before you two rush off to save the world?"

Chapter Twenty-Five

Nic closed the flap on the box she was packing and sealed it with tape. Tossing the dispenser on the bed, she sighed, shoved a hand through her curls, and gauged the progress she'd made over the past five days. Partially filled boxes were scattered around the living room; stacks of books were piled on her pub table and kitchen counter; and clothes, still on hangers, were haphazardly thrown over the backs of chairs and the arms of her couch. It was not like she was cursed with an abundance of belongings; her entire life could fit into one of those small moving containers you hitched to the back of your car. Still, she couldn't conjure enough motivation to pack with her usual speed and efficiency and move out after being there for three years.

She sat abruptly on the nearest cleared surface—the edge of the coffee table. That explained it. She'd lived in that apartment for a long time. Anyone would be in their feelings about leaving a place they'd called home for the past three years.

You had no problems leaving Covington with your deuces up and no looks back. And you'd lived there eighteen years. You were in Charlottesville for eight . . .

Yeah, well . . .

It wasn't because she was also leaving the man who'd lived upstairs that entire time. This wasn't about Ben. In fact, in the time since she'd returned from Martha's Vineyard she'd been incredibly busy. Too busy to think about Ben. To miss him. To see reminders of them together everywhere: in the kitchen, drinking wine while he cooked for her, in the living room as they sat on the couch watching TV, here in her apartment when he'd come to check on her.

Too busy to wonder where he'd been spending his time, considering he hadn't come home.

She'd gone into the hospital to go through out processing, which required signing paperwork and turning in her hospital badges and parking pass. While she'd been chatting with the unit nurses and saying her good-byes, a staff member had told her Dr. Agner wanted to see her in his office.

What a difference two weeks made. The last time she'd been in here, she'd felt as if her life's work had been unraveling before her eyes.

Agner blinked and smoothed his fingers along his bow tie. "You've done wonderful work here at Hopkins, especially in your final year as chief resident."

Uh-huh.

But professionalism reigned. She offered him a tight smile. "It's a great program. I grew a lot here, both academically and surgically."

"I received a call from James Newman at Duke. They're looking forward to having you."

She nodded, while drumming her fingers on her thigh. "I can't wait to start."

Agner cleared his throat. "I— If you were wondering, while you were away, Dr. Whitaker had a . . . difficult time with a . . . couple of patients. He's taking some time off to evaluate his future."

Nic waited for the outpouring of triumph to swell over her.

"We're expecting great things from you. You're an exceptional surgeon, Dr. Allen."

He stood and held out his hand. The triumph hadn't come, but oh, the rage . . .

If I was so great why didn't you stand behind me?

Why was the fellowship, which I'd earned, in jeopardy over someone whose work was clearly subpar to my own?

Why did I need to bolster my case with outside support?

Why wasn't my word, my recommendation, enough?

In the end, she'd stood and accepted his handshake. "Thank you, Dr. Agner."

The encounter still left a bad taste in her mouth, but it didn't mar her feeling of accomplishment. Tomorrow she'd graduate from her residency and at the separate dinner and awards ceremony for the orthopedic surgery specialty she'd accept the award for Chief Resident of the Year.

Feeling restless, she let go of the shirt she'd been folding and headed upstairs. The day was sunny and the kitchen was bright, but it could've been cloudy and rainy. The space felt sad and dreary, a testament to Ben's absence. She hadn't seen him since their argument. True to his word, he'd made sure she had a plane ticket back home and had arranged for transportation to and from the airport.

Still taking care of her. Even in the end.

"Damn you, Ben! Why did you have to go and ruin everything?"

She banged her fist on the counter—cursing when she realized what she'd done—and dropped her head on her folded arms. This was supposed to be one of the happiest times of her life. She'd finished her residency and was getting ready to begin her fellowship! She was on schedule to achieve goals she'd set for herself years ago. Instead, she couldn't think of anything except Ben and his soulful eyes and tousled hair and body made for sin.

"So, you can make compromises when it comes to fucking me, but if I want more, you can't be bothered?"

God it hurt! She missed his presence, his warmth, his laughter. Him. She felt it keenly, nearly every time she breathed. Forget a hangover cure, she wished there was some sort of pill or medication she could take to ease the suffering of her heart. But there was nothing but to endure it.

The chiming doorbell startled her out of her funk and sent her heart free-falling into the pit of her stomach.

Ben?

As fast as her hopes soared, they deflated. Ben wouldn't ring the bell. He'd use his key.

She descended the steps to the foyer and opened the door.

"Mom!"

How did the universe know what she needed?

Dee Allen pulled Nic into a warm hug. Nic had inherited her petite stature from her mother. Within her embrace, she could rest her cheek against her mom's, close her eyes, and inhale the familiar scent of cocoa butter. When she started to feel a little better, she lifted her lashes and stared at the other visitor, whose eyes were hidden behind stylish sunglasses.

"Caila! What are you two doing here?"

"Aren't you graduating tomorrow?" Caila asked.

Jeez, she was right. That's why her mother was here. It had nothing to do with the universe. Nic rolled her eyes at her moment of whimsy.

Another reason to be annoyed with Ben.

Smirking, Nic retorted, "I'm honored you managed to tear yourself away from Mayor McHottie."

"You should be." Caila winked, before stepping forth and giving Nic a hug and brief kiss on the cheek. She leaned back and eyed the writing on Nic's purple T-shirt. "'I Use No Chemicals. Only Juices and Berries'. Ha! *Coming to America*. I love it."

Nic smiled. "Come in."

She closed the door and gestured for them to follow her up into the kitchen, knowing there was a better chance of finding refreshments there than in her apartment.

"How did the two of you connect up?"

"We've been planning this for a while," Caila said, setting her Chanel purse on the counter. "We all wanted to be here to celebrate this with you."

Nic turned wide eyes on her mom. "You knew the girls were coming when I talked to you a couple of weeks ago?"

"I did," Dee said, good-naturedly.

"Ava will be here tomorrow. She's flying in from a judicial conference. And Lacey's going to try, but rehearsals for the tour started immediately and she's not sure if she can get away. She's planning to call, though."

Nic was touched at the effort her friends were making on her behalf. They were all extremely busy people, so she appreciated them taking time out of their hectic schedules for her.

"I'm glad you're both here. It means the world to me."

Dee settled onto a bar stool at the counter and gazed around, her brows raised. "I always thought this was a lovely place. Is Ben still at work?"

"Probably," Nic said, avoiding the question. "Can I get you guys anything? Are you thirsty?"

Caila waved her off. "I'm good."

"Are you sure? Mom, I know what you want, but we also have water, soda, or wine." Nic filled the kettle with water and set about preparing tea for Dee. "Or would you prefer something to eat? If we don't have anything here, we can go out or I can order in with DoorDash?"

When there was no reply, she glanced up to see both women staring at her.

"What's wrong?" Dee asked, furrows appearing in the still-smooth light brown skin of her forehead.

Nic shook her head, as if to Etch A Sketch her expression. "Nothing."

"Nicole Shavonne Allen, I knew who you were before you were birthed from my body. Do you think I can't tell when something is wrong with you?"

She tried to keep it in and if it was anyone else, she honestly believed she would've succeeded. But in the face of her mother's love, support, and compassion, Nic crumpled.

"Oh my God," Dee exclaimed when Nic started to cry.

"It must be bad, Ms. Dee," Caila said, her voice colored with concern. "I can't remember the last time I saw Nic fall apart like this."

In the background of her distress, Nic was aware of both women moving. Of her mother taking her hand and guiding her into the living room. Of Caila opening and closing cabinets and then pouring liquid into a glass.

Dee smoothed one of Nic's curls behind her ear. "What is it, honey? Are you ill? Has something happened with your fellowship?" She gasped. "Are you not graduating?"

Nic took the tissue from Caila's outstretched hand and blew her nose. "Of course I'm graduating."

"Then what is it?"

"It's Ben."

"Is *he* ill?" Dee asked.

"No, I don't think that's it," Caila said in a low, knowing tone.

Nic met her friend's questioning gaze and nodded in confirmation. Caila's gaze softened and her head tilted to the side. "Oh sweetie. What happened?"

She blew out a shaky, shuddering breath. "We got into a huge fight."

Just saying the words aloud and remembering Ben's shattered expression tore at Nic.

"About what? Did he say something wrong? Did he hurt you?" Dee's narrowed eyes and fierce expression reminded Nic of a mama lion protecting her cub.

She had an amazing mother. Great friends, and a prestigious, rewarding career. She didn't need anything else.

"I talked to Ava," Caila said. "Did something happen when you two were on Martha's Vineyard?"

Nic heard Dee's confused "What were you doing on Martha's Vineyard?" but her gaze never left Caila.

She nodded. "He told me he loved me."

It was Caila's turn to be shocked. "Oh! I was not expecting that."

Neither had Nic.

"And that upset you?" Caila pressed.

"Yes!"

Caila frowned. "I don't understand."

Ugh! The Caila of a year ago would've. Before Mayor McHottie!

"You know how hard I've worked to get here. All my life, people have underestimated me, never expecting me to make it. They either told me I wasn't good enough or never stuck around long enough to find out. But I've consistently proved them all wrong. And now, I'm so close and he thinks because he says he loves me . . ." Nic shook her head. "Why would I give up my life, something I can depend on, for meaningless words and something that probably won't last?"

"Did he ask you to?"

"That's what he wants. Some kind of Suzy Homemaker. And that's not me."

"It's been three years. I think Ben knows exactly who you are."

"I support you. I would never ask you to give up your fellowship. And it's only a year. We can make it work . . ."

Nic squeezed her eyes shut, as Caila's logic attempted to make inroads. But something blocked her from fully accepting their meaning.

"It can't work," she said, though to Caila or Ben, she wasn't sure. "My fellowship is in Durham. He lives here. And when I'm done, I'll be searching for jobs. I don't know where that will take me and I won't limit myself just to be where he is."

"Slow your roll! You've raced ahead before the starting gun went off! Calm down. He said he loves you. Has he asked you to marry him?"

"No."

"To live with him?" At Nic's twisted lip, Caila amended, "Officially?"

"No."

"Did he ask you to give up your fellowship?"

The exact opposite actually. He was willing to give up his dreams so she could achieve hers.

"No."

"So where is this coming from?"

Nic opened her mouth to respond when Dee said, "Caila, can you give us a minute?"

Once Caila sensed an issue, she wouldn't stop until she'd figured it out. Nic knew from personal experience that Caila's dogged persistence could be both a blessing and a curse and it didn't take a genius to figure out which one it'd be this time.

Caila started to respond, but then she glanced at Nic. Whatever she saw had her backing down, a rare feat for her friend.

"Sure." Caila stood. "I'll go down and see how much packing Nic has done. Brilliant your daughter is, Ms. Dee. Organized outside of the OR, she is not."

Nic listened as the click of Caila's heels on the hardwood floors grew more faint. When she could no longer hear them, she turned to her mother.

Dee covered Nic's nearest hand with her own. "You know how much I love you, right?"

The nape of Nic's neck tingled. She tensed. "Of course."

"And I'm so very proud of you."

"I know."

"But I made a mistake."

A chill spiraled from Nic's core at the starkness of her mother's words and she pulled her hand away. "I don't want to talk about this."

No child ever wanted to hear their parents wished they hadn't been born. Her father's desertion demonstrated how he felt on that issue, but she couldn't take hearing it from her mother.

"Not you," Dee said softly. "Never you."

Relief made her giddy. "Then what mistake did you make?"

"I gave in to the bitterness. I gave up my plans and instead of taking responsibility I blamed your father."

"He is to blame. He left us."

"Yes, and that was his choice. Everything that happened afterward was mine."

The blood rushed from her head and she suddenly had difficulty breathing. "I don't understand."

"You're still making decisions based on what happened all those years ago."

Nic's heart was beating so loudly she was certain Dee could hear it. "You're wrong. I don't care about him. Or what he did. Or why he's not here."

Her mother looked at her with anguished sympathy. "God, I wish that were true. But I see now that you care about it a great deal."

"Stop saying that!" she raged. "I didn't do any of this because of him."

"Yes you did. You may not even be aware of it." Dee stroked a hand down Nic's hair. "It was always important to me that you had what you needed, that you never went without because of the choices I made."

"'Make a way out of no way.' That was your motto. I just followed your example."

"I can't take credit for that. You blazed your own path. And seeing what you did, I felt ashamed that I didn't do more."

"Are you kidding? You're the best mother anyone could ask for."

"But I was only one person and after your father left, I felt so overwhelmed. And bitter. And angry. I could've gone back to college; looked at nighttime options or took courses online. Hell, I could've taken you and moved to a bigger city where there were more opportunities, but I didn't. I stayed, accepted my lot and let the resentment eat away at me. It never occurred to me that it might infect you, too."

"It didn't."

"Are you sure?" Dee stared into Nic's eyes. "What's going to happen once you achieve your goal? When you finish your fellowship?"

"I'll have the job I want, I'll make a lot of money, and I'll be able to take care of you."

"I don't want you to take care of me. I want you to take care of you."

"What are you talking about? I'm great." Nic waved a hand toward her face. "Recent crying jag aside."

"No you're not. You've based your entire life on your work. It's like building a house on an unsteady foundation."

Nic laughed. "Mom. Stop. It's not the same thing."

"Sure it is. If the foundation collapses, the house is destroyed. If work is your entire life and you can't work, what happens to you then?"

"Am I missing something? Why wouldn't I be able to work?"

"I think what your mother is trying to say is our careers are important to us, but they aren't everything."

Nic started and swung her head to find Caila standing there in her bare feet. "Back so soon?"

"I came to grab my agenda out of my bag. It's chaos down there. Nothing is arranged or labeled. You'll save so much time on the other end by taking a little bit of time to organize now." Caila looked at Dee. "I see she's being her usual ornery self. Do you mind?"

Dee sighed. "Be my guest. Maybe you can get through to her."

Caila, a giantess even without shoes, peered down at Nic. "I've watched you push men away, keep them at a distance. But I can't stand by and watch it this time. Not when I feel like you're going to look back on this and regret it. The fact that Ben even got through your defenses is a miracle. But he did. And he loves you. And he's done nothing but support you. You owe it to both of you to give it a chance. See where it could go."

"Are you and Mom tag teaming me?"

"Maybe. You can be really stubborn. And I know this must sound crazy coming from me, but I've learned you can do your job, chase your dreams, and still be happy with the person you love."

"This is different from what you and Wyatt went through."

"The details, but not the issue. Look, my career was the most important thing in my life until I almost lost it! That's when I realized what really mattered to me. You guys, my family. Wyatt. I still love my work. It's fulfilling and it challenges me and it's a part of who I am. But it isn't *all* that I am."

Nic had seen that change in Caila. Had noticed it during their vacation this year. But she hadn't taken kindly to the transformation, thinking it meant her friend was a hypocrite. What she hadn't known was how much her own life would change in a matter of a month.

"From what you said, Ben wasn't asking you to give up your career or change who you are. If anything, it sounds like he wanted you to, I don't know, just make room in your life for him."

Make room in her life . . .

His parents never having time for him.

His insistence that the woman he married have a flexible schedule and undemanding career.

His refusal to expand his business and increase his client roster.

"I'm just asking you, begging you, to consider making room in it for me."

The realization acted as a tectonic shift in her perspective.

"But what if I make room for him and I'm wrong? What if it doesn't work out?"

"It's not surgery. If it doesn't work out, you move on, Martha, move on. And if putting more distance between you is necessary, you get another job."

"Excuse me?"

"Girl, Ava gave me some tough love and now it's time for me to pass it on. This isn't your mother's situation. You're not a twenty-year-old black woman raising a child on your own in a small Southern town. You're a fucking surgeon. Pardon my language, Ms. Dee. You're not giving up your fellowship, so you're achieving your goals. And if things don't work with Ben, so? It'll be sad. You'll be heartbroken, but you'll keep living your life. And you'll have us." She took Nic's hand. "But Nic, imagine if things *do* work out? You'll have your career and a man who loves and supports you. Isn't the possibility of achieving that dream worth the risk?"

Nic thought of the three years she'd lived with Ben. How he'd supported her, taken care of her, nurtured her. Then she thought of the week they'd just spent together. How becoming intimate hadn't detracted from their friendship, only made it better. What would she give for the chance to have that? Forever?

She covered her face with her hands. "I've been such an idiot."

"There you go." Caila laughed. "That's it. Let it flow over you. Trust me, I've been there. The moment when you realize the mistake you made and you need to fix it? It can be a doozy."

"How do I fix it? And what if he doesn't feel the same way anymore?"

"That man loves you. He didn't stop because of an argument." Caila held up her agenda. "Let's take this one step at a time. We'll figure it out. Do you know where he is?"

"No." Nic smiled, the lightness in her heart threatening to overwhelm her. She loved Ben. It was time to get her man back. "But I know where he'll be."

Chapter Twenty-Six

$\mathcal{I}$ appreciate you coming in," Ben said. "I didn't handle our initial meeting well and that's all my fault. If you'll indulge me, I'd like to have a do-over. You tell me what you want to do and I'll advise you on how you'd go about achieving it. I'll give you my opinion, that would be my job as your financial manager, but it's your money and your decision. If at the end of the session you still believe this won't work, then we part ways, no hard feelings. And you won't sic Mr. Ashford on me."

Quentin Miller rubbed his hands together and then nodded. "Alright."

Ben motioned for the player to precede him into the office and told Ezra, "Hold my calls."

Thirty minutes later, Ben clasped the hand Quentin offered then escorted the young man to the lobby.

"Thanks for giving me a second chance," Ben said, smiling ruefully.

"Thanks for listening," Quentin said, his trademark grin back in place as the elevator doors opened. "Take it easy, BVM."

Looked like he'd acquired a new nickname. Laughing, Ben handed Ezra the iPad he held. "That's the contract he signed. Start a file then call his manager to set up an appointment in two months for all of us to meet."

"Will do," Ezra said, grabbing the tablet.

Ben headed back to his desk, grateful he'd heeded his gut and reached out to Quentin a second time. He hadn't been able to shake the feeling that he'd made a mistake by not listening to the player during their first consultation. Their phone call on the Vineyard had left Ben with mixed sentiments. A positive regard for a young man willing to stand up for himself and the people he cared for and a negative one.

About himself.

Ben had been so certain he'd known the situation, he hadn't looked beyond the surface. Something he'd been doing a lot lately. In this instance, continuing to do so would've cost him the opportunity to work with someone who'd really appreciate his work. The type of client he'd started his business to help.

Ezra poked his head in. "April Ingham's rep confirmed your meeting for next week. Since you agreed to come to her in New York while she works on her latest collection, she's sending her private plane for you. I'll forward you all of the travel information as soon as I receive it."

"Thanks."

Another change he'd made.

By allowing him to back out of their deal, his mother had encouraged him to live his dream. And he couldn't do it halfway. His mother hadn't. Nic wasn't. They were both unafraid to go after what they wanted. He had been living in fear, whether he'd realized it or not. In his personal life, he'd manifested that anxiety by placing restrictions on the type of woman he'd let into his life. It hadn't been because he was concerned about the family they would one day have. He'd chosen women with accommodating lifestyles because a part of him had been afraid that with more rigidity, he wouldn't be chosen.

Professionally, he recognized he'd been operating his business as if afraid it wasn't going to last. As if he, too, hadn't believed that he wouldn't end up back at Van Mont Industries. Keeping things small made them easier to jettison. But now that he knew going back would never be an option, he felt free to give all of his talents to his business without any limitations on its scope and growth. In fact, he was already looking into hiring an associate to help him handle his expanded caseload. And if Ezra was right about athletes talking amongst themselves, that associate would soon have company.

"And Ezra," he called as his assistant was leaving, "the office phones have an intercom system. Feel free to use it. You don't have to physically come in here each time you need me."

"Got it, BVM."

He liked this nickname better than Benji.

Ben's smile faded and he settled back in his chair. If only his love life was similarly trending upward. The pain of his breakup with Nic was immeasurable and it hadn't lessened in the days since he'd left Martha's Vineyard. If anything it had gone from a sharp, radiating spasm to a dull, throbbing ache. Nic wanted space and he wanted to give it to her, so he hadn't gone back to the house when he'd gotten back to Baltimore. Instead he'd stayed at his family's ancestral home in Roland Park. But though they'd physically been miles apart, she'd never been far from his thoughts. He missed her desperately.

At least things were progressing with his parents. His father had called him the day after his talk with his mother. He'd echoed what Fallon had said and Ben was open to seeing if they were willing to put words to actions. Maybe he'd text them to see if they wanted to have dinner at Le Bernardin while he was in New York.

What would Nic think of the situation with his parents? Would she be in favor of their reconciliation? Or would she advise him to be more cautious? He wished he knew. He wanted to talk to her and get her opinion. He didn't just miss touching her, kissing her, and making love to her. He missed laughing with her, cooking for her, sharing his days with her.

He missed his best friend.

He could only hope Nic would accept his feelings and realize he'd meant what he'd said. He wanted only to support her. He'd give her time.

But not too much.

At a certain point, if she didn't come to him, he was going to have to go to her. He was no longer afraid to go after what he wanted and to live his dream. And she was inextricably linked to both.

Ezra buzzed his phone.

Progress.

"You have a walk-in."

He may have stopped constraining the growth of his business, but he still had standards.

"I don't see walk-ins. Give them the paperwork and an appointment. Sometime soon, if you can."

A few seconds later, Ezra buzzed him again.

"She doesn't want an appointment. She said she had to see you today. She told me she was trying to be polite, but she was prepared to go through me if necessary." He lowered his voice. "She's tiny but I'd put money on her."

Ben's heart pummeled his chest trying to break free as if it sensed its other half nearby.

Nic?

He experienced the next few moments as if he were out of his body. Hovering from above, he watched as he jerkily rose from his desk and strode over to the door. When he opened it, there she stood, lovely in a simple hot pink dress that matched the becoming flush on her cheeks and showcased her petite figure to perfection. A small beige bag on a gold chain was slung across her body and her hair was a halo of curls around her gorgeous face.

His consciousness slammed back into his body and he gulped in a huge breath of air.

How had he survived a week without seeing her?

But the first thing he said was, "Your graduation was today."

"I know."

"Congratulations." Before everything had happened between them, he'd planned to be there. He'd been looking forward to celebrating this accomplishment with her. To see the culmination of all of her hard work. He frowned and glanced at his watch. "What are you doing here?"

"I wanted to see you."

"Now?"

What was she thinking? In an hour, her specialty was holding a separate ceremony where she'd be receiving several awards and giving a speech. During this time of day, it'd take almost forty minutes to get to the country club where the festivities were being held.

She took a step forward, her determined gaze meeting his. "We need to talk."

He knew those accolades were important to her. He couldn't let her miss it.

"Wait here." He rushed back to his desk, shrugged into his suit jacket, and grabbed his phone and wallet from the drawer. "We can talk later, after the ceremony. Ezra, can you call down and have my car brought around immediately?"

"Yes, sir."

"Ben, listen—"

With a hand on the small of Nic's back—God, she smelled amazing!—he guided her over to the elevator, hurrying her inside when the doors instantly opened.

She tried to resist his forward motion. "Ben! Stop it! There's something I need to tell you."

"And I want to hear it."

He pushed the button for the lobby and turned to watch the numbers, calculating how to get her across the city on time. If he took 83 North to 695, that would probably be quicker than if he took 695 the entire—

The elevator car jerked to a halt. Startled, he looked around. Nic stood next to the panel, her hands on her hips, the emergency stop button flashing an ominous red. In the distance, a muffled bell chimed.

"Will you listen now?"

He shook his head. "You're going to be la—"

"Ben!" She closed the small distance between them and placed her hands on his cheeks, the beige heels she wore making the feat easier than usual. "I love you."

Hope fluttered to life in his belly. He stared at her, unable to comprehend what he heard, but desperately wanting it to be true.

Her thumbs stroked his skin. "But—"

His heart sank.

"—I want to be clear so that we're both on

the same page. I'm not giving up my career. I've worked too hard for it."

Lightness flooded his being and lifted his heart. She loved him! She wasn't taking the words back!

He needed to address what she said, but she was so close and it had been too long since their lips had been acquainted. He leaned forward and tasted her fully, sweeping his tongue into the heat of her mouth, tangling it with hers. When she moaned, he pulled her body to his, reveling in her softness, her scent, everything that was uniquely Nic. Could she feel his heart churning in his chest? Did she know it beat only for her?

Ending their kiss—reluctantly—he placed his forehead against hers. "I would never ask you to give up your career."

She stared up at him, her lips moist and swollen. "I know. I think I always knew. But I was scared."

"Why?"

"Because I love you so much. There was a part of me that worried what that love could make me do. Could I be tempted to give it up if you asked me to?"

"Oh baby."

He hugged her and felt the shudder cascade through her body. He knew what that admission had cost her. He accepted the gift of her vulnerability and swore to treasure it with the care and respect it deserved.

"*Doctor* Nicole Allen," he said, using her title,

emphasizing it, so she understood the vow he made included *all* of her, "I love you. I adore you. I know you don't need me to take care of you. You're more than capable of providing for yourself. But, if you'll let me, I want to take care of your heart. Protect it and give it shelter. I promise I'll never harm or break it. I'll cherish it always. Do you love me, trust me enough for that?"

Her green eyes shimmered. "You're my best friend, Ben. I trust you with all that I am. I promise that I'll always put you first in my heart. And when the time comes to start our family, you won't be on your own. It may not look the way you imagined, but we'll do it in a way that works for us." She took his hand. "You're going to be a wonderful father."

"And you'll be a phenomenal mother."

Their lips met, sealing their futures together more definitively than any ceremony could ever accomplish.

He straightened and captured one glorious curl, watching it slide through his fingers. "Now that we have that settled, how about we start this elevator again and get to your dinner before management sends the fire department and we miss it entirely?"

"Oh, right."

She threw her head back and laughed and the sound cradled his heart. How lucky he'd been to fall in love with his best friend. He wouldn't have to worry about history repeating itself. With her he knew he'd always be a priority. As she would be for him.

"Did everyone fly in for the celebration?" he asked, as the elevator dinged and the doors opened on the first floor.

"Lacey couldn't make it. It's just my mom, Ava, and Caila. They should be arriving at the country club any minute now."

"Why don't you call Ava and let her know we're on the way? We don't want them to worry."

The last thing he wanted was to have Nic's entire squad blaming him for her missing this important occasion.

"Good point," she said, pulling her phone from her purse. "They wanted me to wait and see you after the dinner, but I couldn't. I needed you there."

He was glad she hadn't listened.

But—

"If Ava's driving," he said, "it's against the law for her to answer her phone. Ooh, I know—"

Nic skidded to a stop on the lobby's marble floors. "Don't you dare say it . . ."

He grinned, stoked to accept Nic's challenge, today and every day for the rest of their lives.

"Why don't you send her a tit pic? From personal experience I know it's how all the cool kids are communicating with their friends these days."

Chapter Twenty-Seven

Six Months Later

To: Ava Taylor <ATay@gmail.com>; Caila Harris
  <CAHarris@us.Endurance.com>; Lacey Scott
  <Lasc@gmail.com>
From: Nicole Allen <NicAl@gmail.com>
Date: March 16, 2021
Subject: Vacay 2021

Ladies—

Another year, another vacay. I know this email is later than usual, but it's been crazy busy finishing up the most important year of my career and traveling between Durham and Baltimore to be with the love of my life.

I have some great news. I accepted a job offer, with a practice just outside of DC, that will start right after my fellowship ends! And my mother finally agreed to leave Covington and move to the DMV! Hallelu!

With all of that said, I can't wait to see you.

I'm so appreciative of your friendship. For years, you've stood by me, supported me, and kicked in a little extra because my budget was so limited. You guys kept me going. Your love for me and faith in me were instrumental in getting me through those long years of school and training.

And I want to say thank you.

I know we agreed to let Lacey plan the next trip, but I talked to her and she consented to wait one more year. (Thanks, Lace.) This year, vacay is all on me! No voting to pick places and allocate points (God, why did we ever let Caila start this?!?) Trust me, it's gonna be lit. We're going to celebrate my new job, Lacey's successful tour, Caila's wedding, and Ava just being fabulous. And it's going to be fucking amazing.

While there have been a lot of changes the past two years, the one thing that will never change is our love for each other. No matter who we may meet or what new things come into our lives, our time together each year must be protected. We'll make it work. Always. (And we'll pinkie promise swear the next time I see all of you.)

Talk soon. To our next vacay, bitches!
Nic

Acknowledgments

When I finished writing this book, I instantly loved it. (And that doesn't always happen.) It features a very strong heroine and the man who cares for her, nurtures her and loves her. It took a while for me to realize I'd created a version of what I'd needed and received during that time in my life.

For ten weeks, my daughter and I left my husband and two sons behind while she underwent radiation therapy for a brain tumor. Other than her original diagnosis, it was the hardest time of my life. I had to be strong for her and establish a new life and routine to help combat her stress, fear and anxiety, all while I was away from *my* support system. From the person who calms and balances *me*.

And, I had to write this book.

While immersing myself in Nic and Ben's world kept me functioning, you wouldn't have read their amazing love story or these words, were it not for:

The wonderful people at St. Jude Children's Research Hospital who made the process as easy as something like that could be. (So, when you have the opportunity to donate, please do. It's so worth it.)

Alvenia Scarborough, Cassandra Williams, Dr. Imani Williams-Vaughn and Tanya Smith Evans, the group of women I based this series on. When I told them I was going to miss our annual trip and explained why, they rearranged everything to come and spend time with me in Memphis. It's easy to write the loving, supportive friendship on the page when it's modeled for me in real life.

My agent, Nalini Akolekar, and my editor, Tessa Woodward, who are full of grace and compassion. Having them as my sword and shield allows me to fight harder and go further than I ever thought possible.

Mia Sosa, my soul sister and fellow resident of this place called Romancelandia. Plot holes and imposter syndrome are no challenge for her ingenious mind and sharp tongue. She kept me sane by bringing order to chaos, brightening my spirits and making me laugh.

Claudine Martinez-Padilla, Sharon McGowan, Ashley Motley, Petra Spaulding, Leigh Florio, Chrissy Kuney, Annette Carillo, Alleyne Dickens, Mary Behre, Sarah MacLean, Tif Marcelo, Pris Oliveras, Nina Crespo and Michelle Arris. They called, texted, emailed AND sent loads of goodies and books to Graysie. Seeing her happy made me happy. And their consistent "check ins" made the experience bearable.

The team at Avon publishing: Elle, Kayleigh,

Pam, Angela, Beth, Stephanie, Guido (for another amazing cover) and everyone else who worked on this book. Their time and expertise made this a better book and ensured more people would experience Nic and Ben's story.

My readers, who continue to show up with each new release. Their support humbles me. They keep on making my dreams come true.

Trey & Will, who never complained about their mom and sister being gone even though our absence affected them, too. They're talented and brilliant and I'm so lucky I get front-row seats to watch them mature into wonderful young men.

Elsie, my mom, who stepped in whenever we needed her, whether it was coming for a visit so I could have a break or driving my car thirteen hours, so I'd have it. Her generosity allowed me moments to breathe.

Graysie, whose smile was created by angels and who shows me every day what it means to push through, persevere and thrive despite what's thrown at you. She is smart, creative, funny and the best daughter a mother could ask for.

And, finally, James, who held down the fort like the spectacular husband and father he is. No combination of words will ever be able to convey what he means to me. He is, quite simply, the best man I have ever known.

Until the next one,
TL

Don't miss out on the first
romance in Tracey Livesay's
wildly fun Girls Trip series

SWEET TALKIN' LOVER

When everything is on the line, surrendering com-
pletely to love is your only choice . . .

Marketing manager Caila Harris knows that
the road to success in the beauty industry doesn't
allow for detours. She's forsaken any trace of a
social life, working 24/7 to ensure her next promotion. When grief over her grandfather's death
leads to several catastrophic decisions, Caila gets
one final chance to prove herself: shut down an
unprofitable factory in a small Southern town. But
as soon as she arrives in Bradleton, she meets one
outsized problem: the town's gorgeous mayor.

Wyatt Bradley isn't thrilled about his nickname,
Mayor McHottie. He's even less happy to learn
that his town might be losing its biggest employer. If he has to, he'll use some sneaky tactics
to get Caila on his side. Yet even as he's hoping
she'll fall for Bradleton, he's falling too—right
into a combustible affair that shakes them both
with its intensity.

Two stubborn people, torn between loyalty, ambition, and attraction. But when you're willing to
give it your all, there's no limit to how far love can
take you . . .